Praise for _The_

'Ayliffe delivers a taut, nail-bit[...]
mark on the modern day Aust[...]

'Bailey is charismatic, sarcastic and broken all rolled into one,
but it's a brilliantly written character starring in a cracking
crime thriller.' _Herald Sun_

'Readers will not fail to enjoy the ride from start to finish.'
**Good Reading**

'A crime thriller with the lot: murder, deceit, corruption and
a hint of romance . . . Ayliffe takes you deep inside the worlds
of politics and the media, with a heavy dose of international
intrigue thrown in.' **Michael Rowland**

'A thriller straight from the headlines.' _Sun Herald_

'Bailey proves nothing is more dangerous than a man who can
fall no further. An absolute cracker of a thriller.' **Chris Uhlmann**

'This novel is energetic, well-written and a good holiday read.'
**Sydney Morning Herald**

'Who needs Jason Bourne when you can have John Bailey?'
Chris Bath

'If Rake were a journalist, with a talent that equals his capacity
to survive being beaten up, Bailey would be him.' **Julia Baird**

For Justine, Penelope and Arthur

TIM AYLIFFE

THE GREATER GOOD

**SIMON &
SCHUSTER**

London · New York · Sydney · Toronto · New Delhi

THE GREATER GOOD
First published in Australia in 2018 by
Simon & Schuster (Australia) Pty Limited
Suite 19A, Level 1, Building C, 450 Miller Street,
Cammeray, NSW 2062
This edition published in 2020

10 9 8 7 6 5 4 3

Sydney New York London Toronto New Delhi
Visit our website at www.simonandschuster.com.au

 A catalogue record for this
book is available from the
National Library of Australia

Cover design: Luke Causby/Blue Cork
Cover image: Thorsten/Adobe Stock
Typeset by Midland Typesetters, Australia
Printed and bound in Australia by Griffin Press

 The paper this book is printed on is certified against the
Forest Stewardship Council˚ Standards. Griffin Press
holds chain of custody certification SCS-COC-001185.
FSC˚ promotes environmentally responsible, socially
beneficial and economically viable management of the
world's forests.

PROLOGUE

Fallujah, April 2004

'I'm done, Bailey.'

Bailey handed Gerald the green army canteen that Captain Alessandro had given him the night before when they were stocking up for the run into Fallujah.

'You just need some water. Drink it.'

Gerald grabbed the canteen and took a long gulp.

'Twelve hours, Bailey. That's how long it's been since we walked into this hellhole. I reckon we've made it, what – two hundred metres?'

'Nah . . . one hundred.'

Bailey took back the canteen and had a swig for himself. It tasted good.

'Where the hell's Bravo company, anyway?' Gerald said.

'They told us to wait here. It's too dangerous out there.'

'Snipers, mortar rounds and that bloody chanting that keeps playing from the mosques like a broken record.'

Gerald was speaking so quickly that Bailey could barely understand him.

'You're just tired, mate. Soon we'll be back in the green zone drinking Buds and laughing about this.'

Gerald stood up. 'I'm going outside to take a look.'

'Careful, mate. They told us to stay here for a reason.'

'Fuck it. I need to see what's going on.'

Bailey watched Gerald walk to the bedroom door and disappear down the hallway. The house they were sheltering in had been almost destroyed by a mortar round. There were so many holes in the battered structure that it looked like a half-eaten block of Swiss cheese.

Bravo company had told them to stay out of sight on the first floor until they had secured the area. It was too dangerous upstairs – difficult to run for it, when the time came.

Bailey got up to follow Gerald. Live or die, they had to stay together. Orders from Captain Alessandro.

There was an explosion down the hallway. Dust filled the air and Bailey lost sight of Gerald. His ears were ringing from the loud bang of the bomb that had landed nearby and he was disorientated. Dust was forming concrete blobs in his mouth, making it difficult to breathe. He tried to wave away the smoke with his hands so that he could get his bearings and figure out what had happened. His disorientation was turning to panic.

'Gerald! Gerald! Gerald!' he yelled.

'Run, Bailey! Run! This way! Get out! Get out!' Gerald's voice echoed back down the hallway.

Relief. Gerald was alive. Now fear.

'Bailey! Get out of there!'

Rapid gunfire was punctuated by the sound of more voices. American, Arabic too.

The wall beside Bailey blew open, knocking him to his knees. He lay there covered by pieces of the shattered wall, coughing, his lungs trying to wrest the oxygen from the dust.

'Gerald! Where are you?'

Pop! Pop pop pop!

The gunfire was moving further away.

No more voices.

He could hear footsteps, someone running towards him.

Bailey pushed away chunks of plaster and brick that had fallen onto the backs of his legs, and clambered up off his knees.

'Gerald?'

Nothing.

The smoke and dust in the air was so thick, Bailey couldn't see more than a few feet in front of him.

'Billy? Mac? Marlon?' He called out the names of the marines he could remember.

The footsteps were getting closer. They stopped in front of him.

Through the dust cloud, Bailey could see a black headscarf and a pair of dark eyes staring at him. Piercing, hate-filled eyes.

'Dog!'

The man raised his rifle and spun it around, knocking Bailey to the ground with the butt. Then, as if in slow motion, Bailey watched as the butt slammed into his head again.

CHAPTER 1

Sydney, Tuesday

On the carpet of a small Rushcutters Bay apartment, near the mouth of Sydney's Cross City Tunnel, a woman lay dead. Her face was a sickening shade of blue and red. The dark welts in her neck suggested that she had been strangled. But that was a problem for the police, not John Bailey.

'I want you on this one,' Gerald had called to tell him earlier that morning.

'Why? Sounds like a murder, and since when did I get assigned to crime and grime?'

'It's more complicated than I'm telling you. You haven't filed a story in months, and I'm not paying you to sit around in late-night bars telling war stories to rich divorcees in Paddington any more. Got it?'

Bailey ignored the insult because he wanted to know more. Maybe the journalist in him was still in there. Somewhere. Still, he couldn't resist having a dig back.

'Right, sounds like it matters. Someone you knew. Anything you need to get off your chest?'

'No, mate. Just go. We'll talk later.'

Bailey could tell that Gerald wasn't up for playing the game, so he backed off. 'Better get moving, then. I'll let you know.'

'Thanks. And Bailey?'

'Yeah?'

'You speak only to me about this one. Right?'

'Okay, boss.'

Gerald hung up.

Bailey knew that his old friend hated being his boss, so he reminded him whenever he could. He also knew that Gerald had been good to him since he'd arrived back from London a broken man.

For the first time in as long as he could remember, Bailey was resigned to doing his job.

Two police cars were parked outside the apartment complex, one marked, the other one of those turbocharged Holdens that plain-clothed cops drove these days. The front door of the building was wide open. This crime beat was easier than he remembered.

Bailey walked along the corridor towards the police tape blocking the entry to apartment 9B. The pungent smell that had alerted the neighbours was stinging his nostrils. The body must have been there for days, maybe longer.

The blue and white strips of plastic crossed the open door in a zigzag that stretched from top to bottom. He peered through the triangular gaps. The apartment was tiny, even by inner-city standards. He could see almost everything. A pristine linen-covered couch by the window, matching armchair, coffee table – all organised neatly in front of a flatscreen television fixed to the wall. Expensive sound system discreetly wired in. Stylish photographic prints of Bondi Beach hung on the walls and a decaying bunch of gardenias sat in a flash vase on the marble kitchen bench. Despite the size, Bailey was in no doubt the apartment had cost a bomb. Sydney property prices were bloody ridiculous.

Two male police officers in blue uniforms stood talking with a woman in a dark suit and a neat ponytail. By the body language of the men in blue it was clear that she was in charge. They were whispering by a window that overlooked Rushcutters Bay Park, occasionally gesturing to the white body bag lying open on the carpet at their feet. Bailey could see one side of the victim's face. She was beautiful. Blonde hair, sophisticated makeup and a large diamond in her ear. She had obviously looked after herself. The discolouration in her skin and the marks on her neck suggested that her death wasn't an accident.

Bailey held his hand to his nose. He could smell the soap from his shower and the booze from last night's session seeping through his pores. Anything to compete with the odour wafting from the corpse.

He swallowed.

It had been a long time since he'd seen a dead body, just not long enough to forget. That smell, always the same. Unless it was burning.

The police officers continued their conversation, oblivious to Bailey's presence at the door. His eyes traced the room for clues. No overturned chairs, no sign of forced entry, no blood on the carpet, no broken photo frames, no marks on the walls. Nothing. If this girl had been strangled, why was there no sign of a struggle?

Bailey knelt down and poked his head through the police tape closer to the floor. A pair of yellow high-heeled shoes were splayed on the cream carpet by the door. The shoes looked expensive. She did, too. A professional robbery she'd interrupted? Maybe the cops had found her lying by the door where she had tried to escape her killer?

Bailey quietly pushed his head further between the tape to take in more of the room, imagining her body on the carpet beside him. The door had been pushed back hard against the wall, denting the plaster. A belt was hanging from the handle, tied at one end to the knob. The buckle end was dangling halfway between the lock and the carpet. Maybe it wasn't robbery, or murder, after all; just some weird sex game gone wrong?

'Can I help you?' One of the policemen had spotted Bailey crouched on his knees by the door.

Bailey didn't answer.

'Mate, I'm asking you a question.' The cop clicked his fingers. 'What're you doing here?'

Bailey casually got to his feet. 'Just seeing if you guys needed any help.'

'Smart arse. How about I –'

4

'Bailey, is that you?' The plain-clothed policewoman turned around.

'Sharon Dexter.' The name came out of his mouth before he could stop it. Same compelling eyes, hard to meet. Same figure, same presence, even more assured than he'd remembered.

He gathered himself. 'Had I known it was you over there I would have pushed all this tape out of the way and let myself in.'

'You almost did. But these days we've got a few more rules to keep people like you away.'

She held his gaze.

'You two know each other then?' The young cop again. Hostile.

His tone reminded Bailey why he disliked cops. Some people just weren't smart enough to wield power. The good ones held it close. Others let the might of the badge define them. It made them impatient and angry. On edge, always.

'A detective in the making you got there, Sharon.'

'Mate, I will escort you downstairs if –'

'He's just stirring you, Rob.' Detective Dexter hated working with hotheads. 'Constable Rob Lucas, meet John Bailey – a man who enjoys taking the piss. It's why he once spent a night in prison. Isn't that right, Bailey?'

'You've got a good memory, Sharon. Although it's not surprising since it was you who put me there.'

'So it was. How're you, anyway?' She started walking towards him.

'Depends what day –'

'More importantly, what are you doing here?' She was standing in front of him now, close enough to clock his shabby flannelette shirt, his podgy middle, sandy hair speckled with grey, and handsome face wrinkled and weathered by a life lived hard. 'Crime beat's a bit beneath you these days, isn't it? Aren't you supposed to be off covering some civil war somewhere?'

'Haven't been doing that for a while now. Prefer the easy life.'

Both of them knew this was a lie.

'This seems like an excessive amount of tape to use on a door. Any chance I can come in?'

'No bloody way!' Lucas said.

'Okay, pal.' Bailey waved his hand at the red-faced cop on the other side of the room. 'Just relax, would you?'

'Rob, I've got this.' Dexter lowered her voice. 'Seriously, Bailey, things *are* different these days. What is it – twenty-five years since you were following cops around?'

'Something like that,' Bailey said. 'One in particular.'

She gave him a steely look – a warning not to go there. 'Yeah, we might have different recollections about that.'

'Gerald's put me on this. Punishment for being lazy, he tells me.'

'The lovely Gerald,' Dexter said. 'How's he doing? Still think journalism's the world's best crime-fighting organisation?'

'That's our Gerald. Although he's virtually on the wagon these days. Boring. Nancy's banned him from seeing me outside of work.'

'She was always smarter than you two.'

Dexter looked like she was about to say something else, then looked away.

Bailey smiled, awkwardly. 'So, what do you –'

'Anyway, no, you can't come in.'

If they were ever going to talk about what had happened between them, now was not the time.

'So, what can you tell me?' Bailey said.

'On the record, this looks pretty straightforward,' Dexter said. 'Accidental death. No sign of an intruder. No sign anyone else was involved. Knickers were on – no sticky stuff anywhere.'

'And unofficially?' Bailey wanted something off the record. Anything that might explain why Gerald had forced him out of bed and sent him to a crime scene.

'Not today, Bailey.'

'C'mon, Sharon, I know you. You must have more than that?'

Dexter paused, moving closer to the tape so she could slip Bailey her card through the plastic strips. 'Highly paid prostitute dies playing choker-sex Michael Hutchence style by the door. Could be anything. I'm looking into it.'

'And?'

'That's plenty, Bailey,' she said. 'You're the only reporter I've spoken to and, as I keep telling you, things are different.'

'Got a name?'

'Catherine Chamberlain. You can print that, but it's all you're getting out of me today.'

'Okay.'

Bailey slipped her card in his pocket and turned to walk down the hall.

'And Sharon, one more thing.'

It was Detective Dexter's turn to stick her head through the police tape.

'What?'

'It's good to see you . . . and you . . . you look good.'

'Don't start that shit with me.'

Dexter fumbled with the tape at the door and disappeared back inside.

Bailey was fifty-three years old and back working the Sydney crime beat like a cub reporter. He had to laugh.

CHAPTER 2

Bailey had to jiggle the key in his car door to get it open. Some idiot had damaged the lock with a screwdriver when they broke into his 1991 Toyota Corolla while it was parked outside his townhouse in Paddington. A meth head, most likely. All they got were the coins stashed in the ashtray for parking. Probably all they needed.

Ice was the new drug of choice in Sydney. Like heroin in the nineties, it was everywhere. And it was cheap. Forty bucks for a point. Users weren't hard to spot, either. Especially when they were coming down. Their gaunt faces, piercing eyes and skeletal builds. Mumbling to themselves and likely to act aggressively towards anyone who dared to look their way.

Bailey felt sorry for the paramedics and hospital staff working on the front line of Sydney's ice epidemic, especially considering users' propensity for violence. But he wasn't doing a story about crystal meth – that was old news. Bailey had just been staring at the body of a beautiful girl, a life snuffed out for no good reason, and he wanted to know why.

The radio blurted alive when he turned on the engine. Talkback, which he hated, but forced himself to listen to from time to time just to check the pulse of the city. The callers didn't bother him all that much. Mostly, he found them amusing. It was the hosts that he couldn't stand. Inflammatory morons masquerading as journalists, purveyors of somebody's truth, the working people's watchdog. They were the nation's best bullshitters. Yet, somehow, they were always talking about the issues that people cared about.

Bailey had been dragged to a dinner party once and sat across from Sydney's top dog of morning radio, Keith Roberts. Hands down the biggest prick he had ever met. The experience was even more unpleasant because Roberts claimed he was Bailey's biggest fan.

Bailey was in a bad way at the time. He had just been summoned back to Australia after two decades as *The Journal*'s Middle East correspondent. The Iraq War, Afghanistan – the Bush years had been particularly damaging to his mental health. It wasn't that Bailey hadn't seen violence before 2001. Beirut in 1989 was especially bad. It was just that modern warfare seemed to be more about bombs than boots on the ground. Drone strikes on one side, homemade bombs on the other. Collateral damage was rising, and journalists and aid workers were left to count the dead and work out how many of them were actually bad guys.

Bailey had counted too many bodies. More than anyone's fair share, if there was such a thing.

Gerald was convinced that the best way to help his friend's recovery was to invite him to as many social functions as possible. Get him out talking to normal people, then maybe he too could be normal again. Bailey knew that it was better than drinking alone so, for a while at least, he had played along.

But Gerald should have known that seating Bailey near Roberts that night at his house in Mosman was a mistake. The moment they sat down Roberts was squawking at the table like he was addressing callers on his show, answering his own questions, spouting his interpretations of the day's news as though they were gospel.

It was almost impossible to challenge the views of a guy like Keith Roberts. When people tried, he simply raised the tone of his voice. The louder he spoke, the more right he was. Heavy with opinion, light on facts. And he was a bully.

The main course hadn't even arrived before Roberts began sharing his personal views about the Middle East – 'A hopeless, barbaric land,' he'd said, 'governed by spear-chuckers with a hateful religion.'

The dinner party was brought to an abrupt end when Bailey stood up and emptied a glass of wine in Roberts' face.

Bailey chuckled to himself as he recalled the night, or as much of it as he could remember. It had happened almost three years ago. He was a calmer man these days, although his disdain for Roberts had never waned.

He played with the dial until he found Roberts' familiar yapping voice so that he could listen to what the punters thought about today's water-cooler issue – whatever that might be – while steering his old crappy car through the traffic towards *The Journal*'s headquarters on the other side of the city.

'They're coming, people. I tell you they are. Michael Donaldson tells us they are too, and he'd know. He was the ambassador in Beijing who spent a long time cosying up to red men over banquets in the Great Hall . . .'

Roberts was in full flight.

'Well, Mr Donaldson has written a book. It's a pile of dangerous hogwash, if you ask me. He thinks we should be best pals with China and forget about America. The old red, white and blue's on the way down . . . the new red's on the way up. Better get in before it's too late. Forget the trenches where we fought alongside Americans against that common enemy!'

Roberts' opening gambits often lasted longer than his interviews.

'So, what do you think about China? Friend or foe? We'll take your calls in a moment. First, let's speak to Michael Donaldson to hear more about his views, which have been splashed across the front pages of today's newspapers.

'Michael Donaldson, welcome to the show.'

'Great to be –'

'So, you say it's time to forget about reds under the bed and let them through the front door?'

Bailey knew Donaldson from when he was ambassador to Israel. He was a career public servant and one of those diplomats who'd done the rounds in top posts in most parts of the world. Bailey couldn't believe that he'd agreed to go on Roberts' program. Although, he did have a book to sell.

'Keith, I don't think you're quite being honest with your listeners. My book doesn't argue anything like what you're suggesting. The world is changing. China's an undisputed economic powerhouse, our biggest trading partner by a long stretch. There's a new president in the White House who's pushing protectionist policies. Australia faces some strategic challenges and –'

'C'mon, Mr Donaldson, speak in a language people can understand.' Donaldson hadn't even finished his first answer before Roberts was into him. 'You think the United States won't be running the world soon, that we ought to ditch DC and buy our guns and warships and fighter planes from the Chinese, cosy up to the bad guys before it's too late!'

'That's not what I am saying at all. Keith, if you'd just let me –'

'No, I think we get your point,' Roberts said. 'You can justify your position further in a moment. Let's take a call to hear what our listeners think. We've got Doris on the line. Doris – how're you, love?'

'Hello Keith. I just love your show, by the way.'

'Thanks, darling. Now, what do you think about this China business?'

'I've got to say I'm really scared by what Michael Donaldson is saying. I mean, the Chinese just aren't like us. They don't share our values –'

Bailey had heard enough. Roberts was still a prick.

He switched the radio to his CD player and blasted the Rolling Stones to clear his ears of Roberts' yapping voice. *Exile on Main Street* – now that was an album.

Bailey was still humming the cool harmonica section of 'Sweet Virginia' when he strolled out of the elevator and onto the fraying blue carpet of *The Journal*'s newsroom.

He couldn't remember the last time he'd been there, and he didn't recognise half of the faces that looked up from their desks at the new guy.

The old guy, really.

He felt like the oldest person in the building. Then he remembered the latest round of redundancies that had cleaned out the place, and the chief executive's note to staff about the need to turn *The Journal* into a digital business. Whatever that meant. Bailey never understood why he wasn't shown the door. Gerald protecting him, most likely.

He nodded at the few people he still recognised and sat down at his desk. It was piled high with old newspapers, magazines and unopened mail. He cleared the clutter off the top of his keyboard and began contemplating the type of story he could write about the death of a prostitute in Rushcutters Bay. Accident or murder? He'd need to report it straight so that he didn't burn Dexter. He owed her a call before publishing. Later.

'Bailey.' A polite, familiar voice sounded behind him. 'Mr Summers wants to see you.'

It was Gerald's assistant, Penelope. She had visited Bailey at home a few times to check up on him during the bad old days. But she never judged him.

Bailey swivelled around in his chair. 'How are you, Pen?'

'I'm good. But you'd better get to it – the boss looks stressed.'

'Summonsed.' Bailey was on his feet again. 'On my way.'

Gerald's office was in the corner of the newsroom. It had a large window that used to have a beautiful view of Darling Harbour before the developers were unleashed on Cockle Bay. These days Gerald looked directly into a twenty-storey hotel and the best view he could hope for was of an unwitting female taking her clothes off without drawing the blinds. It surprised Bailey how often it happened.

'What did you find?' Gerald wasn't in the mood for small talk.

'Dead prostitute. Name's Catherine Chamberlain. Pretty girl, looked after herself too. Guess she was one of those high-paid types. Strangled. Belt hanging from the door handle, looked like a sex game gone wrong –'

'Or made to look that way,' Gerald said.

'I've been at the crime scene, looked at the body. Why do I feel like you know more about Catherine Chamberlain than I do?'

'Ruby Chambers was her working-girl name,' Gerald said. 'And you're right, I do. Shut the door.'

Bailey did what he was told and sat down in one of two stiff uncomfortable chairs on the other side of Gerald's large mahogany desk.

Like always, Gerald was dressed in a smart tailored suit, freshly preened shirt, bright tie and his customary round-rimmed glasses. Conservative and politely spoken, he looked more like a university professor than a newspaper man. But he'd done the rounds – the hard yards – including a stint with Bailey in Iraq.

He stood up, turned his back on Bailey and stared out the window.

'Any lovelies out there, you old pervert?'

'Sorry, no sense of humour today, mate.' Gerald didn't turn around.

'All right. Are you going to tell me what you know?'

'Not much is the short answer, but more than I'd like.'

'And?'

Gerald sighed and turned to face him. 'Last Thursday, I was invited to a love-in at the American consul-general's house in Bellevue Hill. Swanky affair. Ambassador was there with the usual state and federal ministers sucking up to him. Newspaper editors, TV directors, arty types and the odd wealthy banker – we all get invited. When I was leaving, a bloke called Michael Anderson asked me for a lift home. I'd only just met him. He was blind drunk, but eager to get out of there.'

'Michael Anderson?'

'Advisor to Gary Page.'

'The defence minister.' Everyone knew Gary Page – he was a Labor Party heavyweight, one of the government's strongest performers.

'Right. And guess where he wanted me to drop him off?'

'You're joking,' Bailey said.

Gerald finally sat down at his desk.

'He'd probably told me more than a man like him usually would. Given the number of glasses of wine I saw him throw back at the house, I wasn't surprised. Said he was seeing this hot little number called –'

'Catherine Chamberlain.' Bailey finished the sentence for him.

'Right.'

'Surely you don't think he –'

'Who knows? Probably not. But knowing he was in a relationship with her is a story in itself. We could print that tomorrow and sell papers.'

'Why don't we?'

A prostitute who may have been murdered had been seeing an advisor to Australia's defence minister – that was a good story.

'I got a call last night – late, more like morning. It was Page.'

Bailey shifted forward in his chair. 'The minister called you himself?'

'Yep. Anderson must have remembered me dropping him off. God knows how, he was so pissed. Rattled too – about what, I couldn't get out of him.

'Anyway, police had only just found Chamberlain's body and I've got the defence minister on the phone asking me not to put two and two together and print a story with both his and Anderson's names in it.'

'Give a reason?'

'The usual when these guys want to block you – publishing may pose a threat to national security.'

'The only threat I can see here's the veiled one – a late-night phone call from a senior government minister. I say we publish.'

'I know these guys better than you do, Bailey. And you know me.' Gerald's voice was firm. 'We'll pull the trigger on this. I just need more information.'

Bailey regretted pushing him. 'What do you need from me?'

'Get me something we can use.' Gerald paused, a hint of a smile appearing on his face. 'Sharon Dexter's the detective on the case, right?'

'How'd you know that?'

'A little birdie told me. Must be nice for you two to see each other after all these years.'

'Don't start, Gerald.'

'Now, now. Don't be so defensive.'

'She slipped me her card; suggested something, like she couldn't talk in front of the young coppers at the scene.'

'Well, what are you waiting for? Give her a ring.'

'Planning to.' Bailey stood up and headed for the door. 'Some old prick is holding me up.'

'And Bailey?'

'Yep?'

'You've got a real skill for pissing women off, especially this one.' Gerald wasn't smiling this time. 'We need more to run with this, so take it easy.'

'It was a long time ago, Gerald. She's fine.' Bailey didn't like being lectured – by anyone. Especially when they were right.

'If you say so.'

CHAPTER 3

Bailey hadn't eaten breakfast and it was already time for lunch. He took a deep breath and dialled the phone number on Detective Sharon Dexter's card. She answered before the second ring.

'Sharon, it's Bailey.'

'You didn't waste any time.' The tone in her voice was steady, business-like.

'I've got a few questions.'

'And?'

'Not on the phone. Can we meet?' Bailey was trying to sound professional.

'Bailey, I saw you less than three hours ago.'

'Yeah, but I've got something for you too, something that could be connected. How about I buy you lunch in Chinatown?'

Dexter sighed down the end of the phone.

'Nothing cheap and nasty.'

'The Red Emperor? Midday?'

'Sounds cheap. But yeah, I'll be there.'

'I'll surprise you.'

—

Chinatown was almost unrecognisable to Bailey. In the years he had been away the place had been buffed and shined for the tourist dollar with shopping centres, gardens, public art installations and swanky bars, all aimed at gentrifying the streetscape. It was a different place from the one he had ventured out into late at night for a cheap beef and black bean and a bottle of chardonnay after finishing a story just in time for the printers.

The restaurants where Bailey liked to eat – with nylon floors, lazy Susans, murky fish tanks and neon lights – were harder to find these days. But they were there, dotted in among the prime harbourside real estate. The Red Emperor was his new favourite.

Bailey was nervous about seeing Dexter again. They were both caught offguard in Rushcutters Bay – no time to contemplate the past. But that was hours ago, plenty of time for Dexter to remember the selfish bastard who'd walked out on her.

It wasn't like they were destined for the altar – Bailey already had one failed marriage behind him. But he knew they had something good. When Bailey decided to head back to the Middle East to cover the war in Afghanistan, Dexter had understood. It was his job and she wouldn't stand in the way. Especially after September 11. He would fly home when he could and they would talk and email a few times a week. Their relationship was strong enough to withstand a few absent months.

But when the Taliban dug in and George W. Bush set his sights on Iraq, it became clear that Bailey wouldn't be coming home for a long time. Clear to him, anyway. When you're being jolted awake by the sounds of bombs and gunfire – feeling the vibrations – life outside the warzone doesn't seem real any more.

And he was counting bodies again.

The longer he stayed away, the harder it was for him to keep the relationship with Dexter going. He was on the other side of the world and, as the weeks turned into months, it seemed pointless. Weekly calls became monthly. And then Bailey stopped calling altogether.

He couldn't remember exactly how, or when, it ended. Distracted by the war still simmering around him, he had blocked it all out so that he could get on with the job.

That was all in the past now. Forgiven and forgotten, Bailey told himself as he stared out the window, watching the cars and pedestrians pass by. He studied the random faces, wondering about their lives beyond the working day merry-go-round. Everybody had secrets. The journalist in him wanted to know all of them.

Sharon Dexter didn't have any secrets. She was the most honest person he knew. Bailey loved that about her, along with a figure that had made tradies down tools at a construction site. Still would.

Dexter had had a tough upbringing. She was raised in the harbourside suburb of Balmain where her parents, Bruce and Cathy, owned a pub called The Scotsman. Back then, Balmain was a modest suburb with a strong working-class tradition. It was home to the families of miners, dock workers, tradesmen and the men who clocked on and off at the electricity plant before stopping by The Scotsman for a beer.

Balmain was also the birthplace of the Australian Labor Party, and Bruce Dexter liked to tell his patrons that the pub had been one of the favoured meeting places of those early representatives of the working man's movement. No one had the heart to tell him that The Scotsman was built thirty years after those first gatherings took place. It didn't matter. The patrons loved Bruce and, as long as the beer was flowing, they put up with his stories.

Cathy Dexter had fallen victim to the Spanish dancer, as Bruce called it – he couldn't bring himself to say the word. The cancer had started in her lungs before rapidly spreading to her brain. She was dead within twelve months. It was the year that Sharon started high school. Bruce tried to be strong for his daughter. But most of the time it was Sharon who took care of him.

Bruce never recovered from the death of his wife. Every week until the day he died he would place a fresh bunch of lilies – Cathy's favourites – by her gravestone, dutifully clearing the previous week's wilted bunch away. He never remarried. What was the point? No one would ever be good enough.

Bruce didn't like many people, but he liked John Bailey. And Bailey liked him too. He liked drinking with him and talking about the world. Publicans knew more about life than anyone because of what went on in their pubs – anger, violence and tears when times were tight; celebrations when they weren't.

The most accurate take on the health of the economy was always from the bloke who poured the beers, especially in a country like Australia.

The Scotsman had made Dexter a tough young girl. Men could turn into monsters after too many beers and Bruce made sure his daughter knew how to defend herself. Although he didn't need to teach her much. Dexter had a strong sense of right and wrong and wasn't afraid to dish out a little justice. She once broke a man's hand when she caught him trying to steal money from the cash register. It was the only time she used the small wooden baseball bat she kept hidden under the bar, the only time she needed to. Sharon Dexter's little bat became legendary.

But Dexter was determined to move on from Balmain and do something different with her life. The police force made sense. She was one of only three women to graduate from the New South Wales Police Academy in the class of 1987. It was a boys' club back then. Still is.

Bailey met her for the first time at a crime scene at Kings Cross sometime in the late eighties. It was before he went to Beirut and Dexter was still feeling her way through the murky underworld of policing in one of the dirtiest decades of law enforcement.

Bailey was hated by the men in uniform because his reporting had put some of them behind bars. It didn't matter that they were corrupt. The force was tribal in those days. Bailey was despised for investigating cops, instead of the real criminals still out on the streets.

Dexter was instantly drawn to Bailey when he approached her that day in Kings Cross, notepad in hand, with questions for his story. The young crime reporter, hungry for the truth. He was polite, charming, and his thick gravelly voice and leathery tanned skin made him popular with the ladies. But he wasn't chasing skirt in those days. He had a young wife and baby at home. Not that he saw much of them. For Bailey, it was all about the job. He was tough and had wanted justice as much as Dexter did. He just had a different way of doing it, different tools. A pencil instead of a gun.

Dexter started paying close attention to Bailey's stories in *The Journal* – the ones that questioned the tactics and actions of her dubious colleagues. As a rookie policewoman, she had felt powerless to do anything about it. The bad guys in blue were more dangerous than the crooks they were chasing.

When the corrupt underworld of policing reached out to bring her into its fold, Dexter knew she had had enough. She called Bailey. They became friends, trusted each other. Dexter helped Bailey bring down a number of crooked cops with his front-page *Sin City* scoops. Then, suddenly, he was gone. Dispatched to the Middle East, his wife and baby daughter in tow, to fulfil every reporter's dream of becoming a correspondent.

—

A giant fish tank separated the kitchen from the bar at the Red Emperor. Inside the glass, Bailey counted six sad looking lobsters, claws tied, moving in slow motion in the cloudy water.

He looked past the lobsters to the kitchen staff on the other side. They were all dressed in white, prepping the food for the lunchtime rush, if it came. Right now, it was just Bailey, the barman and about thirty empty chairs.

He resisted the temptation to order himself a drink. It was only midday and if he really was getting back to work, he couldn't start drinking at lunchtime. At least, not in front of Dexter.

The bell sounded at the door when Detective Sharon Dexter walked into the restaurant. The barman looked up from his post and stared a fraction longer than was appropriate. Bailey had clocked her too. She smiled at the barman while he ushered her to where Bailey was sitting by the window.

He hadn't paid much attention to her appearance that morning. He did now. She was dressed in a dark suit, practical and conservative, nothing too flash, somewhere in between expensive and cheap. He couldn't help noticing that her body still pushed her clothes in all the right places. Middle age could be brutal. But Sharon Dexter was one of the lucky ones. Other than the crow's feet around her eyes, she looked much the same as she did when she'd dropped Bailey at the airport more than a decade ago.

He stood up when she approached the table, tucking in the front of his shirt.

'See – all class, Sharon. A nice restaurant and a table with a view.'

'Don't get carried away, Bailey,' she said. 'All I can see is a building site, a busy street and a window of skinned chickens across the road.'

'Ducks.'

'What?'

'They're ducks,' he said. 'And my apologies. They'd promised a view of the harbour.'

'This restaurant would need to be twenty storeys high to see the water from here.' She paused. 'Anyway, what'd you have for me? I can't stay for lunch.'

'You still know how to cut me down.'

'Don't be cute. I'm here on business. From my reading, it could be serious business.'

'Okay, okay, just messing around,' he said. 'Let's talk – just like old times, hey?'

It wasn't going well.

Dexter looked like she was about to say something, but she paused and stared out the window instead.

'It wasn't suicide. I'm sure of that.'

'Figured. Why didn't you tell me that this morning?' Bailey was relieved that they'd moved on to the case.

'Couldn't. Not with the other coppers around me. Didn't want them getting excited and running to the boss about a new murder case for us to solve.'

'Have things become that political in the force?'

Dexter was turning her mother's engagement ring on her finger.

'Sharon?' Bailey could see that something was unsettling her and he hoped it wasn't him. 'Not like you to go quiet?'

'There's something . . . something strange going on, Bailey.'

'What do you mean?' Bailey realised they were talking about more than a murder investigation. He wanted to reach across the table and hold her hand, reassure her that he was still someone she could trust.

'The commissioner has shown an unusual interest in laying this case to rest as soon as possible.'

'And?'

'When I was on my way to Catherine Chamberlain's apartment he called me to get my thoughts about what had happened.'

'Weird – you hadn't even seen the body.'

'There's more. He wanted to read my report before I put it in and –'

'Is that even legal?'

'He can do what he wants – he's the police commissioner. But that's not the issue. Can I just get this out?'

'Sorry.'

'He told me the victim's name was Ruby Chambers.' Dexter pronounced the name slowly.

'She had two names – not unusual for a prostitute?'

'Yeah, but how'd he know it? The girl's name was Catherine Chamberlain. It's the name that appeared on the mail in her letterbox. The name that all the people we spoke to in the building knew her by.'

'So, what do you think it means? The commissioner was a client?'

'I strongly doubt it. I've known David Davis for almost

thirty years and he isn't the type.' Dexter's voice hardened, along with the expression on her face.

'I don't think you can ever know the type. Most men –'

'He's *not* sleeping with prostitutes!'

They sat in silence, the seconds ticking by, waiting for each other to say something.

'Don't tell me?' Bailey sat back in his chair. Surprised, disappointed too. He couldn't hide it.

'Not any more. Usual story. Unhappily married, kids are grown up and his wife spent most of her time at their place on the Central Coast.'

'Shit, Sharon. I never would have picked you for –'

'Don't you dare lecture me!' She yelled across the table, face flushed with anger.

The barman looked up, startled, from polishing wine glasses at the bar.

'Sharon, I'm sorry . . . I was –'

'You were what, Bailey? Going to give me relationship advice?'

He was struggling to dig himself out of this one.

'Seriously, I'm sorry. I was going to make a joke.'

'Don't.' Dexter stood up, slinging her jacket and bag over her shoulder. 'Your jokes were used up a long time ago.'

'Yeah, I guess so.' He looked at her. 'You weren't joking about not staying for lunch.'

'No, Bailey, I wasn't.'

'Fair enough.'

Dexter made to walk away, then hesitated. 'You know, Bailey, I'm not upset with you, not any more. But that's all I've got for you about Catherine Chamberlain.'

'Don't you want to hear what I've got?'

'Okay. Go for it.'

'Michael Anderson.'

'Am I supposed to know that name?'

'He's an advisor to the defence minister. Gerald met him at a function last Thursday night and dropped him at Chamberlain's place afterwards, late.'

'Thursday?' Dexter looked surprised. 'The medics reckon that's around the time she died – best guess, anyway. That's the timeframe we're looking at.'

Bailey tapped the menu on the table with his finger.

'Surely that little nugget of information has increased my chances of you staying for lunch? The spring rolls here are to die for.'

'Don't push it.'

'It's a sad old man who eats alone,' he said.

'You did that.'

'Yeah, guess I did.' Trauma and loneliness had, at least, made an honest man out of him.

Dexter stepped back to the table and their eyes met in the uncomfortable silence.

'Bailey?'

'Yep?'

'Have you seen much of Miranda?'

'I've got a bit of work to do there. Any advice is welcome!' He made another unsuccessful attempt at humour.

'How long have you been back?'

'Three years, give or take.'

'Three years! What have you been doing?'

'I don't know how to answer that.' The shame of depression, post-traumatic stress, or whatever it was that his psychologist had diagnosed, wasn't something that Bailey knew how to talk about, or wanted to.

'What do you mean?'

'The desert banged me up this time. I made dysfunction an art form.' But Bailey wasn't much for analysing himself. He preferred to focus on real things, like his relationship with his daughter. 'Miranda's the one good thing I have going.'

'She was always a lovely girl.'

Dexter had gotten on well with Miranda.

'A lawyer now. Can you believe it? Her mother did well there.'

'You didn't do too badly, either.'

Bailey shrugged. 'I never quite mastered how to be a father. But we're talking regularly now, catching up when we can.' It was the one thing he was determined to make right.

'You're a shit. But there was never a shortage of love with you. You just forget how to show it sometimes.'

He knew that Dexter wasn't talking about Miranda any more.

'It's a long way back from where I've been.'

'Believe me, I know.'

'Why don't you stay for lunch, just for old time's sake?'

Dexter threw her jacket on the chair and sat down opposite Bailey.

'A quick one.'

CHAPTER 4

Bailey had stuck to black tea during lunch. Wine was off the menu because Dexter was on duty, so he'd played along. Sitting at the table with Dexter reminded him of the life he had chosen not to have. He wanted to show her that he'd changed or, at least, that it was possible for him to change.

He had nervously drunk so much tea that when he arrived back at work his bladder had puffed up like a blowfish. It was sending painful signals, urging him to get to a urinal. Quickly.

He limped past the reception desk – oblivious to the tall man loitering in the foyer – and charged into the elevator, headed for the toilet on level one.

When he came out, Penelope was waiting for him. 'Mr Summers knows you're back and he wants to see you.'

'Has he got a tracking device on me?'

'Dunno, Bailey. Don't shoot the messenger!'

'Sorry, Pen, only kidding around.'

'Forget about it. He's just on edge today,' she said. 'Maybe he's in shock after hearing you're in the office for the second time in one day?'

Penelope had spunk. Bailey liked it. 'Guess I deserved that.'

'Anyway, Mr Summers also wanted me to give you this.' Penelope handed him a small computer bag with a laptop inside. 'Now that you're back on the job.'

'Thanks.' Bailey took the bag and peered inside. 'These things get smaller every day.'

'It's called tech-nol-ogy.' She sounded out the word. Cheeky.

'Yeah, yeah. I'm an old man, we've been here before.'

'You're a popular boy today. A bloke downstairs has been waiting for you ever since you went to lunch.'

Strange. It was Bailey's first day back at work and he hadn't told a soul.

'Give a name?'

'Ronnie someone. American accent, or maybe it was Canadian. I can never –'

'American, thanks.' Bailey knew exactly who it was, but what was he doing here? He turned and started walking towards the elevator.

'Hey, Bailey! What do I tell Mr Summers?'

'Tell him I've gone to get a haircut. Part of my new serious approach to the job, look the part, you know?'

'Bailey! That's not going to fly –'

Penelope's plea was cut off by the elevator doors.

Ronnie Johnson was sitting on a cracked leather sofa near the reception desk, reading a newspaper with an unlit cigar in his hand.

'Thought you'd given up on those things?'

'I have, bubba.' He stood up, towering over Bailey. 'Like a pretty blonde, I just like to hold one from time to time.'

During the almost three decades they'd known each other, they always started with banter.

'Yeah? When's the last time you held a blonde?'

'I only remember the cigars these days, bubba.' Ronnie grew up in Oklahoma and his thick southern accent had survived his intrepid lifestyle.

'Been a long time.' Guys like Ronnie Johnson didn't stop by just to say hello and Bailey was struggling with the old pals routine. 'What brings you to Sydney?'

'That all I get?' Ronnie looked offended and shoved his cigar into the corner of his mouth. 'Almost three years and all you can say is what're you doing here?'

'C'mon, Ronnie, don't get all sensitive on me. It's good to see you.'

'You too, bubba.' He clutched Bailey in a bear hug. At six feet four inches and weighing more than a hundred kilograms, Ronnie Johnson was a barrel of a man. His big hands were like catcher's mitts. When he gave you a hug, you felt it.

'Okay, big guy.' Bailey patted him on the back. 'Time to let go.'

Bailey didn't have many friends, other than Gerald. He and Ronnie had seen a lot together, most of it not good. Whatever the reason for his visit, it was good to see him.

'You're a long way from the action, Ronnie. Or have you finally given up on the Mid East?'

'You mean settled for the easier life, like you?'

It didn't feel so easy for Bailey. 'Could say that, but yeah, have you?'

'Let's not talk here. I presume you know somewhere quiet for a chat between two old buddies?'

The look in Ronnie's eyes gave him away.

'Friends can catch up anywhere, mate,' Bailey said. 'This really isn't a social visit, is it?'

'I don't want us to be seen together, bubba.'

'What is it with you?' Bailey was shaking his head. 'Whenever we see each other you've got trouble clinging to your shoe like chewing gum.'

Bailey started walking towards the elevator. 'My car's downstairs.'

'Your car? Please tell me you've upgraded from that old bomb you were driving when you picked me up at the airport for Gerald's sixtieth?'

'Same old bomb. And just like me it gets more interesting with age.'

Ronnie was still laughing when they stepped into the elevator, headed for the underground carpark.

—

When a CIA agent wants a quiet conversation, you don't take him to your favourite watering hole. Bailey drove them to The Duke in Kings Cross, a 24-hour bar that was popular with the late-night crowd and dead by day.

They sat down in a quiet booth in the corner, the kind

where hookers and drug dealers plied their trade in the early hours of the morning. Hopefully the cleaners had been in.

'Nice place, bubba.' Ronnie peeled a sodden beer coaster off the table.

'I wasn't about to introduce you to my local. I like it too much.' Bailey also didn't want to take Ronnie to a place where everyone – literally everyone – knew his name. Ronnie didn't need a rundown of Bailey's life for the past three years.

'This isn't your local?'

'Good one.' Bailey held up his glass of whisky to cheers Ronnie across the table.

Clink.

'Now, what are we talking about?

'Catherine Chamberlain.' Ronnie took a sip of his whisky. 'Or, Ruby Chambers. Not sure how much you know.'

Bailey put down his glass. 'You're kidding me, aren't you?'

'I'm not here to play games with you. This isn't just some dead hooker.'

'And why does the great and wonderful United States of America care so deeply about a dead Australian prostitute, apart from the fact that your new president is rumoured to have enjoyed a little party time –'

'I didn't vote for him.'

'Someone did, but let's not get off track. Why do you guys care about a prostitute who may, or may not, have killed herself?'

'She didn't kill herself. I think you know that.'

'Suspected as much,' Bailey said. 'Can we go back to my original question?'

Ronnie took a long drag of his single malt, emptying half of his two-finger pour, and placed his glass back on the table. Bailey followed the American's eyes as they darted from one corner to the next, surveying the room. Old habit. The place was empty, apart from the middle-aged barman studying the form guide, sipping from the beer he was hiding on a shelf under the cash register. The colour of his nose suggested that he'd been drinking too much of what he was selling.

'You know I can't go into the detail,' Ronnie said.

'Not good enough.' Bailey wasn't in the mood to mess around. It was mid-afternoon and he should have been drunk by now. He raised the tumbler to his lips until he could see the bottom of the glass, swallowed and waited for the warm sting to subside.

He held Ronnie's gaze across the table for a few seconds before opening his mouth again. 'For once, mate, I'd like you to tell me something that's not part of some grand charade, like half the bullshit you fed me in Baghdad.'

'I have a job to do too.'

'And you're very good at it.' Bailey held up his empty glass and tried to get the attention of the barman, who was busy staring at the television, dreaming about the thirty-to-one shot that was finally going to turn his luck.

'Don't make this personal, you grumpy old son of a bitch,' Ronnie said.

'Hey, who's getting personal? I just want to know why we're here. It wasn't my idea. And you want to know who's grumpy?' Bailey held up his phone, which was vibrating with Gerald's name lighting up on the screen. 'Gerald's sitting in a big leather chair staring at the hotel some rich prick built in front of his harbour view, wondering why I'm ignoring his calls.'

'Okay, okay.' Ronnie showed Bailey the palms of his big hands.

It was all an act, one that Bailey knew well. Ronnie knew exactly what he was going to divulge long before they'd walked across the sticky carpet at The Duke.

'Don't get me wrong,' Bailey said, 'I enjoy having a drink with you. We are, after all, old friends. Aren't we? It's just that I know you better than you'd care to admit. So, why don't you cut the shit and tell me what it is you want to get off your chest?'

'We're worried about an intelligence leak.' Ronnie ended the charade. 'More to the point, we suspect someone very senior in Canberra may be squeaking like a barn full of mice.'

'What does that have to do with Ruby Chambers – or Chamberlain – or whatever the hell we're calling her?'

'I'm not sure, bubba. I was hoping you might enlighten me on that score?'

'You think a washed-up journo who has barely written a story in three years would know more than the CIA? You guys really are losing your edge!'

Bailey was almost as good at playing the game. Almost.

'Don't toy with me. I'm being straight with you. I'd appreciate the same courtesy.'

'Straight? Yeah, if straight could turn a corner.' Bailey enjoyed holding the cards for a change. 'You still haven't told me what you're doing here?'

'I've told you, I want to talk about Ruby –'

'No, dummy,' Bailey said. 'What you're doing *here* – in Australia? Surely this is a job for your local people?'

'I am the local people, bubba. I've been working for the American ambassador on his security detail.'

Bailey laughed out loud at that one. 'Do you really expect me to believe that?'

A guy like Ronnie Johnson working on the ambassador's security detail was like the head chef waiting tables.

'Believe what you like. Us older fellas get planted in the embassies when they take us out of the main game. Iraq was it for me. My obsession. It all turned to shit after you left, bubba. Ruined my life, my marriage.'

Bailey nodded – the curse of Mesopotamia stayed with you. He had an ex-wife too.

'I spent almost eight years in and out of Baghdad after Bush's war, even tried a desk job at Langley,' Ronnie said. 'Sitting around analysing data wasn't for me so they sent me here.'

'I know what that place does to you.' Bailey didn't expect to be going down this path. 'You saw what it did to me. And I'm sorry for you. Believe me, I know.'

'Yeah, well, shit happens.'

'But do you seriously expect me to believe you're on the American ambassador's security detail?'

'Didn't have much choice, bubba. They talked about it as a promotion – like they could do with more experienced ops managing the security detail of our top people overseas. It's really a stepping stone to retirement. I never had the patience for the Ivy League geniuses at State and in the White House. They never listen.'

Maybe Ronnie was telling the truth. It was the foreign policy wonks that made a mess of the reconstruction in Iraq. They never understood the hate and the history. Bailey knew Ronnie Johnson would never last in a desk job alongside them.

'Anyway, bubba, they also know what that place did to me. You know better than anyone. We're all pawns on the ground, positioned to fit the narrative.'

Ronnie suddenly looked much older than the man Bailey had first met in 1989 at the scene of a bomb attack in Beirut. His eyes were missing the laser focus that would strike fear into anyone who found themselves sitting opposite him at a negotiating table. Bailey had seen that side of Ronnie in action.

'Yeah, I'll leave that to the historians. You and me – we're the here and now. If what you suspect is true, it doesn't sound like you're retiring just yet.'

'I didn't expect to get drawn back this far into the game either, and it's changed. New tactics, different players.' Ronnie paused. 'Anyway, what can you give me? I need to get moving.'

Bailey paused for a moment, distracted by the vibration of his phone. Gerald again. He didn't answer.

'Bailey?'

Swapping notes with the CIA carried great risks, ethical and professional. The trick for Bailey was to give with a guarantee that he would get something back. Everyone liked the power of telling a secret. The problem for Bailey was that he didn't have much to barter.

'I don't know what to say, Ronnie. The first time I heard the name Catherine Chamberlain was about eight hours ago when I was staring at her body.'

Ronnie sat back and folded his arms without saying a word.

Pretend you have nothing, then give him something. The game.

'There's one lead that I'm looking into but, as yet, no luck,' Bailey said.

'Yeah? And what might that be?' Ronnie's grey bushy eyebrows were pointing at the ceiling like the blunt tip of an arrow.

'Michael Anderson.'

'And?' Ronnie said.

'That was your cue to tell me what you know about him.'

'Nice try, Bailey.' When it came to the game, Ronnie could still run rings around anyone. 'I know about Michael Anderson. What have you got?'

Bailey gave up playing and decided to show his hand. 'Well, it appears that Anderson knew our Catherine Chamberlain, knew her in a way that'd make it okay to drop around at midnight pissed as a parrot.'

'We're talking the night in question?'

'Possibly. That's all I know.'

'That fits.' Ronnie stood up to leave.

'Fits what?'

Ronnie ignored Bailey's question and shrugged on his jacket.

'Fits what?' Bailey raised his voice.

'I presume you know our friend Michael Anderson is missing?'

'Since the night he dropped in for a late-night cuddle at Chamberlain's house?'

'You tell me.'

'That's the first question. Aren't we still talking?'

'Don't worry, bubba, we'll talk again soon.' Ronnie winked and started walking towards the door.

'No doubt,' Bailey said. 'And Ronnie?'

Ronnie stopped and turned around. 'Yeah?'

'What happened to paying for the drinks? I'm used to you turning up with a duffle bag filled with greenbacks!'

'Good one, bubba. Time heals, huh?'

'Sure.'

The awkward smile on Bailey's face was gone before Ronnie had even reached the door. Time didn't heal everything.

—

Bailey decided against going back to the office.

He reached into his bag and pulled out the laptop that Penelope had given him. He would tap out ten pars and send them to Frank on the subs desk.

First, he needed another drink.

'Oi! Mate!' Bailey gave up on waiting for the barman to spot his empty glass. 'Get me another double, would you?'

The barman waited for the race to finish before he turned in Bailey's direction. 'Same again?'

Bailey gave him a thumbs up.

'Any luck on the ponies?' Bailey asked when the barman finally came over with his whisky.

'Nah. Got any mail?'

Asking for tips from a stranger, this guy had a problem. By the fraying collar of his stained white shirt and the plastic shine on his trousers, he wasn't good at hiding it, either.

'Yeah, I've got a tip for you,' Bailey said. 'Don't bet.'

'So they keep telling me. Presume you'll want another one of those shortly?' He pointed at the glass he had just deposited on the table.

'You guessed right.'

'Looks like we both have our demons then, hey mate?'

There was a lot about this guy not to like.

'Looks like it.' Bailey skolled his drink and handed the man the glass. 'The same.'

He switched on his laptop. Better start typing while he could still see the keys. That window was closing, fast.

There wasn't much of a story today. A high-class prostitute named Catherine Chamberlain is found dead in a Rushcutters Bay apartment. Police are investigating.

Time for another drink.

CHAPTER 5

Bailey knew it was a bad idea from the moment he staggered into his car parked out front of The Duke. It must have been Ronnie's reference to his ex-wife that planted the seed.

With each whisky he drank, the better the idea became. Anyway, it was too late now.

He knocked on the front door of his ex-wife Anthea's posh house in Hunters Hill, which was actually more like a castle. Surrounded by immaculately kept lawns, a tennis court and lush English gardens, it was the type of estate you'd expect to find in the countryside, not ten kilometres from the city centre.

The mansions were lined side by side around here, with his and hers Mercedes parked in double garages, street after street. Anthea and her husband, Ian, had the pick of them.

Luckily, it was Anthea who opened the door.

'John?' She was the only person who never called him Bailey.

He was swaying on his feet and squinting at the bright sensor light on the balcony. 'I'm sorry, sweetheart. I was just in the neighbourhood and I –'

'My God. How many drinks have you had?'

She leaned back, probably trying to escape the alcohol on his breath.

'Enough to be able to read that expression on your face.' He was also painfully aware that he was slurring his speech. 'But not enough to have forgotten it by tomorrow.'

His timing was always off with Anthea.

She stepped onto the porch and closed the door behind her. 'Seriously, you can't be here. We've got people coming over shortly. You know how Ian gets.'

He knew all about Ian, the bloke who had rescued his wife after her divorce from the man who could never grow up. Fifteen years older than Anthea and filthy rich, he may as well have had the word *safe* tattooed to his forehead. Yeah, Ian was a saint.

'How is old Ian and the philanthropic world of merchant banking?' Bailey regretted the words as soon as he heard them slur from his mouth.

'Don't be a condescending prick, John. At least he's here.'

Bailey also had an uncanny ability to get under her skin.

'I deserved that.' He was speaking slowly now, trying to sound sober. 'Sorry.'

'No, you're not. Now, why're you here?'

'You're the doctor, you tell me.' He was teasing her, trying to invoke memories of happier days when he would call her 'doctor' in recognition of her PhD in history.

'Yeah, yeah. If I'd been a shrink, I would've given up trying to psychoanalyse you years ago. Trying to understand what goes on in that impenetrable fortress you call a brain is like trying to explain the origins of the universe to a Catholic.'

Bailey started laughing. He loved how she could make him laugh, even when she was angry.

Anthea's lips widened with her smile. She had never managed to stay mad at him for long.

'Anyway,' she said, 'I'm going back inside. We really do have people coming around, so, unless there's something important you want to discuss, I think you should go.' She turned and reached for the door.

'Anthea!' Bailey suddenly remembered why he'd come. 'I went back to work today.' He sounded like a child telling his mother he had been a good boy at school.

She let go of the door. 'Really?'

'Don't look so surprised!'

'I'm not,' she said. 'I'm just happy for you.'

Anthea had seen him at his lowest, heard his screams in the night, then watched him try to silence his demons with the bottle. He knew that she had wanted to help him, even after the divorce. But the thing about John Bailey is that he didn't want, or need, anyone's help.

'Step one.' He shrugged. 'Haven't quite mastered the other steps yet.'

'Anthea darling!' Ian's voice echoed from inside the house. 'Who's there?'

Anthea turned around and poked her head through the crack in the door. She was dressed in a singlet and a pair of skin-tight pants that highlighted her sporty physique.

'Wow, Anthea,' Bailey said, 'that yoga routine's paying off.'

'Oh, shut up.' She turned around with a smirk on her face. 'Don't give Ian another excuse to punch you.'

'It's just Cheryl from across the road,' she called back to her husband. 'I'm giving her my hummus recipe!'

'Okay, darling. Please hurry and get ready – they'll be here any minute!'

Bailey raised his eyebrows. 'Hummus?'

'Oh piss off, will you. It's all I could think of. It's great about your work. Really, I mean it. But it's time to go.'

Anthea stepped over to Bailey and hugged him. There was still love there, not just because of Miranda, but because they genuinely liked each other. They'd married when they were both twenty-two and their daughter had arrived the next year. Anthea knew him in a way that no one else could. It was why he had wanted to tell her he was working again.

She took a step back and stared at him.

'I'm not angry with you,' she whispered in his ear. 'You know that, right?'

'Yeah.' This was a hard truth for Bailey, because she should be. He had left her alone to raise Miranda. No job was that important. It hadn't felt that way at the time though. Clinton had managed to get Yasser Arafat and Yitzhak Rabin to shake hands at the White House. Peace was finally coming to the Holy Land. Bailey had to be in Jerusalem to cover the story.

'And I'm not judging you – really, I'm not. But you need to get off the booze.'

'Yeah – work one day, booze another. Baby steps.'

Anthea touched his shoulder gently and went back inside.

Standing on the steps in the dark, Bailey felt lonely. He stood there for at least a minute after the click of the front door, listening to the sounds of domesticity inside, before heading off down the street. He looked at his watch – it was only eight o'clock, too early to go home, especially for someone who didn't sleep. There was only one place left to go – the place where no one ever judged him, not to his face, anyway. He was going to his local.

CHAPTER 6

Iraq, unknown location, 2004

Click.

Bailey's eyes had been glued closed by a mixture of sweat and dust. He was too disorientated to force them open, not ready to confront the reality of being a prisoner in this sea of sand and hate.

Click. Click.

He was tied to a hard wood chair inside a dark humid room. The air was so stale he could taste each anxious breath that rushed into his lungs like a punch to the chest.

Click. Click.

'Mr Bailey . . . Mr Bailey . . . Mr Bailey.'

The man clicking his fingers was speaking calmly in Bailey's face. He could smell the stench of forgotten gums in the warmth of his breath.

'Welcome, Mr Bailey. You are our special guest.'

His accent was like that of the Oxbridge elite – posh and refined, but frightening. What was it doing here?

Bailey feared he had been blinded until finally his eyelids won the battle against the blood and dirt and peeled open.

All he could see was darkness. He tried to speak but his throat was so dry that it hurt to swallow.

'Here.' The man passed him a cup of water. 'Drink. It must have been many hours since you last had any water or sustenance.'

Bailey tried to take the cup but his hands were tied to the arms of the chair.

'I'll help you.' The man held the cup to Bailey's lips and poured.

The water felt like sandpaper, scraping down Bailey's throat, but he kept swallowing, desperate to get the precious liquid inside. Water was the only thing that mattered.

The sting of dehydration began to wane and was replaced by a rising panic. Then anger. His wrists and ankles were aching. The rope, or whatever had been used to restrain him, was cutting into his skin. A wave of pain shuddered through his body. The bruising in his torso, his right shoulder, the pulsating headache and the constant ringing in his ears. The explosion in Fallujah. The man with the piercing eyes. It was all coming back to him.

Fuck!

'Where am I?'

'That is not important right now.'

'Who the fuck are you and what the fuck am I doing here?' Stockholm syndrome was never going to be an issue for Bailey. He'd stopped caring long ago.

'Now, now. Is that wise, Mr Bailey?' The man's voice was disturbingly calm.

A lamp in the corner of the room was the only source of light and the man was hovering over Bailey like a shadow, close without touching. The darkness made it difficult to distinguish the features of his face, other than his eyes – large, soft and almost comforting, were it not for the circumstances.

Bailey's sight was adjusting. He peered over his shoulder to survey the room. It was more like a cave. In the corner, next to the lamp, a camera was fixed to a tripod.

'No fucking way!' he said to his captor. 'No way!'

'This is an entirely natural reaction, Mr Bailey.' The man knelt down in front of where Bailey was sitting, strapped to the chair. 'Perhaps not so wise. You see, I'm your new best friend. And we can be friends, can't we?'

Bailey was bouncing up and down on his chair, trying to break free.

'Just kill me, arsehole.'

'No, no, no. That's not why you're here, Mr Bailey.'

Bailey had never felt so helpless. His captor had absolute control.

'We don't see you like them – the Americans, that is. You're a respected journalist. You may not believe this, but we have many mutual friends.'

Bailey could see the off-white of the man's teeth through his smile. 'I doubt it.' He could count his friends on one hand. 'I'm not into your games. And that video recorder, no way, no fucking way.'

Bailey was in shock. He was so dehydrated that his tear

ducts couldn't spill the water that would ordinarily have come with terror. Ignoring the pain, he jolted the chair up and down again, trying to free his wrists and ankles from his restraints. It was no use.

'Calm down, Mr Bailey.'

'Stop talking!' The man's calm voice and smooth accent was distressing Bailey more than the room, the heat, even the camera in the corner. The educated fundamentalist was the worst kind, someone who has studied and arrived at an irrational end where violent intolerance, and killing, was found to be God's work – the sacred path.

There was no reasoning with this man. He had a plan for Bailey and there was nothing he could do to change it.

'Bring him in!' The man shifted his focus towards the darkened corner of the room.

An overweight man, dressed in black with a dark bushy beard, came through the door. He was holding the arm of a skeletal figure – head down, feet dragging – leading him across the room. Bailey could see that the figure's wrists and ankles were shackled. He could hear the metal restraints clanking together.

'Over there.' The man in front of Bailey climbed off his knees, pointing to the camera in the corner.

The captive was directed to sit and the man in black switched on the camera. The prisoner's head and face were cleanly shaven. He looked gaunt, like he hadn't eaten a proper meal in months. He turned his head to the side, squinting and troubled by the light.

'This day has regrettably arrived, Douglas.' The man was standing behind Bailey.

Douglas McKenzie.

The US soldier who had been kidnapped in Mosul six months ago, presumed dead.

'Today, you must give the message you have been practising, now that you see the injustice of what your country is doing.'

McKenzie, hopeless and weak, nodded his head.

'You can't do this, you fucking barbarians!' Bailey shouted.

'Please, Mr Bailey. Such foul language from an educated fellow like yourself.'

Bailey had volumes of bloody images reluctantly stashed in his brain, but he'd never witnessed an execution. 'Don't do it. Don't! This isn't how you get what you want!'

'Enough!' The calm, polite tone of his captor's voice was gone. 'You're here as an observer, Mr Bailey. Don't make me change my mind.'

Nausea climbed from Bailey's stomach into his chest and throat, burning acid that made him gag. He closed his eyes, not wanting to be in the room. Not wanting to see what they wanted him to see.

'Go on, Douglas ... we're recording.' The man behind Bailey instructed the shell of a man on the other side of the room.

'The United States ...' Weak and despondent, McKenzie faltered as he began to speak. 'The United States —'

'Don't do it!' Bailey shouted at him.

'The United States and its allies have the blood of the innocents on their hands. Women ... children ... ordinary Iraqis ... wanting to lead a pure life, free of the decadence of western culture.'

McKenzie sounded like someone who had given up on life a long time ago, alone in the horror they had prepared for him.

'I know now, Mr President. We came in the name of freedom, but it's that very freedom ... we're depriving. I now know the wicked ways –'

'Don't do it!' Bailey couldn't listen any more. He yelled for McKenzie to stop. 'They'll kill you anyway! Don't do it! Don't –'

He was silenced by a punch to the stomach that forced the wind from his lungs. Just as he tried to take a breath, gaffer tape was slapped on his chin, across his lips and around the back of his head, round and round until he could no longer make a sound.

'It's America that's doing wrong here ...' McKenzie's vacant, faltering declaration continued. 'And I pray to God for forgiveness ...'

Bailey had closed his eyes, hoping the darkness would switch off the noise.

'Do you hear him?' the man whispered in Bailey's ear. 'You can close your eyes, John Bailey, but you can hear him. He knows the wrongs of his people. He knows what they have done. What he has done. He understands now, and he will pay a very high price.'

The room fell silent. Maybe Bailey's wish to numb his senses had worked.

'Watch!' Someone was clawing at his eyelids, forcing them open.

He tried to look away, but he couldn't. The man in black shoved a blade into McKenzie's neck. Small like a kitchen knife, sharp enough to eventually kill him. McKenzie had enough time to scream, but all he could manage was a sickening gurgling sound.

—

Bailey sat up in bed, woken by a vibration somewhere in his room, sweat streaming down his face and stinging his eyes. An empty bottle of whisky was dumped, clumsily, on the bedside table.

He let out a deep sigh and turned his body until his feet hit the floor.

Fucking Fallujah.

Bailey recognised the vibrating noise – his phone. He walked around the room, trying to get a sense of where the sound was coming from. His pants.

Just as he reached into his pocket the phone stopped. He looked at the screen – twelve missed calls from the same number. A number he didn't recognise. The phone started vibrating again.

'Yeah?' His voice was husky from the whisky.

'John Bailey?'

He didn't recognise the voice. 'Yeah.'

'It's Michael Anderson. We need to meet.'

'Who?'

'Michael Anderson.'

Michael Anderson. Michael Anderson. Bailey knew the name but his brain was struggling to process information. Whisky will do that.

'I want to talk to you about Catherine Chamberlain.'

Michael Anderson.

Bailey was wide awake now and the rush of adrenalin helped his brain to catch up. 'I'm listening.'

'Not on the phone.'

'Mate . . .' Bailey swallowed. His throat was so dry that he was struggling to speak. 'Mate, I don't even know you.'

'Yeah, well, you're just going to have to take that chance.'

'Why?'

'Because someone is setting me up ... because I know things.'

'What things?'

'You're just going to have to trust me.'

Bailey rubbed his eyes with the palm of his hand. Fuck it.

'Okay, when?'

'Now. Palm Beach. South end, near the pool. Park your car there. I'll find you.'

'Palm Beach?' Bailey looked at his watch, it was just after two o'clock. 'I'm in the east. It's going to take me a while.'

'Shouldn't be more than an hour at this time. See you soon.'

Anderson hung up.

Bailey put on his pants, grabbed yesterday's shirt and rummaged around on the floor in the dark until he found his car keys. He wasn't in great shape to get behind the wheel. But this guy had a story to tell and Bailey wanted to hear it.

CHAPTER 7

Sydney, Wednesday

Palm Beach was a good place to hide out in autumn. More than half of the houses nestled in the bushy hills were holiday homes, so when the cooler months arrived only the permanent residents remained.

The locals were a private bunch. Half of them were families who had been there since the days when Barrenjoey Road was still a dirt track. The rest were either running from the city hustle or eastern suburbs yuppies who just had to have a weekender.

Bailey didn't know anyone who owned a holiday house at Palm Beach, but he knew the place well from the days when his parents would take him and his younger brother, Mike, there as kids. Sometimes, they would take a ride on a seaplane and, afterwards, the boys would chase crabs on the rocks and eat fish and chips by the ferry. Good times, happy memories.

The boys were everything to Ros and Jack Bailey. John didn't make it easy for them. He was the wild one, always in trouble at school. Fist fights in the playground, chasing girls, drinking and smoking marijuana. Bailey had infuriated his father when he decided against going to university and instead slung a rucksack over his shoulder and headed overseas for an adventure. He loved watching and experiencing the world beyond the one that he knew. It was why he became a journalist.

Mike was only a year younger than Bailey and, even though they did most things together, somehow Mike had kept out of trouble. When he wasn't surfing, he was playing rugby or studying. He was humble, and everyone, including his teachers, would say that he was destined to do something special with his life.

Mike had gotten into medicine at Sydney University and was out celebrating with his mates when their car lost control and hit a tree on a winding stretch of Mona Vale Road on the northern beaches, not far from the cemetery where he lies today. Three of the boys died instantly. Mike had hung on for two weeks. Bailey was working in a bar in Lagos when he heard the news. He came home in time to watch his brother die in hospital.

It had been almost an hour since Bailey had left Paddington headed for Palm Beach. He knew that he was getting close to the rendezvous point with Anderson when the traffic lights disappeared and Barrenjoey Road narrowed and started to wind through thick bushland along the edge of the Pittwater.

Driving past the ferry wharf, Bailey couldn't stop thinking about Mike. Kicking a footy on Concord Oval after watching the Waratahs take down the Reds, and later, sharing their dreams about one day being good enough to wear a blue rugby jersey in that stadium. For thirty years Bailey had lived without his best mate, the guy who'd understood him, the one person whose advice he'd listen to. Maybe Bailey wouldn't have been such a selfish bastard had his little brother not been ripped out of his life when he was still figuring out how to be a man.

Bailey rounded the bend past the golf course on the surf side of the peninsula. He could hear the crunching waves of the Pacific smashing into the sandbank. The street lamps were dangling along the beachfront, beaming an orange mist of sea spray across the road.

He kept driving until he reached the dead end at the southern end of the beach that the locals called kiddies corner, and parked beneath one of the giant pine trees that lined the sand.

Bailey looked out the window. It was a clear night and, away from the smog of the city, the stars were burning brightly. The beach was empty, which wasn't a surprise given it was three o'clock in the morning. This end of the beach was protected from the wind, and the sea was still, with only the slightest breeze licking the tops of the small waves that rocked into the little cove.

He got out of his car and walked towards the rocks by the pool.

There was no point looking for Anderson. He would find Bailey.

It didn't take long. His phone vibrated – a text message.

Turn around and walk up the path behind you.

Bailey did as he was told. A street lamp showed the way to the start of a pathway that wound up the hill away from the beach and into darkness. He started walking, his eyes slowly adjusting to the night. Aided by the shimmer of the moonlight, he weaved around the branches reaching across the track.

'Bailey!' A loud whisper. 'Over here.'

A man wearing jeans, a hooded sweater and a baseball cap stepped out from behind a bush and into the moonlight. As he drew closer, Bailey noticed the stubble on his chin.

'Long way to come for a quiet chat.' Bailey extended his hand and Anderson shook it.

'Had to be this way.' He sounded more nervous than on the phone. 'I saw your article online last night and remembered your Iraq reports. Thought I could trust a bloke like you.'

'You can.' The compliment made Bailey rue the three years he had wasted. It didn't matter because he was back at work. One day down. 'Let's talk.'

'How much do you know?' Anderson asked. 'I presume it's more than I read online.'

'I always know more than I write. But you first.'

Bailey had driven a long way in the middle of the night and he wasn't about to risk not getting anything for his trouble.

'Okay.'

'I'm listening.' Bailey was surprised by how easy this was, although it was Anderson who had requested the meeting.

'Catherine was murdered and I . . .' He paused.

'Take your time, mate.'

'I think it . . . I think it was because of me.'

'Why do you think that?'

'I'd been seeing her. Started as a call girl thing,' Anderson said. 'You know what it's like in a job like mine – no time for real life.'

'Not really.' Bailey instantly regretted sounding judgmental.

Anderson didn't seem to care. 'She told me to stop calling her Ruby Chambers, call her Catherine, and stop paying for visits. I wouldn't call it your conventional relationship.'

That's one way of describing it, thought Bailey. But he kept his mouth shut this time.

'For the past six months we went out from time to time. It wasn't always about the sex, either.'

Bailey felt like a priest in the confessional and he was becoming irritable as he sobered up. 'This is all interesting to know but –'

'Wait.' Anderson held up his hand. 'It's important for what happened next.'

'Which was?'

'Work stuff. Gary Page – he's not all he seems to be.'

'You mean an arrogant politician who's had a lick of the power lolly and wants his own candy store?'

Anderson laughed. 'Funny. Not untrue, either. Page is a very powerful man within the party. He's also an ideologue. A man wedded to ideas.'

'I know what it means.'

'Sorry. Just trying to make the point that it's not just about power for Page. He's not one of those MPs who just wants to be prime minister.'

'I've never met one who didn't – and I've met a lot.' Bailey also struggled to recall a politician that he liked. 'But you know him better than I do.'

'Page had been disappearing for regular meetings that he wouldn't tell me anything about, the type of meetings that didn't get recorded in his diary.'

'Know who with?'

'I'm getting to that.' Anderson stepped closer. 'I knew he was meeting with someone off the grid, not uncommon for a senior minister. It could be polling stuff, cabinet reshuffles – who's in and who's on the nose inside the party. I didn't ever question him. Then one day after we'd knocked off the best part of a bottle of scotch in his office, he asks me what I think about allowing Chinese military exercises up in the Northern Territory, a permanent rotation to let them build support infrastructure to regularly move in and out.'

'Boots on the ground? A permanent presence? Seems odd to me.'

'Odd's an understatement. We're already copping shit from the Americans about leasing the Darwin Port to a company linked to Chinese Defence, given we'll soon have two and a half thousand American marines training up there as part of a deal we struck with Washington.'

Anderson was good on the detail.

'So, what'd you say?'

'I thought he was joking! We're America's little brother in the region. An agreement like that would severely damage our relationship with the United States and send a fairly blunt signal about where our future priorities might lie.'

'I'd say that would be a fair interpretation.'

'Page wasn't laughing. He said I needed to think about the geopolitics of the Asian century, and how Australia fitted in.'

'What happened next?'

'Not much, really.' Anderson shrugged. 'Never mentioned it again.'

'I don't get it. How does Ruby – I mean Catherine Chamberlain – fit in? And you haven't got to these secret meetings yet. Off the grid or not, it doesn't mean anything unless you know who these people are.'

'Person – singular,' Anderson said. 'The Chinese Ambassador, Li Chen.'

'Okay, now you've got my attention.' This really was worth the two-hour round trip in the middle of the night. 'Go on.'

'Six private meetings in four months, and they're the ones I know about.'

'And?'

'Since when does a defence minister meet with an ambassador without the knowledge of the PMO?'

'Not often, I'd imagine.' Official meetings are always recorded and sanctioned by the Prime Minister's Office. Bailey had sifted through enough Freedom of Information documents to understand the protocols.

'Never.'

'What about Catherine Chamberlain?'

'She's the only person . . .' Anderson's voice changed whenever the discussion turned back to his dead girlfriend. 'She . . . she was the only one I told about this.'

'What'd you tell her?'

'And now she's gone.'

Bailey could see that he was losing him.

'It wasn't your fault, mate.' He tried to sound supportive, but he needed more information. 'What'd you tell her?'

'Sorry.' Anderson's cheeks were glistening. He wiped his nose with the back of his hand. 'This isn't easy for me.'

'It's okay, mate, take your time.'

Anderson turned his back on Bailey to collect himself. They'd stepped off the track and were standing beside a thick bush that had been clipped back to keep the path clear.

'Meeting with Li was one thing,' Anderson said. 'But hearing Page sound off about military exercises and the Asian century – I had to tell someone. I had to say it out aloud, just to check that it was as crazy as it sounded in my head!'

He paused again, this time to look up at the stars.

'This next bit's off the record. Actually, all this is off the record.' He turned back to Bailey. 'I just wanted to tell you in case anything happens to me.'

'I'm in no hurry to print any of this.' Bailey knew that he didn't have a story. It couldn't just be Anderson's word against the world.

'I presume you know your boss dropped me at Catherine's flat?'

'Yep. We talk, from time to time.' Bailey couldn't resist having a dig at Gerald, even though he was tucked up in bed with Nancy.

'We were at the consul-general's house in Bellevue Hill and Page pulls me aside, tells me I'm fired.'

'He sacked you?'

'As good as.'

'On what grounds?'

'He said I'd been talking too much. Tells me to take some leave and consider my position.'

'Say anything else?'

'Just that he couldn't trust me and that I didn't understand the future. So I'm thinking, is this guy bugging me? I mean, I hadn't told a soul. Not one person! Other than Catherine, this stuff had been inside the vault.'

'And then I thought, no.' Anderson was shaking his head. 'He couldn't have put a tap on me. No way – too risky. It had to be the Chinese.'

'This is all pretty speculative, mate.'

'Yeah, I thought so too. Then Catherine turns up dead and my house has been turned over like a bomb's hit it!'

'When?'

'Not sure, exactly. I'm guessing it must have been at some point that night.'

'You didn't go home?'

Bailey was quick with his questions, leaving no time for Anderson to think about what to hold back.

'No, not straight away. I walked up to the Cross, had a few more drinks. When I eventually made it home, the sun was coming up. After I saw the mess, I grabbed what I could and cleared out in case they came back looking for me.'

Bailey was still unclear about the *they*.

'What're you going to do now?'

'What do you mean? Until the police realise I was the last person to try to see Catherine and put out a warrant for my arrest?'

'I was getting to that. I would've been a bit more subtle.'

But Bailey didn't think Anderson was a killer. Other than that, he didn't know what to believe.

There was a noise in the bushes that made both of them shudder.

'Probably just a possum.'

Possum or not, Anderson looked like he was readying to leave.

'I'm staying out of sight, but you'll hear from me again. The people who messed up my house were looking for something – something that will bring Page down.'

'Something that'll back this theory of yours?'

'Documents.'

'Any chance you were planning on passing them to me?'

'Sorry, Bailey. That information stays with me – for now.'

'Then what am I doing here?'

'I wanted to meet you. Decide if I could trust you.'

'And?'

'I've got to go.' Anderson started walking up the hill.

'When will I hear from you?'

'I'll contact you when I need to.' He stopped on the track. 'And Bailey?'

'Yeah?'

'I didn't even see Catherine that night. I'm sure the autopsy will point to it as the night she was killed. She wouldn't let me in. Too drunk, she'd said.'

'That's going to be difficult to prove.' Especially if Anderson was seen going into the building. But Bailey didn't want to tell him something he already knew.

Anderson walked back so that he was standing face to face with Bailey.

'Maybe. I sat on her buzzer, talking into the intercom, trying to get her to open the door.'

'And?'

'She wouldn't. So I kept hitting random buttons until, finally, someone let me in.'

'Then what'd you do?'

'Banged on her front door. She refused to open it. Told me to go home.' Anderson's voice was quivering again. 'Something wasn't right . . . I never should have left her.'

'What do you mean?'

'I heard a male voice inside. I know what you're going to say – could've been a client. But I'm the only one she let into her home. She was a pretty girl – she wasn't stupid. Someone else was there. That's who the cops should be looking for.'

'Let's hope they work that bit out for themselves.' Bailey was thinking about Dexter.

'Yeah. Let's hope.'

Anderson walked up the path and into the darkness.

CHAPTER 8

Bailey's phone was flashing and vibrating on the table beside his bed. It was the sixth call that woke him. When he saw the name on the screen, he knew he had to answer.

'Gerald.' Bailey's voice sounded like a car skidding on a dirt road.

'Bailey! Where the fuck have you been and why haven't you been returning my fucking phone calls?' Gerald abhorred foul language. The fact that he had sworn – twice – left Bailey in no doubt that he was furious.

'I can explain, mate –'

'Don't you fucking *mate* me!'

Three.

Gerald wasn't interested in Bailey's excuses.

'Gerald, calm down.' Bailey instantly regretted trying to appease him. Don't poke the beast.

'Don't you fucking tell me to calm down!'

Four.

Bailey's throat was dry, he had a throbbing headache and Gerald's voice was pounding his brain like a boxer.

'I've been trying to speak to you ever since you disappeared yesterday afternoon – and what is Ronnie Johnson doing in Sydney? I need to know what's going on, and I need to know *now*!'

'Okay.' Hangover or not, there was no avoiding Gerald this morning. 'We can't talk on the phone.'

'I know,' Gerald said. 'I'm standing outside your front door. Let me in.'

It was seven o'clock in the morning. Bailey had managed to sleep for another couple of hours after the long drive back from Palm Beach.

He grabbed the empty bottle of whisky from his bedside table and dropped it in the garbage on his way to the front door. Gerald didn't need to know everything about last night.

'Good morning.'

Gerald charged past Bailey and into the house without saying a word. He was walking from room to room, a manic look on his face, as if he was searching for something. Or someone.

'Gerald? What are you doing?'

'Not here.' He was flustered. 'Get some clothes on. We're going out.'

Bailey looked down at his bare chest and the comfort layer concealing his six-pack. At least he was wearing boxer shorts. 'Give me a minute.' He disappeared into his bedroom to throw on some clothes.

Gerald was in a hurry. He marched out of Bailey's house, almost knocking over the tired, dehydrated fern in a pot by the front door, and up the street. Bailey trailed after him, squinting and rubbing his eyes, adapting to the morning light.

The traffic started early in Sydney and a steady stream of cars was flowing down Oxford Street. The smell of freshly ground coffee was wafting from nearby cafés, their machines already humming to cater for the morning rush. It was a work day and, apart from a few random hipsters staggering home from a night out, most of the foot traffic belonged to the bankers and lawyers racing to be the first good soldier at work.

A stroll in the cool morning air should have been good for Bailey's hangover. But he didn't need exercise, he needed sleep, and the smell of coffee was taunting him.

'C'mon, Gerald.' Bailey was struggling to keep pace. 'Are you going to say something?'

Gerald was looking over his shoulder, nervously, as he led them up the street towards Centennial Park. When they reached the gates, he gestured for Bailey to walk in first. Always the gentleman.

'What were you doing back at my place?' Bailey tried a different tack.

'I don't know what we're getting into, but it's something . . . something big.'

He steered them away from the early birds exercising on the jogging track and onto the lush grass towards the cover of the evergreen oaks and Australian fig trees that towered throughout the park.

The cold morning dew was seeping into Bailey's shoes and dampening his socks, adding to his discomfort. 'I could've told you that back at my place over a bloody coffee!'

Gerald stopped by the trees. 'I was checking your house to see that you didn't have company. God knows, you often do!'

Bailey didn't bother responding to that one. He couldn't deny it. The only constants in his dysfunctional life were women and booze.

'And stop asking questions,' Gerald said. 'You'll get your turn.'

Gerald's beige trenchcoat was buttoned so that the top of his blue tie and white shirt could be seen beneath. No matter what time of day, he was always dressed like he was headed somewhere important. But he looked even more rattled than the day before – so Bailey waited.

Eventually, Gerald took off his glasses and massaged the corners of his eyes. 'The police commissioner dropped by my house last night.'

'He *what*?'

'Around ten o'clock,' Gerald said. 'Rude prick rang the doorbell and woke Nancy.'

'He's off the Christmas card list, like me, I presume?'

'Nancy loves you, Bailey, you know that.' Gerald was calming down. 'She just doesn't trust you.'

'Smart woman. I've always said it.'

'Anyway, Davis wanted privacy, said he had something important to tell me. So I pour two glasses of whisky and we sit in the study.'

'I think I know where this is going,' Bailey said.

'Probably. But let me finish.'

'Go on, then.'

'He starts asking me questions. What do we know about the Catherine Chamberlain case? Who've we spoken to? Have the neighbours told us anything about what they saw?'

'Isn't that what the cops are supposed to be doing?'

'That's what I said, but Davis laughed it off, said he knows how thorough reporters can be. He suggested we should share information from time to time.'

'Eh?'

'Then he goes on this weird tangent.' There was no one within a hundred metres of where they were standing amongst the trees, but Gerald had lowered his voice to a whisper. '"Gerald," he says, "I want to share something with you. I want to tell you – off the record – that I'm going to be running for the seat of Grayndler in a by-election later this year –"'

'Why's he telling you?'

'No idea.'

'Isn't that Doug Smith's seat?' Politics wasn't Bailey's thing, but he knew enough. 'I didn't even know he was standing down. I guess he must be in his seventies now.'

'Doesn't matter. It's the blue-collar heartland and Davis is assured the win if he gets preselected. Good story too, although we can't print it yet.'

Bailey's eyes wandered to the morning mist drifting across the lake in the middle of the park. He could just make out a parade of ducks waddling across the road, forcing a fluorescent peloton of lycra-clad cyclists to stop. Everyone was into cycling, it seemed. Bailey smirked at the thought of the rounding middle-aged men sitting around in their matching spandex, sipping coffee after barely raising a sweat on their minted bicycles.

'Bailey! Are you even listening to me?' Gerald was clicking his fingers.

'No offence, but is this why you got me out of bed?' Bailey said.

Gerald sighed. 'No, dummy, there's more. I also expect you have a few stories of your own, or you wouldn't have been screening my bloody calls for most of yesterday.'

'When you're done delivering *War and Peace*.'

Gerald ignored the jibe. 'Davis tells me he's already started raising money for his campaign and that, with Gary Page's help, he's going to pick up one of the safest Labor seats in Sydney.'

'Okay, Page's involved, it's getting more interesting.'

'He wouldn't tell me much more. We all know Page is the numbers man for the New South Wales left faction, and Grayndler falls into that category.'

'And?'

'Just when I thought he was about to leave, he asks whether we – *The Journal* – had had any contact with Michael Anderson.'

'What'd you say?'

'Of course not! But what do I know? I'm just the editor. Are you about to tell me something different?'

'And why would you think that?'

'Because David Davis asked me whether I'd spoken to you recently, and whether you had been speaking to Anderson.'

Gerald was pointing his finger at Bailey as he spoke. 'It was a direct question. Why would he ask me that?'

'Let's back up a minute. Why would Davis directly connect Anderson to Catherine Chamberlain in a conversation with you? He must've been talking with Page.'

'I'm getting to that –'

'What did you say about me?' Bailey could see that Gerald had had enough of the interruptions.

'I told him that neither of us had heard from Anderson.'

'Good answer.'

'He tells me that if we do hear from Anderson, we'd better pass that information on to the police immediately.'

'Give a reason?'

'They're preparing to charge him with murder. Davis said he was happy to give us the jump on the story – a downpayment, he called it, for later.' Gerald looked like he felt grubby repeating the words. 'They're releasing a statement in an hour.'

It was Bailey's turn now.

'That's why Davis decided to pay a visit to your house – he wants you to print it. Anderson was expecting as much.'

'So, you have spoken with him?'

Bailey was thumbing through his phone until he had *The Journal*'s website open. Michael Anderson's photo was on the front page – 'Wanted for Murder'. There was no byline on the story.

'Who'd you get to write it?'

'I wrote it. I told you I wanted you on this, so I left my name off it. I didn't want to confuse our readers, or your sources.'

'Fair enough.'

'Which brings me back to Anderson. When did you speak to him?'

'Last night – actually, only a few hours ago.' Trust was the bedrock of Bailey's relationship with Gerald, he wouldn't hold anything back. 'Met him up at Palm Beach. The guy's scared shitless.'

'You've been busy.'

'Too busy.'

'Yeah, well, it's about time.'

'There's so much we don't know. Anderson's got some theories that, if true, will destroy the careers and lives of many people.'

'What'd he say?'

Bailey recounted Anderson's theories about Gary Page and his secret meetings with Ambassador Li Chen.

Bailey could see his friend's expression change as his mind processed the ramifications. 'We can't tell anyone about this, Bailey. Not until there's proof. Even then, I don't know if it's something that we could ever fully substantiate. Where's Anderson now?'

'He wouldn't tell me – the bloke's terrified. He says he'll contact me again.' Although Bailey wasn't certain that he would. 'He says he has documents.'

'Documents?'

The word sounded like something else when Gerald repeated it. It sounded like *proof*.

'Didn't say much, only that they're damaging. Not just for Page; the government too.'

'And there's that other thing that's been bothering me,' Gerald said.

'Which is?'

'Ronnie Johnson.'

Bailey smiled. 'It's been a while.'

'Sure has. And a CIA agent doesn't just drop by to say hello.'

'No, he doesn't. Ronnie reckons he's working for the US ambassador on his security detail.'

'Yeah, right.'

They both knew Ronnie Johnson about as well as anyone gets to know a man like him. Enough to know that he always had an agenda. Ronnie also had a habit of arriving at a place either just before the bombs landed, or immediately afterwards to clean up the mess. He was also the world's best liar.

'The Yanks are good at listening in. Careful what you tell him,' Gerald said. 'And keep him close.'

But Bailey was already thinking about the next dig. 'I need to speak to Dexter about her boss.'

'Careful, Bailey.' Gerald lowered his voice again. 'We're back in the corridors of power and we're the expendable ones.'

'Just like old times.'

CHAPTER 9

The pocket of Bailey's coat was vibrating as he walked down Oxford Street towards his house. It was a text message from Miranda.

Dad are we still on for breakfast? xx

Bailey hated the touchscreen on his phone because his fat fingers could never hit the right letters. As a stubborn old journalist, he also didn't like a machine subbing his work so he refused to activate the auto-correct program. He could live with the typos and figured others could too.

Og vourse, sweethest. See yoi at 8.

He had just enough time to shower and put on some clean clothes. The walk with Gerald had fixed his hangover, and the excitement of working on the type of story that had once helped to define his career made him forget about his lack of sleep. He was running on adrenalin and his hunger for answers was growing.

But nothing would make him cancel his breakfast with Miranda. The rehabilitation of John Bailey was reliant upon winning back the love of his daughter.

—

Ralph's Espresso Bar in North Bondi was one of those cafés where all the trendy kids wanted to work. Places like this barely existed when Bailey was young, and they certainly weren't called bars. That was just misleading.

The décor looked like it had been salvaged from a decrepit Balinese restaurant. Pinewood tables, aluminium chairs, and walls adorned with obscure artwork and photography created by local artists and fixed with obscene price tags.

It was a weekday morning and the café was already packed with beautiful people – the tanned and tattooed – enjoying a slow start to the day, while others tapped away on laptop keyboards in their mobile workplace, which was anywhere these days.

Everything about Ralph's bothered Bailey, not least the juicer vibrating loudly on the counter, churning vegetables he had never heard of, like kale.

He spotted Miranda sitting at a table by the window. She had chosen the café so he would pretend to love it.

'You look beautiful.' Bailey always greeted his daughter with a compliment. It was his way of addressing the burning guilt of the lost years.

Miranda was dressed in a slim-fitting navy suit, looking every bit the corporate lawyer. Luckily, she had inherited her mother's looks – blonde hair, blue eyes and the body of an athlete.

The male eyes in the room followed her as she stood up from the table she had reserved with a view of the ocean and kissed her father on the cheek. The sun was flickering on the water and it was one of those days that made Sydney seem like the best city in the world. But the view outside was lost on Bailey.

'Dad, if I was thirty kilos heavier and dressed like a goth you'd tell me I looked beautiful.'

'That's true,' he said. These catch-ups were getting less uncomfortable with time.

'I was in the Middle East during your gothic phase. I missed all the black outfits and piercings.' Bailey regretted harking back to the years when he wasn't around and tried to recover with a joke. 'How're those tattoos?'

'Very funny. I was always too straight for rebellion. All you missed out on were the teenage mood swings. Probably more frightening, actually. My arguments with Mum were legendary.'

'How is your mum?' Bailey wasn't about to admit that he'd called around to Anthea's place, drunk, the night before. Miranda and her mother were tight.

'She's great. Ian may be a boring banker, but he's good to her. One extreme to the other, when you think about it.'

'Fair enough.'

The expression on his face gave him away.

'Dad.' Miranda reached out and held his hand across the table. 'I'm joking.'

'I know, sweetheart.'

But the pain was still raw. The pain of letting her down. He remembered how his daughter had refused to speak to him on the telephone when he called from whatever country or conflict he had chosen over her. She had even stopped calling him Dad for a while. Like her mother, Miranda had simply called him John.

But Bailey was back to being Dad again, and they were both desperate to keep it that way.

'We're past all that, aren't we?' she said.

'Yeah, yeah, we are.'

'G'day groovers!' A tanned bloke with skin-tight jeans and dreadlocked hair appeared alongside their table with a notepad in his hand. 'What can I get you guys?'

He was way too happy for Bailey. Cocky too.

Miranda let go of her father's hand and looked up at the waiter. 'Poached eggs and a skinny flat white for me. Dad?'

Bailey was desperate for caffeine. 'Long black, mate. And make my eggs fried with bacon.'

'Sweet as!'

Bailey watched the bloke with the knotted hair walk away before turning to his daughter. 'Please don't date a bloke like that.'

'Don't worry, Dad. I'm into grown-ups.'

'Good.' Bailey hadn't met many of her boyfriends. 'You sure we're okay?'

'Seriously, Dad, we're all good. Mum, on the other hand . . . Well, I know her. She'll always love you.' Miranda paused for the truth. 'But it won't stop her being pissed at you from time to time.'

'We're lucky to have her.'

Anthea may have moved on from Bailey but she had never cut the cord.

'You should drop her a line.' Bailey knew Miranda had given up fantasising about her parents getting back together years ago but she knew they still had a connection, not just because they shared a daughter. 'She'd like seeing you getting back on your feet.'

'Yeah. We talk.'

'Glad to hear that.' Miranda held out her hand again and he took it. 'Although, Dad, I hate to say it but you look exhausted.'

'I'm working on a story that has required a few late nights.'

'The one about Catherine Chamberlain? I read your article.'

'Really?'

'I read *The Journal* every day. I'm just not used to seeing your byline these days.'

Anthea had once told Bailey that Miranda used to search for his stories in *The Journal* when she was a child. It was often the only place she found him. Another painful reminder from his daughter.

'Not a pleasant story.'

'What happened to her?'

Bailey wasn't sure whether his daughter had read the update from Gerald about the fact that police thought Catherine Chamberlain was murdered, with a federal government employee the chief suspect.

'It's complicated, Miranda. There's a lot more to that poor girl's death.'

'Like what?'

'She was murdered, for a start.'

'Oh my God! I actually knew her. Not well, but I knew her. I was going to tell you yesterday, but I thought I'd leave it till we caught up this morning.'

Bailey shifted in his chair.

'You knew her? How on earth did you get to know a prostitute?'

'Dad, you make it sound like she was a criminal. She wasn't,' Miranda said. 'It's the oldest occupation in the world, right? Or so they say.'

'I suppose –'

'Anyway.' Miranda kept talking. 'Catherine was studying law at Sydney Uni. She's in . . . or, bloody hell, she *was* in . . . the tutorial that I run on Wednesday nights.'

'How well did –'

'It's not that uncommon, you know.'

'What's not uncommon?' The caffeine hadn't quite kicked in and Bailey was struggling to keep up.

'A girl paying her way through university by doing that type of work.'

Bailey still didn't like it. 'How'd you find out that she was working as a prostitute?'

'Quite random actually. I bumped into her in a bar in the city. She was with a much older man and looked uncomfortable seeing me, so I left her to it.'

Bailey wanted to gauge whether Miranda might be in danger. 'How well did you know her? Were you friends?'

'I didn't see her socially, if that's what you're getting at. She was a nice person and she always handed in her assignments on time.'

Miranda paused for a moment. 'I saw you quoted Sharon Dexter in the article. That's the woman you were living with before you went back to Iraq, right?'

There was an awkward pause.

'You've got a good memory.' His daughter was forensic – no wonder she was such a good lawyer.

'She's the only woman you ever introduced me to after Mum. I figured she was important.'

'She is. I mean, she was.'

'What does that mean? Are you seeing her again?'

Bailey and Dexter had shared a lunch that had ended up being professional and personal. But there was nothing to it.

'No. I don't think she'd put up with me a second time round.'

'A little hesitation there –'

'We're not seeing each other. Haven't been on the dating circuit for a while. Do old guys even do that any more?' Bailey was caught offguard. He was rambling.

'You should think about it,' she said. 'You're not that old. It's about time you had a nice woman in your life again. Better than the divorcees of Paddington!'

Bailey's face slumped. 'What?'

'I bumped into Gerald in the city the other day. He made a joke about your dating habits. Secretly, I think he's jealous.'

'Bloody Gerald!' This wasn't a topic of conversation he was keen to explore with his daughter. 'How's work? Got any news?'

'I'm working on a big merger at the moment. I can't talk to you about it, of course. This one would be of great interest to your readers.'

Bailey couldn't believe his daughter was a corporate lawyer. 'Have I told you how proud I am?'

'Every time we see each other, Dad.' She blushed. 'You need a new line.'

It had taken a long time for Bailey to reach this point with Miranda after the months, sometimes years, he had spent working in the Middle East. She had a forgiving heart, like her mother.

They finished their breakfast and a second – third for Bailey – round of coffees.

'Dad, I have a question for you,' Miranda said.

'Sure – shoot.' The caffeine had finally kicked in.

'Years ago, when you came over to Mum's house for dinner, you said something that I just can't get out of my head. It worries me and I wanted to ask you what you meant.'

'Okay, sounds cryptic. Remember, I was probably loaded up on whisky back then, you made me so nervous.'

'I asked you about the Middle East and you said it was like living on beautiful sands littered with scorpions and, no matter how hard you tried, you could never get the sting out.'

Bailey knew exactly what he'd meant. But sharing pain didn't make it go away, despite what the shrinks told him. There were some things his daughter never needed to know.

'I don't know, Miranda,' he said. 'As I said, I was probably drunk. I carry a bit of baggage from those days. I'm trying to move on. And, honestly, it's one of those things that talking about doesn't help.'

'I don't believe that, Dad.' She looked disappointed. 'Talking always helps.'

Bailey didn't know where to go next so he said nothing.

Miranda wasn't the type of person who needed to fill the silence. She let the sound of the waves enter their moment and followed her father's eyes out the window to the sea.

The minutes passed until Miranda finally said something. 'Is that guy ever going to light that thing?' She was pointing at a man standing across the road sucking on a cigar. 'I'll never understand how much people pay for cigars.'

Ronnie Johnson was standing by the edge of the road admiring the ocean, while disrupting the view of the father and daughter sitting in the window.

Bailey pushed his empty coffee cup away. 'Filthy habit indeed.'

'Anyway, Dad.' Miranda looked down at her watch, missing her father's change in mood. 'I've got a meeting. Better go.'

She leaned over the table and kissed his cheek. 'I love you – and one day you're going to tell me about those scorpions.'

'I love you too, sweetheart.'

—

Bailey waited for Miranda to leave before he paid the bill and walked outside towards Ronnie.

'What're you doing here? I can't see the ambassador's car anywhere . . . you got the day off?' Bailey was annoyed about his breakfast being interrupted.

'Trendy place, bubba.' Ronnie pointed back across the street at Ralph's Espresso Bar.

'Don't ask.' Seventy dollars for two serves of eggs, bacon and a few rounds of coffees. Bailey couldn't believe it. He'd felt like asking the kid with the dreadlocks if breakfast came with one of the pictures on the wall.

'Walk with me.' Ronnie kept his eyes fixed on the water and started towards the children's playground by the esplanade.

They were past the greased-up body builders doing chin-ups at the outdoor exercise area before Ronnie reached into his pocket and pulled out a photograph and handed it to Bailey.

'Who's that?'

'Victor Ho, taken two years ago for his student ID card.'

'And?'

'He's been studying economics at Sydney University.'

'Why're you showing me?'

Ronnie handed Bailey a second photograph.

'He *was* studying economics.'

'What the . . .' Bailey flinched at the sight of Victor Ho, his face beaten so badly that it was almost unrecognisable.

'That's what young Victor looks like now,' Ronnie said.

'Why're you showing me these?'

Ronnie took back the photograph of dead Victor. 'You can keep the other one – you might need it.'

'What happened to him?' Bailey folded the picture and put it in his pocket.

'Body was found in an alley down by the casino at Darling Harbour two days ago. Bashed, wallet stolen. Cops said it was a robbery.'

'Okay. Again, why're you showing me?'

Ronnie's eyes were skirting the area.

'We've been watching young Victor for a few months – suspect he's been working for Chinese intelligence.'

'Does this have something to do with Catherine Chamberlain?'

Ronnie nodded. 'This has everything to do with Catherine Chamberlain.'

'So, you've made a connection?'

'No.'

'What does it mean then?'

'Nothing.' Ronnie paused. 'Yet.'

'I still don't understand why you're showing me, unless you want something.' Ronnie always wanted something.

'C'mon, bubba!' Ronnie put his cigar in the corner of his mouth, leaving it there. 'Don't be like that!'

'Don't play me. What do you think I can give you?'

'Anderson.'

'What about him?'

'You met him up at Palm Beach. Lovely spot, but a hell of a drive at three o'clock in the –'

'You were following me?'

'Not quite, bubba. I was sound asleep. I attached a little tracking device to that shitbox car of yours, which told me you went for a long drive when you should have been sleeping.'

'You've been tracking me? You're unbelievable!'

'Keep your voice down.' Ronnie grabbed Bailey by the forearm and looked around. 'It was for your own good.'

'How'd you know I met Anderson?' Bailey didn't care that he was speaking loudly. 'Were you listening in too? Bugging me?'

'Listen here, bubba. You don't know what you're putting yourself in the middle of with this.'

Bailey pushed Ronnie's hand away. 'Answer the question.'

'I didn't put a listening device in your car, I just guessed it was Anderson. The stupid fool should have spoken to the police. I'm hoping you can tell me why he's chosen you.'

'He said he read my story in *The Journal*. Other than that, I've got no idea.'

Bailey wasn't even sure that Anderson would get in touch again. What was stopping him from disappearing? He wasn't stupid. He just had trust issues. And so did Bailey.

'So, what did he say?'

Bailey looked at him without answering.

'Answer the question.'

Bailey wasn't going to be pushed around. 'We go back, Ronnie. There's a raging river under our bridge, at least that's how that saying goes for me. And don't get me wrong,' he lowered his voice. 'I'm forever grateful for the day you pulled me out of that hellhole. But I'm not going to be played by you.

I'm not going to be dangled on some line so you can catch whatever fish it is you're after.'

'I'm not playing you, bubba,' Ronnie said. 'This is some serious shit you've stepped in. I've shown you my aces, now give me something.'

They may have been working different angles, each with their own way of doing things, but Bailey knew Ronnie was one of the good guys.

'The police commissioner,' Bailey said.

'What about him?'

'Don't know, except that he made a discreet visit to Gerald last night, told him he's preparing to make a play into federal politics.'

'Interesting, but I can't see how it's connected.'

'Gerald said he's been showing an unusual interest in the case. That was confirmed by my contact in the police.'

'Sharon Dexter? Your ex-girlfriend?'

'Does everyone feel the need to keep reminding me about that? Sharon said Davis has been trying to control this one from his office.'

'That all?'

'He asked specifically about Anderson, whether I'd been in contact with him.'

Ronnie stepped closer, towering over Bailey. 'Think he's listening in on your calls?'

'A tap . . . on me?'

'Anderson, more likely.'

'He called me about a dozen times before I finally picked up.' Bailey thumbed through his phone so that he could see the call times. 'First one came through around nine o'clock last night – that's a few hours before Gerald says Davis dropped by his place.'

'What did Anderson tell you?'

What didn't he tell me? thought Bailey. 'He thinks Page's spying for the Chinese.'

'That's quite an accusation against the Defence Minister of Australia.'

'I didn't say I believed him.'

'You should.'

'You think he's telling the truth?'

'Yes, bubba, I do.'

No wonder Anderson feared for his life.

'What else did he say?' Ronnie said.

'That Page had half a dozen meetings in the past few months with China's Ambassador, Li Chen.'

'Half a dozen? That's more than we thought.'

'So you knew about the meetings?'

'Some of them.' He looked at Bailey. 'Bailey, we've shared an awful lot of information here. I know we have trust issues but you may need to get over them. This has the potential to be very dangerous for you.'

'I've been around the block a few times.' And Bailey had the scars to prove it. 'Don't worry about me.'

'It's different, bubba, not like before.' Ronnie was talking about Fallujah. 'You won't see these guys coming.'

Bailey hadn't seen the last guys coming, either. 'Yeah, yeah. I've got to go.'

'Where?'

'Petals – it's time I met Ruby Chambers' boss.'

'Hard-hitting journalism.' Ronnie shoved his cigar back in his mouth. 'Readers will like that angle – law student doubling as a prostitute to pay the bills. Murdered.'

'Maybe you should write it?'

Ronnie's big grin put a dent in his cheeks. 'I'll leave the poetry for the poets.'

'One more thing before I go,' Bailey said.

'Yeah?'

'Take that bloody tracking device off my car!'

Ronnie reached into his pocket and picked out a tiny black square that looked like a fridge magnet. 'Already done, bubba.'

'Good. Don't do it again.'

'Sure, bubba, promise.'

Bailey sighed and shook his head. 'Whatever that means.'

CHAPTER 10

Dexter

'The guy's hammered, so I shine the torch right in his eyes and I'm saying, "Look at me! It's not that hard. Here . . . no . . . here!"'

Constable Rob Lucas was recounting a story to three rookie cops as Detective Sharon Dexter walked past his desk. She was carrying a mug of instant black coffee on her way back from the station's crummy kitchenette.

Lucas hadn't noticed her and he continued with his story, growing more animated by the second.

'I can't see, officer, you're shining it right in my eyes!' Lucas was pointing a torch at one of the other cops and raising the pitch of his voice, mimicking the drunken man.

'I grab the breatho, tell him to blow into it, while I'm still shining the torch in his face the whole time, blinding him!'

Lucas was holding a breathalyser in his other hand and waving it from side to side. The three rookies listening to the story stopped laughing when they noticed Detective Dexter standing beside them.

Lucas kept going. 'Sad prick couldn't see a thing. I keep moving the breatho around, his head's going from side to side out the window of his Porsche, his lips open like he's trying to give someone a blow job, still chasing the breatho!'

Dexter had heard enough. 'Sorry to interrupt your story about some obviously fine police work, Constable Lucas.'

'Seriously, Sharon? I'm just having a laugh with our new recruits here.'

'And setting a fine example, no doubt. You can call me Detective Dexter in front of the first years.' She nodded to the young graduates, who sheepishly returned the gesture.

'We've got more important things on our plate, don't we, Constable Lucas?' Dexter knew that he had never liked taking orders from a woman so she made a point of letting everyone know who was in charge.

'What might that be, Detective?' Lucas was playing up to the rookies.

'I would like the security camera tapes from Catherine Chamberlain's apartment building in Rushcutters Bay.'

'Why? We reviewed it. You've seen Anderson's mugshot. Clear as can be at one o'clock in the morning. Open and shut, right? Just need to find him and charge him.'

Dexter perched on the edge of his desk. 'You're a smart guy, Rob.' She lowered her voice and smiled, letting him know that she really didn't think he was a smart guy. 'And you're probably right. But I'd like to take a look myself, unless you have any objections?'

'Course not.' Lucas leaned forward, opened the cabinet drawer and produced a clear plastic evidence bag with three

VHS tapes inside. 'Knock yourself out. The tape you're after is the one with the yellow sticker on it – covers the midnight to three block.'

Dexter took the bag and walked down the corridor until she found a spare room with a tape deck. She wasn't surprised that the apartment complex's security surveillance system still used old VHS tapes. There were plenty that did. It actually made it easier for her to spool through the vision using an old-fashioned remote control. Trying to fast forward and rewind digital recordings was a nightmare because computers skipped entire sequences, while film spun on small cogs, like a conveyor belt, allowing you to inspect a roll frame by frame.

She thumbed open the bag and selected the right tape. Lucas may be an idiot, but knowing that Anderson had arrived at the apartment block sometime after midnight would have at least made him examine every frame of the tape that placed him at the scene of the crime. Lucas's evidence log noted that Anderson stood outside for around ten minutes, pressing the buzzer and staggering around, suggesting that he was drunk. At one stage, he hit every button at the front entrance until, finally, someone let him in. Eleven minutes later he stumbled out of the building and left.

Dexter started watching the recording from earlier in the evening and took a sip of her coffee. She had made it too strong. She'd drink it anyway. The caffeine would help her to concentrate.

The view from the camera was fixed on the foyer. Mario Monticello, the manager of the complex, had told Lucas that it was the only way in and out. Every five or ten minutes, someone different strolled through the doors. Some were holding hands, others were drunk and swaying, and there was an old woman walking her dog. They looked like they were simply going about their business. Nothing suspicious.

At eleven o'clock white lines appeared on the screen. It looked like the recording had been hit by electrical interference. The lines turned to snow and then the picture went black. The clock in the corner of the screen kept ticking over, which meant the recording was still rolling, but somewhere along the line the feed from the camera had been corrupted.

Dexter watched the darkness for a few minutes before spooling forward until the picture came back after another crackle of white at 11.15 pm. She rewound the tape and watched it through again. Same problem. It was an old system and she wondered whether there were similar black spots on the other tapes, so she spooled through them from start to finish. Both were fine.

She called Mario Monticello to find out if he had any other copies and if he was aware of the black hole in the middle of his recording. He didn't answer. She left a message and went back to her desk.

Kings Cross Police Station had an open plan design, with the desks lined side by side to maximise the office space. But it was in desperate need of renovation. The grey carpets were worn and stained, the venetian blinds were caked with dust, and the fake plants positioned around the room to add character just looked cheap. The only decent furnishing in the place was the leather chair that Dexter had wheeled in off the street after finding it discarded outside an apartment building around the corner. It wouldn't have looked out of place in a boardroom. It was comfortable too.

She was leaning back in her chair, bouncing on the springs and contemplating her next move, when the idea came to her.

'Constable Lucas!' she called out across the room. 'Could you please come here for a minute?'

Lucas took his time walking over to Dexter's desk by the window. 'What's up, Detective?' He made sure to emphasise her title.

'Did you go through all three tapes when examining the evidence?'

'No. Once we saw Anderson, we didn't feel the need.'

'Who's the *we*?'

Lucas smiled at her. 'Me and your boss – the police commissioner.'

Dexter knew that rumours about her affair with David Davis had spread around the station but she wasn't going to let a weasel like Rob Lucas get to her. 'So did anyone go through all three tapes? And by anyone – I obviously mean you.'

'Obviously.'

'So?'

'Again, that would be a negative,' he said. 'Maybe you should take it up with the commissioner?'

'Thank you, Rob, I might just do that. You can go now.'

Dexter was flabbergasted. They were preparing to charge a man with murder and key pieces of evidence had not been properly analysed.

Davis had made it clear that he'd wanted this case dealt with quickly, which explained why he'd signed off on the arrest warrant for Michael Anderson. But Dexter was unnerved by his involvement. She was the lead detective and the one who had issued the warrant that morning without, it now seemed, considering all of the available evidence. She did things by the book. Slicing off corners left a bad taste in her mouth. It was bad practice from another era. She needed to speak to Davis.

She called his mobile, hoping that he'd see it was her and pick up. It worked. 'Commissioner, it's Detective Dexter.'

'Sharon, why so formal?'

'You know why.'

'Okay, okay. Let's not go back there.' Davis was smug, but he wasn't stupid. He would never cross his former mistress while trying to – apparently – repair his marriage. 'What can I do for you?'

'Something's puzzling me about the Catherine Chamberlain murder and the case we're building against Michael Anderson. I think we may be moving a little too fast.'

'Why?' He sounded irritated. 'Seems open and shut to me.'

'Could be. Probably is, to be truthful.' Dexter was careful not to contradict her boss. No matter how many nights she'd spent at his Maroubra apartment, he was still the police commissioner.

'Well, what's the problem?'

Davis was also a renowned bully.

'It's just that I've been through all the security vision from the apartment complex and there's a black hole in one of the tapes from earlier in the evening.'

'That's strange. Constable Lucas said he went through those tapes and that Anderson was the only suspicious thing on them. Are you telling me he's wrong?'

'Well ...' Dexter stumbled, contemplating words that might prove costly later. 'Constable Lucas told me you and he discussed the tapes yesterday. He said you were satisfied.'

'Aaaahhh, yes. We did have a discussion about your investigation. I think you were off having lunch with that reporter from *The Journal*. What's his name? Bailey?'

'I was and ...' Dexter was thrown offguard, not sure what Davis was trying to suggest. 'Bailey is an old friend, and –'

'I'm sorry, Sharon, we're done here. I need to get to a meeting.'

'Okay. But, Commissioner, I think we may need to dig a little deeper on this, just to be sure.'

'I don't. We have our man at the scene and inside the building. He's been missing ever since Ruby Chambers was murdered. Tell me – if he's innocent, why didn't he come in?'

Ruby Chambers.

The call girl name sounded like an alarm bell in Dexter's head. It was the second time Davis had referred to Chamberlain in this way.

'I don't know.' She pretended to ignore it.

'Answer that question for me, then I'll be all for your plan to dig a little deeper. Goodbye, Sharon.'

He hung up.

Dexter stared at her phone, wondering what had just happened.

'Spoke to the commissioner then, I take it?' Lucas was standing over her desk.

'Yeah, I did.'

'And how'd that go for you?'

'A few questions – a few questions we still need answered.' Dexter's heart was pounding, her mind was racing. She needed to calm down.

'Well, the boss wants me to stick with you on this one. Told me last night after he signed off on the warrant.'

The commissioner's errand boy.

Dexter stared at her blank computer screen.

'Detective? Are you even listening?'

'Sure, Rob. Do as I say and we'll get along fine.' She was back. 'And I'm not interested in your little crime-fighting stories like the one you were telling the kids this morning. Got it?'

'No wonder no one wants to work with you, Sharon – sorry, Detective Dexter.'

'And why is that, Constable?'

'Because you're a bitch – and you don't know how to have a laugh.'

Dexter glared at him. 'Don't pretend you know me.'

'It's like that, is it?'

'Yeah, it's like that,' she said. 'But we still have work to do, so get your shit together – we're going out.'

'Where?'

'Back to Rushcutters Bay. There's a fifteen-minute black hole in one of those tapes from earlier in the night and I want to know why.'

'Bullshit!'

She could see that he was regretting calling her a bitch now.

'No bullshit.' Dexter stood up. 'And you know what else's bothering me, Constable Lucas?'

'What's that?'

'For some reason those missing minutes don't appear to concern anyone but me.'

'I actually did mean to look at all of the tapes but –'

'The commissioner told you not to worry about it, right?' Lucas was on the back foot and Dexter wanted to keep it that way.

'He never actually gave me an instruction. He just, he just said that –'

'We had identified our man?'

'Yeah. And, he . . . I guess –'

'Surely you're not suggesting the police commissioner thought it'd be okay to ignore the other tapes when they could hold vital evidence in a murder investigation?'

Dexter had Lucas exactly where she wanted him.

'Yeah, well . . . no . . . I may have misunderstood something along the way, and –'

'Forget about it.' She slapped his shoulder, patronising, like she was one of the boys. 'No need for me to be a bitch about this. Let's move on, shall we? Gather your things. Let's see if we can find Mario Monticello.'

CHAPTER 11

Bailey inspected the outside of his car to see if Ronnie had been telling the truth about removing the tracking device. He got down on his knees, rolled onto his back and slid his head underneath the tailgate to get a good view of the chassis. He figured this was where a little magnetic square would ride if Ronnie had been lying. But, really, he had no idea.

Remembering he was in Bondi Beach, where binge-drinking backpackers routinely pissed on the street, he abandoned the inspection. He wriggled out from underneath the car and stood up, brushing the dirt and sand from his shoulders, and taking a precautionary whiff of his clothes. If the CIA wanted to track his movements there was nothing that he could do about it.

Bailey started the engine and the stereo came on. Mick Jagger was singing a story about a woman lying in a hotel room with a smiling face and a tear in her eye. Bailey hummed along, his mind wandering down into the basement of Villa Nellcôte, imagining Mick and Keith arguing, singing, strumming and writing their finest album while living as tax exiles in the south of France. Bailey had never tired of the Rolling Stones and *Exile on Main St*, with its songs and stories about a place and a time, was his pick. He could see the celebrities and hangers-on mingling upstairs, the band huddled inside the sandstone hollows below, where the music bounced around and landed in an imperfect jumble that would be dismissed by the same critics who later lined up to embrace the words and the sounds of a band at its mighty and decadent best.

He stopped at a red light and closed his eyes when the song kicked up and the perfect chemistry of the gospel blues backing singers, Mick's unmistakeable voice and Keith's guitar sent a rush through his veins like a shot of morphine. It was moments like these that Bailey loved, where he escaped in sounds and forgot about life for a while.

A car horn interrupted the moment and his eyes jolted open. The light had turned green. It was too early for *Exile* and hearing those songs made him want to head back home and nestle a whisky. He switched off the CD player and his AM radio blurted alive to the sound of Keith Roberts proselytising to the world.

As if on cue, Roberts was railing against the Chinese menace.

'You mightn't have heard of the Uighur peoples, my dear listeners. They're Muslims who have, for as long as time remembers, lived in Northern China. Now, just like with Taiwan, just like with Hong Kong, the Chinese Government does not like people holding different views, they don't like them having different customs.'

Bailey was surprised. Roberts actually sounded like he knew what he was talking about today.

'They don't like anything about these Uighurs – and quite frankly, my dear listeners, neither do I.'

Bailey was mistaken.

'I don't like the fact that they're Muslims because we all know what old Islam has done to the Middle East and what some Muslims – and I say some, I'm not a bigoted man, I don't say all – are trying to do here too. But I've got to say it like it is – between the Uighurs and the Chinese – I can't say I feel very comfortable about a battle raging on our doorstep.'

Not really a battle, thought Bailey. Certainly not on our doorstep.

'Now, my point here, my dear listeners, is that if the Chinese keep monstering these Uighurs and they need a new home, guess where they're coming?'

Click.

That was enough for Bailey. Silence was often the best antidote.

—

The mid-morning traffic was moving slowly on Oxford Street. Bailey was less than a kilometre from his house, but he couldn't go home. He was like a pinball bouncing around the eastern suburbs, from one destination to the next. And the next stop was one he would much rather have avoided, only he couldn't. It was part of his deal with Gerald.

He reached into the glovebox and rummaged around until he found the bottle with the inch of brown in it – for emergencies, like now. He unscrewed the lid and emptied the bottle. By the time he got out of the car the warm sensation in the back of his throat had spread to his head and the task ahead suddenly felt less daunting.

—

'How're you feeling, John?'

The sessions always started with the same question, and Bailey was ready with his standard response.

'Pretty shit thanks, Doctor Jane.'

And he looked like shit too. He could tell by the expression on her face. Or maybe she could smell the whisky he'd just thrown back in the car.

'C'mon, John, do we have to go through this every time? You know the deal.'

'Yeah – doesn't mean I have to like it.'

'No, you don't, but it's only half an hour.' Jane pointed to the brown leather couch, palm open. 'Have a seat, talk to me. You know I'm a good listener.'

'We're talking, aren't we? What do you want to know?'

'How 'bout we start again?'

'You can do what you like.'

'Okay, okay. I hear you're back at work?'

He tossed his keys and phone on the couch and sat down. 'News travels fast.'

She smiled at him. 'You know I talk to Gerald.'

'Inquisitive fellow, that one.'

'Seriously, how're you doing?'

Bailey avoided her calm, welcoming eyes. They'd trapped

him before and he wasn't up for the deep dive into his brain today.

'I'm fine.'

Jane picked up her notepad from the coffee table and clicked her pen.

'Tell me about this story you're working on.'

'Can't do that, I'm afraid.'

Jane scribbled something in her notepad. 'Why not?'

'It's confidential.'

'Everything we talk about in this room is confidential. That's the idea.'

'I'm not talking to you about the story.'

After a long pause she tried again. 'How're you sleeping?'

'Good,' he lied. 'Whisky helps. Amazing how it makes you nod off.'

'Funny.'

It went on like this for the next fifteen minutes, with Bailey deflecting each question like he was swatting away flies. Jane kept writing, always taking notes.

He leaned forward and tapped the paper. 'You must have enough for a bestseller by now?'

'Depressing read – so far.'

Bailey laughed. 'Good one.'

'Why don't you get yourself a hobby? Something to take your mind off things.'

'I have a hobby.'

'I don't think you can count drinking at the pub as a hobby.'

'What about drinking at home?'

'C'mon, John. Tell me about something you like doing. You once told me you like listening to seventies music. What else do you do?'

The sessions in Jane's tiny office always went for thirty minutes. He had to tell her something, if only to keep the clock ticking.

'I watch rugby.'

'Really?' She looked up from her notes. 'What kind?'

'The only kind – union.' Bailey hated rugby league – it was a thug's game.

'Watch the Wallabies?'

'Used to. Not much at the moment.'

'Why not?'

Bailey wasn't sure that he could be bothered answering the question. But he didn't want to go back to the sessions where he would just sit and stare, without saying a word. He looked at the clock on the wall – fourteen minutes left.

'Prefer the grassroots.' Rugby was easier to talk about than war.

'How come we haven't discussed rugby before?'

'You never asked.'

Bailey had been coming to see Jane for almost three years. Part of Gerald's return-to-work plan, or something. It had taken a little longer than anyone had expected.

'Tell me, why don't you like the Wallabies?'

He looked up at the clock again. Thirteen minutes.

'Because the team's been ruined by a bunch of Gen Y dickheads.'

Jane was scribbling in her notepad again.

'Surely that's not going to make the book?'

'Very funny.'

What didn't Bailey like about the Wallabies? He didn't like the way they played the game, for starters, and the word team didn't seem to mean much any more. It was all about money. He especially didn't like the way the players referred to themselves as brands.

Today's crop had nothing on the legends of 1991. The boys who brought home the William Webb Ellis Trophy when nobody believed they could. Farr-Jones, Horan, Lynagh and Campese. Campo! Those guys threw the ball around with passion and grace. Never gave up. Beating Ireland on the bell in that quarterfinal was a case in point. The hardheads like Willie-O and Poidevin, the backrowers who bounced off defenders and tackled anything that moved. And who could forget that giant-killing front row of McKenzie, Kearns and Daly – three blokes plucked out of second grade to represent their country – who overpowered the mighty All Blacks to make the Rugby World Cup final at Twickenham. In an era when every player needed a day job to pay the bills, these guys played rugby for the love of the game.

Bailey had all but given up on today's Wallabies. He would occasionally catch them on television, but he couldn't justify paying for a ticket. He preferred watching free-flowing rugby where he could smell the grass, which often led him to Coogee Oval on a Saturday afternoon to see the colts run around. The girls played there too, and they were getting good. Young players lacing up for the fun of it. Pure.

'John? John?' Jane was tapping Bailey's knee. 'I'm still here, you know.'

'Yeah. Sorry.'

'You were telling me about rugby, how you like to watch a game, now and then.'

'It's a beautiful game.' Bailey shrugged and winked at her as he noticed the last minute tick over. 'I'm afraid time's up, Doctor Jane.'

She fumbled with her watch and when she looked up, Bailey was already on his feet.

'Got to run. Next time.'

'Okay – and John?'

He paused at the door. 'Yeah?'

'You seem different this week. And I'm not talking about the rugby.' She paused. 'You look tired. Do you feel like you're getting better?'

'You really want the truth?'

'Of course.'

'I'm done looking backwards.'

'Okay.'

'All this . . .' He pointed at the couch, shaking his finger. 'It's all about the past and, no offence, because I like you, but I'm done with it.'

'We can work with that.'

Doctor Jane might call that progress.

CHAPTER 12

The escort service that had employed Catherine Chamberlain had a registered address in Double Bay, one of Sydney's most exclusive suburbs, ten minutes drive from Paddington.

Bailey parked his car and chuckled to himself as the Corolla settled like a hobo in a fine-dining restaurant beside the Mercedes and BMWs that lined the street. The business, offering 'something special for Sydney's discreet elite', was called Petals and the address that Bailey had scribbled on his notebook was a large gunmetal-grey townhouse. It could have been a family home.

Bailey rang the bell and the door buzzed open. His phone was vibrating in his pocket. It was Dexter. He'd call her later.

'Hiya sir, what can I do for you?' A young and, not surprisingly, beautiful receptionist looked up from the type of desk you might expect to find in a doctor's surgery.

'I'm wondering if I might be able to speak with someone about one of your former employees, Catherine Chamberlain? Or you might remember her as Ruby Chambers?'

The girl burst into tears and hurried away, disappearing into a room out back. Not a good start. At least Bailey knew he was in the right place.

He could hear voices in the back room before an older woman appeared. She too was beautiful, wearing a fitted dress – sleeves to the elbows, stylish, with plenty of cleavage and a hem short enough to show off her legs – no doubt bought from some overpriced Double Bay boutique. Her black heels made her tower over Bailey and her asymmetrical hairstyle didn't move, neither did the skin on her face.

'How can I help you, sir?' She was confident and direct, holding his gaze, leaving him with no doubt who was in charge.

'I'm sorry about the intrusion.' Bailey was doing his best to be charming. 'John Bailey from the –'

'And?'

'I'm a reporter from *The Journal*, and I –'

'We don't talk to journalists.'

It was her place, her terms. Bailey's pleasantries were pointless.

He tried playing it straight. 'As the young girl out back may have mentioned, I was wondering if you could answer a few questions for me about one of your former employees, Catherine Chamberlain?'

'I'm not sure that anyone here can help you, Mr Bailey. As I explained, we don't talk to the media. And we're certainly not in the business of talking about our clients, or our girls.'

'Even the dead ones?'

The woman reacted to the provocation with silence, her piercing eyes daring him to insult her again.

Bailey knew that if he was going to get anywhere, he needed to make a friend.

'That was a bit insensitive, I apologise.'

'Yes, it was.' She paused. 'Murder isn't something we've had much experience with here at Petals.'

'Didn't expect you would.'

She was older than him, more experienced. Bailey couldn't help imagining what her body was like beneath that dress. A night with a brothel madam – that would be something else. But she wasn't flirting, she wanted him gone.

'As you can see by the reception you received when you arrived, we're all still coming to terms with this horrible, horrible tragedy.'

'It's truly awful, Miss . . .'

'Francesca.'

'Sorry, is that your first name or last?' Full names – a journalist's habit. You never knew when you would need them.

'Both.'

'Okay, Francesca, I really don't want to add to your grief or cause any more problems. I'm just trying to understand who might've wanted to hurt Miss Chamberlain, or Ruby Chambers, as she was known here.'

'Her name was Catherine,' Francesca said. 'Her friends called her Catherine, her clients called her Ruby. I'm not sure where you fit into that equation. I'd guess neither.'

'Never got to know her, you're right. But that's the tragedy of it, right? She was also a law student and my daughter knew her as Catherine when she taught her at Sydney University.'

'I see. I'm sorry, Mr Bailey. I presume your daughter was as shocked as we were here at Petals.' Francesca's voice softened, but not the hard look in her eyes.

'Yeah, she was. I'm trying to find out why someone might've wanted to hurt Catherine.'

'At least the police know who's responsible. The sooner they catch this man, the better we'll all feel. An advisor to the defence minister – who would've thought?'

'Well, Francesca, that's the thing.' Bailey was sure she knew something. 'I have some new information suggesting there may be another suspect.'

Francesca raised her eyebrows, gesturing for Bailey to go on.

'Did Catherine have any other regular clients?'

'As I said to you, Mr Bailey, we don't discuss our clients.'

'Not even if it might help find the person who killed her?' He knew it was a cheap shot, but he was running out of ideas.

'A job for the police, no?'

Francesca was done. She wasn't interested in talking about Chamberlain's death with a reporter.

'I understand this is very distressing for you, Francesca, but –'

'If you wouldn't mind, I have some work to do. Please leave.'

'Could I ask one more question about a potential client? Was there a young Chinese gentleman, perhaps?'

'Goodbye, Mr Bailey.' Francesca gave him a blank stare, turned and walked away before he had a chance to show her the photograph of Victor Ho.

Bailey watched her disappear into the back room, wondering how she had ended up running a brothel. It wasn't on the list of prospects at his high school career night. But life was complicated. Of all people, Bailey understood that much. And Francesca was smart, wily too. Observations – the only things he was taking away from Petals.

The young girl from the reception desk reappeared and told Bailey she would escort him out.

'Francesca was very close to Catherine.' She opened the door. 'All the girls liked her.'

'Thanks,' he said. 'It's awful . . . Miss?'

'Scarlett.'

'Everyone just calls me Bailey.' He held out his hand and she took it. 'I'm sorry to have upset you earlier. You girls were close?'

They were standing in the doorway.

'Yeah. She was a good mate. And I'm just –'

'Scarlett!' Francesca's voice sounded from inside. 'I need you!'

'I should get back inside, Mr Bailey.'

She closed the door.

—

There was no point loitering outside. Francesca had two cameras pointing at the footpath and she was probably watching right now, waiting for Bailey to leave. But Scarlett had looked like she wanted to tell him something. With no leads other than the picture of the dead bloke in his pocket and Michael Anderson's conspiracy theories, he didn't have many options. He needed to do this the old-fashioned way.

Bailey walked across the street, grabbed a tabloid and a tired looking pre-made sandwich and headed for his car, parked just up the street. He sat on the bonnet, eating his ham and cheese sandwich while thumbing through the pages, without paying much attention to the words. Tabloid newspapers stopped reporting real news stories about the same time they stopped leaving ink marks on your fingers. Anyway, his focus was on the people coming and going from Petals. Every fifteen minutes or so, someone walked in or out, old and middle-aged men mostly. Some of them looked like they'd just attended a business meeting, others wore big coats and hats, and walked with their chins almost touching their chests.

A group of young blokes in chinos and bright polos walked out together, backslapping each other, having just paid for something that Bailey would have thought they could have had for free. He had just skimmed over a column about sexting – which he didn't really understand – and how kids these days had a distorted view of sex. Paying for it at Petals probably didn't help, either. Whatever happened to dinner and a movie? Crossing your fingers that if you played your cards right, after a few more dates, you might just get lucky?

Bailey looked at his watch. It was almost two o'clock, but it felt like five. He folded the newspaper in half and placed it on the bonnet beside him. There was nothing left to read.

The clock ticked past two.

Scarlett appeared on the steps, alone. She crossed the road and walked into the pub on the corner. A watering hole that Bailey knew well.

—

The Sheaf had been in Double Bay for as long as Bailey could remember. As a cub reporter, he used to drink there and watch the rugby on the big screen. It had probably been renovated five times since those days and, apart from the gaming machines, it still looked and smelled like the pub he remembered, minus the cigarettes.

Bailey watched as Scarlett ordered food at the window in the courtyard, then walked into the public bar, sat down at an empty table and started thumbing through her phone.

The public bar was littered with red-nosed locals. The private school boys in their tight fitted t-shirts were playing drinking games in the courtyard under the big oak tree, and the smell of a busy hotplate was wafting from the kitchen window.

Bailey ordered two glasses of orange juice.

'Mind if I join you?' He pointed at the empty stool beside Scarlett.

She looked up from her phone. 'Uuuummmm . . . sure.'

'Didn't mean to startle you,' Bailey said. 'Ordered us a couple of orange juices – they're on the way.'

'Just juice?'

'Mate!' Bailey called out to the bartender. 'Put a nip of vodka in those drinks, would you?'

The bloke behind the bar gave him a thumbs up.

'One thing we've got in common.'

'Midday rule, right?'

'Yeah.' Bailey lied.

'I never say no to a drink at lunchtime.' Scarlett smiled. 'Especially when someone else's buying.'

'You looked like you wanted to tell me something back there, about your friend.'

'She was a good person, Mr Bailey. She didn't deserve this. It's not right.'

'I'm trying to find out what happened to her.'

The barman arrived at their table with the drinks. 'Here's those screwdrivers, guys.'

'Good man.' Bailey handed him a twenty and took a long sip of his drink. Hungover, operating on very little sleep, it was just what he needed.

'How're you, babe?' The barman touched Scarlett on the shoulder.

'Good, Pete. How about you?'

'Surviving, babe. No surf today, so, only just.'

She shrugged at Bailey when Pete had left. 'What can I say? I'm a local.'

'A popular one, too.' Bailey noticed every bloke in the room checking her out. 'I know this is tough on you – and I really am sorry for your loss.'

'It's okay.' Thankfully, Francesca's hard-bitch routine hadn't rubbed off on her staff.

'I didn't mean to react the way I did back there,' Scarlett continued. 'In this line of work we're kind of like a family. We look out for each other. It's why Francesca was so short with you.'

'It's okay, I get it.' Bailey was determined to make a friend this time.

Scarlett gestured to the courtyard. 'See those boys out there?'

'Yep. Private school boys, I'm guessing.' It was obvious to a state-educated kid like Bailey.

'Arrogant little trust fund babies, no idea how to treat women. Some of our biggest clients.'

'That doesn't surprise me.'

'See the blond one?' Scarlett was pointing with her chin. 'Looks like a footy player, the one in the pink shirt?'

Bailey nodded.

'He comes in with his dad sometimes. Reckon he was fifteen the first time.'

Bailey had known guys like that and he didn't like them either. 'Different life.'

'Mine or theirs?'

He didn't know how to answer that.

'I'm joking,' she said.

'I'll try to keep up.' Bailey laughed awkwardly. 'Now, you okay to talk?'

Scarlett put down her drink and leaned back on her stool. 'We were close, Catherine and me.'

'I'm sorry.'

'It's good money, what we do. For Catherine, it was just for a while. For me too, I guess. But I don't have a grand plan like she did. She was going places, going to be a lawyer.'

'I know. My daughter says she was a smart girl.'

'Real smart. A good friend too – looked out for me.'

'How?'

'You really want to know?'

'Yeah, I do.'

'There was this one client of mine who liked it a bit rough. Catherine once hid in a hotel bathroom just in case he really hurt me.' Scarlett's eyes were filling with water. 'She really cared for people, Mr Bailey. I mean, who'd do that for someone?'

'Sounds like you lost a good mate.' Bailey was speaking as softly as his voice could go.

'I did. Shame I couldn't . . .' Scarlett was fighting back her tears. 'It's a shame I couldn't do the same for her.'

Scarlett looked like one of those people who only knew how to be honest. She was a straight talker and Bailey liked her.

'I don't think there is anything you could have done,' he said. 'I'm guessing whoever did this was a professional.'

'Professional? What do you mean?'

'I don't know anything for a fact. All I know is that it wasn't Michael Anderson.'

If Scarlett was going to share the truth, Bailey was too.

'I never thought it was, to be honest. He was a nice bloke, maybe a little jealous but tell me a bloke who isn't? He loved her, you know.'

'I'm sure he did.'

'Sure, it started out as a trick but it was real by the end.'

'Know how long they'd been seeing each other?' Bailey needed to find out as much as he could about Anderson – whether he was someone who could be believed – in case he got in contact again. Scarlett was his best chance.

'Months. Maybe six? Can't be sure.' She shrugged and took a sip of her drink. 'Long enough that she knew she wanted to be with him. He was trying to get her to quit Petals. He even said he'd pay for her tuition.'

'What did Catherine think about that?' Anderson wasn't sounding so crazy.

'She was a proud girl, and she wasn't keen on relying on someone.' Her voice was cracking up. 'But she was smart. She knew they couldn't last if she was still getting paid to sleep with other men. She was thinking about it.'

'That's good –'

'Careful not to judge us here, Mr Bailey,' Scarlett said. 'We know what we do, and it's okay, as long as you stay in control.'

'I'm sorry, I –'

'Forget about it. You've got a daughter and it's hard to imagine a girl wanting to do this. Right?'

He leaned forward on his stool. 'I'm not here to judge you, Scarlett.'

'It's actually not that bad, and the money's ridiculous, especially for a girl from Penrith with folks who gave me more beatings than hugs.'

Bailey didn't know how to respond to that.

'Sorry – you don't need my back story. I'm just saying that if you play it right, you can do all right. A grand a day. Who else's going to pay me money like that?'

'That's good money. Got an opening for a washed-up reporter?'

Scarlett patted his arm playfully. 'You're a handsome man, Mr Bailey. But girls only.'

Bailey's phone was vibrating – Dexter, again.

'Anyway, Scarlett, recall any customers a bit out of the ordinary the past few weeks or months?'

'In my game, there's no ordinary. Anyone in particular you're looking for?'

'A young Chinese bloke, a student.'

'We get plenty of them – fat wallets.'

Bailey put his elbows on the table and rested his chin on his knuckles. 'Go on.'

'Frustrated they can't seem to pick up Aussie girls in nightclubs, they come to us instead. A bit more expensive, but money's never an issue.'

'Any of them behaving strangely?'

'Maybe. Sorry, you've put me on the spot here.'

'Can I show you a photo?'

'Sure.'

Bailey reached into his pocket, unfolded the photograph of Victor Ho that Ronnie had given him at Bondi Beach and handed it to Scarlett. 'This guy one of them?'

Scarlett stared at the photograph.

'Yeah, he's been around.'

'What can you tell me about him?'

'I think he started booking with us a month or so ago.'

'Anything else you remember?'

'Bit creepy. Probably made five or ten appointments in the space of only a few weeks. A lot of money – and I mean, a lot – flashed it around and talked about his rich family back in China. And he always asked for Catherine.'

'This is really helpful.' Bailey threw back the rest of his drink and slid off his stool. 'I've got to get moving.'

He scribbled his phone number on a piece of paper and tore it from his notebook. 'If you think of anything else, give me a call.'

'Thanks. And Mr Bailey?'

'Yep?'

'What are you going to write?'

'Haven't figured it out yet. I don't have enough on the Chinese bloke in the photo other than that he might be a person of interest.'

'Francesca would be pissed if she thought I was a source.'

'Don't worry. Nothing I write will lead back to you.'

One dead prostitute was enough.

'Thanks. And I'll get back to you once we start recruiting old blokes to turn tricks!'

'For the money you make, I'd do anything!'

'You're a nice guy, Mr Bailey.'

He liked how she kept calling him Mr Bailey. It made him feel responsible.

'You take care of yourself, Scarlett.'

He walked across the stained carpet and out the door of the public bar. His phone vibrated again in his pocket. This time he answered.

'Sharon, I'm sorry I haven't called you back.'

'We need to talk – now.'

'Okay, what've you got?'

'Not on the phone. I'm in Rushcutters Bay – at the apartment.'

'Chamberlain's?' Bailey stopped alongside his car.

'Yes, dum-dum. Where else?'

He deserved that.

'Be there in ten. And I've got . . .' He jiggled the key in the lock, trying to get the door open. He really needed to get it fixed, or buy a new car.

'Bailey? Bailey – are you there?'

'Sorry. I've got something for you too.' The door finally clicked open. 'What are you wearing? Just in case –'

'Just shut up and get here, John.'

John.

Dexter had never called him by his first name, even when they were together. It was always Bailey. Something was wrong.

CHAPTER 13

Bailey called Gerald on his way to Rushcutters Bay.

'I've just had an interesting discussion with one of the girls at Petals.'

'Find out anything new?' Gerald sounded just as irritable as when he'd stormed into Bailey's house that morning.

'Yeah. Not exactly sure what it means yet.'

'And?'

Bailey could tell that Gerald wasn't himself. 'Are you okay, mate?'

'I'm fine. Let's meet.'

'My place. Give me forty minutes.'

—

A run of giant Moreton Bay figs lined the road across from the apartment building where Catherine Chamberlain had been killed. It was unseasonably warm for May and Bailey was relieved to have found a parking spot under the trees away from the glaring sun. On hot days it was almost impossible to get the heat out of his car because the air conditioner hadn't worked since 2000. He used to tell people that the millennium bug had killed it, until Miranda reminded her father that his car was too old to have a computer.

Dexter was waiting for him at the entrance of the building. He didn't know whether to hug her, give her a peck on the cheek, or shake her hand. Amidst the uncertainty he avoided all options and settled for a smile. 'Detective.'

'Don't be cute, Bailey. I'm not in the mood.'

Keeping his distance was the right decision. 'Okay. Why're we meeting here?'

'The building manager, a bloke called Mario Monticello, won't pick up his phone. I thought I'd try knocking on his door.'

'Any luck?'

'No one home.'

'I presume we're here to share information then. Got something for me?'

'Yeah, I do.'

'Are you going to start, or should I?'

'The security tape.' She pointed at the little camera in the roof above the entrance.

'What about it?'

'It's got a black hole in it.' Dexter was still looking up at the camera. 'We don't know who walked in and out of this building between eleven and eleven-fifteen on the night Catherine Chamberlain was murdered. Looks like some static interference knocked out the signal.'

'Interesting.'

'Interesting how?'

Bailey didn't want to hide anything from her, but he wasn't sure this was a good time to be sharing. He was a journalist, not a cop.

'Bailey? If you know something, then please do me the courtesy of –'

'Hold on, hold on.' He held up his hand. 'I just need you to agree that I won't be divulging any sources.'

'You think you need to explain that to me of all people? Give me a break.'

'Fair enough.'

'And right now I couldn't give a damn about police protocols, so spit it out.'

Bailey reached into his pocket and withdrew the photograph of Victor Ho.

'That's Victor Ho,' he said, pointing to the picture. 'Could be a professional hit man, foreign spook – who knows?'

'Chinese intelligence?' Dexter gave Bailey a sarcastic smile. 'C'mon, you're not trying to tell me we've got a modern-day Profumo Affair on our hands?'

'I'm not saying anything – just laying it out and trying to make sense of it.' Bailey didn't like Dexter's dismissive response, especially given Catherine Chamberlain had most likely been strangled to death because Michael Anderson had spilled his guts to her. 'And what are you talking about? This is nothing like Profumo!'

Bailey was hit by a sudden pang of tiredness. Maybe Scarlett's tears had got to him. Or maybe it was the vodka.

'Bailey – it was a bad joke. Calm down, would you?'

He knew he was being ridiculous. 'I'm sorry.'

'No worries,' Dexter said. 'Now, how's the guy in the photo connected?'

Bailey was struggling to concentrate. 'The photo?'

'In your hand?'

'Yes, yes . . .' Bailey shook his head as though he was warding off a fly. 'For starters, he's already dead.'

'What?'

'Bashed for his wallet, apparently. Pyrmont, two nights –'

'Down by the casino. I heard about it. It's being investigated as a robbery. You about to tell me it's not?'

'You tell me. You're the cop.'

'And how'd you get all this?'

'Got a source.'

'Police?'

'No, because that would be you.'

'Then who?'

'Nice try.' Bailey wouldn't even know where to begin if he was going to tell Dexter about Ronnie Johnson. Not that he would anyway because Bailey never gave up his sources. 'I thought you weren't going to press me about this.'

'Can't blame me for trying.'

'What I can tell you is that it appears our Victor Ho was a client of Catherine Chamberlain.'

'I'm listening.'

'He had a bunch of bookings with her in the weeks leading up to her death.'

Bailey didn't need to interpret the incredulous look on Dexter's face to know that it was all sounding too simple.

'You don't book an hour with a prostitute to kill her.'

'As I suggested earlier, I'm not trying to join dots for you. I'm just throwing them on the page and, right now, there are lots of dots.'

'I've got another dot for you, then,' she said. 'David Davis. He's been going around me and instructing the cop who's supposed to be helping me with the investigation.'

'How so?'

'Hard to pin. Gave me the impression he knew about the black hole in the videotape.'

'We've got to find out what that black hole's all about.'

'To point out the bloody obvious.'

'Thank you, detective,' Bailey said. 'After all these years, you and me, working the same murder.'

It had been a long time since they'd laughed together. A lot of tears in between.

'I can't hang around, Bailey. And neither can you.'

Bailey was disappointed, but she was right. They couldn't stand in the street all afternoon. 'Yeah, of course, jobs to do.'

'I sent the cop I was talking about, Rob Lucas, up the street to see if any other shops around here had cameras pointing at the footpath. I don't want him seeing us together.'

'I'm a bad influence.'

'Yeah, you are.'

He couldn't tell if she was being serious.

'I told him I'd meet him at the Cross. I need to get going before he doubles back looking for me.'

'Dinner tonight?' Bailey said.

'No.'

Shutdown.

'Some other time, then?'

'I'll say maybe.'

'And I'll say that's good enough for me.'

'One more thing before I go –'

'Yes, detective.'

'Monticello might have gone away somewhere. Let me know if you hear anything.'

'Sure. What're you going to do?'

'I'm going to head back to the station and find some contacts for his family. He must be around somewhere.' She was already walking away.

'Okay. Let's talk later. And Sharon?'

'Yep?'

'I'm going to hold you to your maybe.'

'Part of me hopes you do. But there's also a little voice that wants me to tell you to piss off.'

'Don't listen to it, even though I probably deserve it.'

'Yeah, you do.' She was standing on the street talking to him over the roof of her car. 'But ask me again sometime. When this is over.'

'That's a promise.'

'See you, Bailey.'

—

He watched Dexter drive away, feeling a buzz inside that he hadn't experienced for years, and walked over to where he'd parked his car under the fig tree. A familiar figure was loitering and chewing on a cigar.

'I'm starting to think you've got a thing for me.'

'I do, bubba,' Ronnie said.

'Well, I'm not interested. You're too tall.'

'Have you been back to your house today?'

'No time. Why? And is that bloody tracker still on my car?'

'No, bubba, took it off, like I told you.'

Problem was that Ronnie had told him lots of things over the years. 'You sure?'

'Positive.' Ronnie obviously had other things on his mind, which was why he was waiting under the fig tree in the first place. 'You've had visitors, and your house looks a little different to how you left it this morning.'

Bailey rested his elbow on the roof of the car. 'Don't tell me some druggy prick has robbed me?'

'I'd say pricks, plural,' Ronnie said. 'They've worked it over good and proper, and I doubt they were drug addicts.'

'What makes you say that?'

'TV, toaster – all the good stuff's still there.'

All Bailey could think about was his vinyl record collection. 'Better go and check out the damage. I'm due to meet Gerald. You coming?'

Ronnie tapped the roof. 'Was planning on riding with you.'

'Easier than sticking that tracking device under my car again, right?'

'Why's it so bloody hot? Isn't it almost winter?'

'Global warming, mate. Apparently it's real.'

Bailey used his key to unlock the passenger door for Ronnie.

'Please tell me your air conditioner's working.'

'Hasn't since January, the year 2000 when –'

'The millennium bug attacked this piece of junk's computer?' Ronnie finished the sentence for him. 'You need some new material, bubba – and a new car.'

Ronnie climbed in and chuckled as he watched Bailey fiddle with his key to unlock the driver-side door.

He reached over and lifted the latch. 'Having trouble?'

'Shut up, hillbilly.' Bailey climbed in and fastened his seatbelt. 'And as for the air con, pretend it's June – in Baghdad.'

'Might as well be.'

After a few pumps on the accelerator, the car spluttered to life.

'Now, let's go see how my renovation is looking.'

CHAPTER 14

Gerald was smoking a cigarette on the front porch when Bailey arrived home with Ronnie. 'Are you two going to tell me what the hell's going on?'

'Not even a hello for your old pal?'

Gerald glared at them through a cloud of smoke. Bailey hadn't seen him light up for more than a decade but he resisted making a quip about telling Nancy.

'You walk into my newsroom yesterday and out the door with Bailey without giving me that courtesy, Ronnie. Don't expect niceties from me.'

'Okay, bubba.' The big Oklahoman extended his right hand and Gerald shook it, reluctantly. 'You're going to love me again soon, just you wait.'

'It's going to take more than that bullshit charm of yours.'

'Look, you two,' Bailey said. 'I'm the one who's just had his house done over. Get a grip.' He turned to Gerald. 'How bad is it in there?'

'Not good. They're looking for something, Bailey. I was hoping you could tell me what?'

Bailey ignored the question, pausing at his front door and shaking his head at the shattered window on the porch. The glass had spread across the tiles inside and it crunched under the soles of his shoes as he stepped inside.

'That's where I climbed in to take a look. Hope that's okay . . .'

Gerald's voice trailed off as Bailey checked out the damage inside. His belongings were scattered everywhere, ripped out of cupboards and thrown on the floor. Bookshelves overturned, picture frames smashed, lamps broken and tables lying on their sides. Anything with cushions or fabric had been sliced open – chairs, his couch and even the mattress on his bed.

He walked over to where his vintage Pioneer turntable had been tipped on its side in the lounge room beside a half-empty bottle of Talisker. His beloved vinyl collection was spread out in a mess on the carpet. Pink Floyd, The Eagles, Dylan, The Who, Ziggy Stardust, The Clash and every Stones record he'd ever purchased were now a jumble of cardboard covers, plastic sleeves and black discs on the floor. None of the records looked broken, thankfully. It was just a matter of how many were scratched.

'Fuck me.' Bailey bent down and picked the bottle of single malt off the carpet, unscrewed the lid and took a long swig. 'This is about as thorough as you get.'

Buying the Paddington townhouse after his divorce was the only responsible thing Bailey had ever done. He did it so that Miranda would have a place to call a second home, not that she'd spent much time there. But he loved the house and it was unsettling seeing it trashed.

'Any idea what they were looking for?' Gerald asked again. He and Ronnie were following Bailey from room to room.

'Who knows? I don't have much, only that –'

Ronnie grabbed Bailey's elbow and raised his index finger to his lips. He gestured towards the roof and then touched his ear. 'Outside.'

'What's going on, Ronnie?' Bailey said when they were all back on the porch.

'It looked professional in there.'

A guy like Ronnie must have messed up a few homes in his time, so he would probably know.

'Someone could be listening.'

'You mean a bug? In my house?'

'These guys knew what they were doing. Who knows what they left behind?'

'Arseholes.' Bailey took another swig from the bottle.

'Let's go somewhere we can talk.' Ronnie patted Gerald on the shoulder. 'Just like old times.'

Bailey was still staring at the mess through the window. 'Sure. House is stuffed and the cleaner isn't due till Friday.'

'Okay then,' Gerald said. 'But I hope this is nothing like old times.'

Bailey looked at his watch: it was just after four o'clock.

'I know a place.'

—

The Old Hen was only a short walk up the hill from Bailey's townhouse. Sydneysiders had been drinking there for more than a hundred years. Bailey liked it because it still resembled a place where blue-collar workers mixed with lawyers, bankers, advertising execs and the footy players who went searching for a beer after stepping off the grass down the road at Moore Park.

In reality, the Old Hen wasn't so inclusive any more. The clientele was mainly business types, retirees and the occasional rich divorcee tired of sitting home alone. The only thing these people had in common was the fact that they had cash to burn and most of them liked to show it.

Bailey led them through the door and they settled at a table in a quiet corner of the pub.

'Nice,' Ronnie said. 'Better than the dump you took me to yesterday.'

'At least you got invited,' Gerald said.

'I'm going to get a round of drinks while you two sort out whatever it is that you need to sort out.' Bailey pointed at the bar. 'You've got the time it takes for me to walk over there and back. Whisky?'

Both men nodded.

The carpeted floor muffled Bailey's footsteps when he returned with the drinks. Gerald and Ronnie sounded like they were only just getting started.

'Bubba –'

Gerald held up his hand, gesturing for him to stop.

'I'm nervous, Ronnie. I've got to be honest with you . . . the last time we worked together, Bailey almost got killed.'

They hadn't noticed Bailey standing beside them with a handful of tumblers. Bemused, he just stood there and listened.

'C'mon, Gerald!'

'No, I'm serious.'

'I thought we'd moved past this? There was no master plan in that place and, yeah, it got hairy. You knew the risks.' Ronnie raised his big right hand and pointed his index finger at Gerald. 'And don't you forget, bubba, we got him out.'

'It took almost a year as you dangled him like a carrot in your backroom game playing with the Sunni and Shia militias –'

'We got him out.' Ronnie repeated the words, as if they were all that mattered.

'Yeah, we did, but not without that bag of cash I gave you.'

'Everything comes with a price, and it was better than Bailey starring in a movie where he gets his head cut off.'

Gerald leaned forward across the table. 'And how did the money get spent?'

Ronnie shifted uncomfortably in his chair.

'Go on, answer me that. Ronnie?'

'Bubba, why are we even talking about this? It was over a decade ago! I was at your goddamn sixtieth birthday party a few years back.'

'Why?' Gerald said. 'Because it looks like you're knee-deep in something on my doorstep. I don't like it.'

'Bubba, this isn't Iraq.'

'Too right. This is my livelihood, my reputation, and my family is here.' Gerald was raising his voice. 'I run the largest newspaper in the country –'

'You've got nothing to worry –'

'Let me finish. You're right, this isn't Baghdad. We have rules here and one of them is that journalists don't work with people like you.'

'Since when?' Ronnie's face was starting to go red. 'And what do you mean – people like me?'

'Enough!' Bailey slammed the glasses on the table – all doubles, neat – along with a small jug of water that almost tipped over. 'What is it with you two?'

The two men looked up, startled.

'Do we need to keep going over this old ground? I know I don't. We're all friends, aren't we?'

Gerald and Ronnie were eyeing each other across the table, waiting for the other to blink.

'Boys?'

Ronnie sat back, a smirk on his face. 'I never understand why you insist on adding water to a perfectly good glass of whisky.'

'You know it releases the flavour,' Gerald said. 'We've had this discussion a thousand times, you uncultured Oklahoman.'

'That's my boys,' Bailey said. 'One happy family again.'

'Not quite,' Gerald said.

'Come on, Gerald, let's stop this.' Ronnie sounded like he was pleading.

'If we're going to start sharing information,' Gerald said, 'I don't want any games.' Gerald lowered his voice and eyeballed first Ronnie, then Bailey. 'And I want to make something crystal clear – we can share information but we're not working together. Got it?'

'Bubba, I'm going to surprise you here. I'm happy with those terms. This isn't Baghdad, as you've been reminding me.'

'I'll drink to that.' Bailey downed his whisky in one.

Bailey started by telling them about the black hole in the security tape and the police commissioner's ongoing inter-ference in the case.

'You said you talked to a girl at Petals today too?' Gerald asked Bailey.

'The girl said she was a good friend of Chamberlain's, and guess what?' Bailey unfolded the picture of Victor Ho, laid it on the table and turned to Ronnie. 'I showed her the picture you gave me and she says he was a client of –'

'Catherine Chamberlain,' Gerald finished.

'Here's the other picture I've got of Victor,' Ronnie told Gerald, 'taken a few days ago.'

'What the . . .?' Gerald was staring at Victor's bloodied, lifeless face. 'Who is this guy?'

Bailey waited for Ronnie to answer the question.

'We think he's an agent, working for the Chinese Govern-ment,' Ronnie said. 'One of their so-called student spies.'

'Students?'

'Yeah, agents in universities, an old tactic they learned from the Russians. Student visas are the easiest way to get your people in. I'd be lying if I pretended we didn't do it too.'

'You wouldn't want to be caught telling fibs now, would –'

'The Chinese started doing it in the seventies.' Ronnie ignored Gerald's sarcasm. 'They're getting more organised and aggressive.'

'How's it work?' Gerald asked.

'Countries play the long game with these moves. It's about establishing contacts, influencing opinion, tapping future business leaders and politicians. Unless you get lucky.'

'How so?'

'A few years back, this one Chinese kid at Brown got close to the son of a sitting congressman. They were friends, probably more. Anyway, he gets invited to his new pal's home and manages to plant a bug inside the congressman's personal computer. From there, you can probably guess. Chinese hackers get a window into committee rooms on Capitol Hill.'

'And how come we never heard about this?' Gerald said.

'Never got out. We shut it down. Sent the kid home – with a limp.'

'And now students are killing people?' The leap from intelligence gatherers to murderers sounded a bit far-fetched for Bailey.

'A thousand dollars says young Victor here is the star of the missing fifteen minutes on that security tape,' Ronnie said.

'Maybe, maybe not,' Bailey said. 'But here's a question for you – who killed Victor?'

'Can't answer that. Looks like someone's cleaning up,' Ronnie said.

'Let's put his picture out there. It can be a follow-up story about Victor's death down by the casino. We don't need to say much. Just that police are investigating a link with Chamberlain,' Gerald said. 'Reckon Sharon Dexter might play ball?'

'I'll send her a message.' Bailey tapped his fingers on his phone slowly. No typos this time.

We want to publish the photo. Investigating link to the Catherine case. No direct source. OK?

'I reckon she'll play.' Bailey knew Sharon Dexter better than anyone. Despite the baggage between them, she trusted him. 'We'll put it under my byline. Anderson's reading my stuff online, so it might flush him out again.

'Now, old boy.' Bailey turned to Gerald. 'You've been in a foul mood all morning and I'm guessing you've got something for us?'

Gerald's frown returned. 'I do, but not in front of him.'

'C'mon, bubba. I thought we were good.'

'Changed my mind.'

'He's right, Ronnie.' Bailey wanted to show Gerald where his loyalties lay. 'How can we trust you? We've been down this road. And I'm not talking about my time in the dark room with the mad sheikh. I'm talking about the drip, drip of misinformation you fed us –'

Ronnie's fist crashed on the table, startling the few people sitting at the bar. 'I'm tired of the lectures from you two sons of bitches! They were classified operations with people's lives at stake. You two sit here sounding all righteous, but you've never got it, have you?'

'What, Ronnie? What haven't we got?' Now Bailey was the one sounding defensive.

Ronnie took a sip of his whisky.

'The bad people out there – they're smarter than you. You may not see it like I do, but there are many ways to do right, to do good. The world isn't pure. You dig down deep and you'll see it's all mud.' Ronnie stood up to leave. 'It doesn't matter where you live, bubba. It's all mud underneath. People like me keep it down, keep that shit from rising up . . . for the greater good.

'I always figured you two got it, that you understood the grey area. Maybe you just forgot. But I'm too old for the damned lectures.'

Ronnie grabbed his whisky and finished it.

'Sit down, mate.' Bailey knew they'd pushed him too far. He also knew they couldn't do this alone.

Ronnie didn't move. 'Why? So you can lecture me again? Accuse me of screwing you over? That isn't what happened. You've got no idea how many times I saved your skin in that hellhole. And you'll never know because that's my world.'

'All right, all right,' Gerald said. 'Sit down, Ronnie, please.'

Ronnie stared at them for a few more seconds before finally settling back in his chair.

'It's all going to be on the table,' Gerald said.

'Why don't we cut the bullshit, then?'

'At the moment, we can't print any of this. When it goes off, we print what we want. Got that, Ronnie? There'll be no interference from your people and no bullshit stories about national security, compromising assets, and any of that other legal injunction crap you and your mates at ASIO like to slap on our stories.'

Ronnie shrugged his shoulders. 'They're the last people I'll be talking to. Anything we discuss is yours. Best I can do.'

'Okay, here goes,' Gerald said. 'Gary Page called me personally today to tell me that Michael Anderson is wanted on suspicion of spying for the Chinese Government – off the record, of course.'

'And he's telling you because Anderson's been speaking to me and they want us to turn him over?' Bailey said.

'Fair assumption. But turning him over is something that we, of course, won't be doing.'

'Clever,' Ronnie said. 'He's backed you into a corner. Page has linked you to a crime that could get you locked up for questioning without the slightest case against you – put you in a cage without charge. He must know something we don't.'

Gerald looked confused. 'What do you mean?'

'Just talking to Anderson compromises you. Any communication could be interpreted as helping him,' Ronnie said. 'Aiding and abetting. Accessories after the fact. Remember, he's a wanted man.'

Bailey sighed, shaking his head. 'Sneaky bastard.'

'It's how you play it from here that matters, bubba.'

'What'd you say to Page?' Bailey asked.

'I said you hadn't had any contact with Anderson.'

'How'd he take that news?'

'Wasn't happy. Warned me to be careful, that Anderson was dangerous.' Gerald nudged Bailey with his elbow. 'Then he told me to pass on his concerns directly to you. I get the feeling they know you met him.'

Maybe it wasn't such a crazy idea that Bailey's house had been bugged after all. 'Either someone has been following me or they're listening in.' The thought made him feel sick.

'I'd say that's very likely,' Ronnie said.

'The bloke called me about fifteen times before I answered.' Bailey held up his phone and showed them the long list of missed calls. 'Can you trace a number from a missed call?'

'If his phone's on, he's traceable,' Ronnie said. 'Everyone leaves a mobile data trail these days. The phone transmits a signal to, or from, the nearest tower. If he's smart, he'll have gotten rid of it altogether.'

Bailey remembered the recent headlines about privacy laws. The federal government was making it easier for authorities to get hold of people's data by making telecommunications companies hang on to customer records for years. Not that the spooks needed any more help.

'But there's a simpler explanation,' Ronnie said.

Bailey knew where he was going. 'Don't tell me – it's my phone.'

'You're not running from anyone, or anything,' Ronnie said. 'I'd keep using it but be careful what you say. Turn it off or leave it behind when you need to.'

The conversation reminded Bailey about his message to Dexter. He looked down at his phone – still no response.

'Let's presume they know he was in touch. Let's also presume they have something on Anderson, concocted or real – something that'll stick.'

'I'd bet Anderson has something even bigger on them,' Gerald said. 'And we need to get it.'

Bailey's phone vibrated. 'Sharon says publish. Line is: *The Journal* understands that Victor Ho is a person of –'

'Thank you, Bailey. I've done a few of these in my time.' Gerald stood up to leave. 'Now, if you gentlemen will excuse me, I'd better get back to the office.'

'Okay, boss.' Bailey winked at him.

Gerald ignored Bailey's cheek and walked out of the Old Hen without turning around.

'Back in a minute, bubba.' Ronnie was on his feet too. 'Nature.'

Drinking with Gerald and Ronnie made Bailey think of the years he'd spent in the Middle East. About the man he was back then, when he was spending more time trying to escape from life than running towards it. War correspondents were like that – they thrived on the adrenalin rush. As a young cadet sitting in the back of a courtroom, or chasing ambulances, no one ever warned him about the highs and lows of the job, how to deal with them. Whisky was the only way that Bailey knew how.

He stared into the bottom of his empty glass, wondering how many more it would take today. He hadn't always been a heavy drinker. At least, not in those early days in Beirut when he was a young hack trying to make sense of Lebanon's civil war. Ronnie Johnson was there, on the scene of almost every violent attack – the type of bloodshed that people would simply call terrorism these days.

Bailey remembered the day he first met Ronnie. Blood and body parts were scattered on the street in West Beirut when a car bomb was detonated next to the motorcade of newly elected President René Moawad, in the last days of the war. It was November 1989, and the moderate Maronite Christian leader was one of almost two dozen people who died. The screams from the families of the innocent victims were sounds that Bailey would never get out of his head. He remembered seeing Ronnie chipping residue from the wrecked cars. Later, he shared a beer with the CIA agent, who told him about the 250-kilogram bomb that did all that damage. Bailey even remembered the story he wrote that day under the headline 'Beirut Bloodbath'.

The hard times for Bailey weren't the days he'd spent documenting the horrors and the evils of war. Those were the times when the feeling of doing something important brought the highs. The darkness set in when everything was normal. It was why Bailey always found somewhere else to go, which meant leaving someone behind. There was always someone.

Ever since he'd lost his brother, Mike, Bailey had been on the run. He lived by the rule of motion: never turn around, keep moving. He had to keep the adrenalin pumping, which meant more days in conflict zones, on the scene of the latest bomb attack, walking past the wounded with nothing to offer them other than a paragraph in a story. For two decades, it was the only life he knew how to live.

'Another whisky?'

Bailey hadn't noticed Ronnie standing beside their table.

'Why not?'

The warm fuzz of forgetting.

CHAPTER 15

'Get your fucking hands off me!' Bailey screamed.

'Bailey. Bailey! Wake up.'

'Let me go!'

'Wake up, bubba. Wake up.'

Bailey jolted upright in his bed.

'It's okay,' Ronnie said. 'It's just a bad dream. It's me – it's Ronnie.'

The sweat was stinging Bailey's eyes and he had a dry, smoky taste of a long whisky session on his tongue.

'Ronnie?'

'Yeah, bubba, your old pal.'

The smell of coffee brought Bailey back to reality.

'Some nightmare, hey, bubba?'

Ronnie was standing over him, balancing two steaming cups in his hand.

Bailey rubbed his eyes. 'One of those for me?'

'Irish – thought you'd need it. Know I do.'

Ronnie had forgotten what it was like to go drinking with John Bailey, now he had a pounding headache to remind him.

'You know me too well.' Bailey took a long swig. 'That's good.'

His head was throbbing, but at least his heart rate was slowing.

'Nightmares.' Ronnie paused. 'We all get them. What was it – Beirut? Kabul? Iraq?'

It was always Iraq.

Bailey pretended not to hear the question and switched on the television.

'You've got to be joking.'

Ronnie followed his eyes to the flatscreen fixed to the wall. Two men were patting each other's backs and waving at a friendly crowd.

'Page and Davis.' Bailey couldn't decide which face he wanted to punch more.

'What's this about?'

'Australian politics, mate. The sport of cronies. I need to call Gerald.'

Bailey picked up his phone and prepared to piss off his boss.

'Wait.' Ronnie tossed his phone on the bed beside Bailey. 'Use mine.'

Bailey did as he was told and walked outside to the courtyard at the back of his house before typing Gerald's number into Ronnie's phone.

He answered after two rings.

'It's Bailey. Switch on your TV. That exclusive Davis was promising you is on the ABC right now. Breaking news, apparently. Looks like a town hall function last night.'

'Duplicitous bastards,' Gerald grumbled down the line.

'Don't tell me you're surprised?'

'I need to watch this. Call you back.'

Bailey walked back inside and turned up the volume. The presenter was part way through her commentary on the story.

'. . . it's a departure from a thirty-five-year career policing criminals in the state of New South Wales. But Commissioner Davis says he's ready for a new challenge.'

Davis had an earnest look on his face that made Bailey groan.

'It's time for an exciting change,' he proudly declared to the cameras. 'I'm just happy that an opportunity to continue to serve the great people of New South Wales, the great people of Australia, has become available.'

'Become available?' The words sounded more incredulous when Bailey repeated them.

'I've always been a proud supporter of the Labor Party, the values of fairness and making sure we can grow prosperous, while helping the little guys at the same time.'

'What a wanker.'

Bailey hit the mute button. He had already reserved a special dislike for David Davis, largely because the man had slept with Dexter. Add a free ride on the political gravy train and he was close to topping Bailey's shit list.

'These guys get better at lying by the day.'

'You've got nothing on American politics, bubba.'

'At least some of your guys do the hard work to get elected.' Bailey had met enough congressmen to know the difference.

'Even when someone gets an office on the Hill, they spend twenty hours a week on the phone, speaking to constituents, trying to raise money for re-election. Here it's a wink and a nod from some union or faction boss and the door swings wide open.'

'Power and privilege, bubba, same story everywhere.'

'Yeah. Anyway, the stakes just got higher.'

Bailey was still staring at the two smug faces on the screen when his phone rang. He looked down at the screen expecting it to be Gerald. It was Miranda.

'Sweetheart.' He was instantly in a better mood.

'Dad, are you watching the television?' Miranda was speaking quickly, like something was wrong.

'Yeah.'

'The police commissioner's on now, talking about resigning and going into politics.'

'I'm watching. What's wrong?'

'He was the bloke I saw with Catherine Chamberlain that night in the city.'

The skin on Bailey's forehead rippled with concern, his brain trying to process what it meant.

'You sure?'

'As sure as I can be. I knew I'd recognised him from somewhere, at the time. Frankly, you see so many familiar faces on television, they all blend in and you forget who's who.'

'Sweetheart . . .' Bailey had walked back out to his courtyard, worried that someone might be listening. 'Don't tell anyone what you've just told me, okay?'

'What do you think it means?'

'Not sure.' Bailey wanted to get off the phone. 'I think we should talk in person. Can we meet later?'

'Dad, you're scaring me.'

Bailey hated himself for letting Miranda get this far involved. 'I'm just being cautious. When can we meet?'

'I'm in court till four.'

'Call me at the office when you're finished. I'll be there. Can you come by?' If she said no, he'd be waiting outside the courtroom.

'Sure. It's a short walk.'

He wanted to respond with something that would make her feel safe, make her smile, but nothing came. 'Take care, sweetheart.'

Inside, Ronnie was still watching the television. Before Bailey could speak, his phone rang again. It was Gerald.

He answered. 'I'll call you back.' And hung up, feeling ridiculous.

Bailey grabbed Ronnie's phone and walked back outside for a third time. This time, Ronnie was following him.

Gerald answered before the first ring.

'Are you there?'

'Of course I'm here!'

'I was talking to Miranda.' Bailey lowered his voice. 'You're not going to believe this – she says she saw Davis with Catherine Chamberlain in a city bar a few weeks ago.'

'He was a client?'

'It's possible. Leave it with me. I need to speak to Sharon.'

Bailey hung up the phone for the third time in less than five minutes.

He turned to Ronnie, who was hunched over, his face next to Bailey's so he could hear both ends of the conversation. 'Get all that?'

'Loud and clear, bubba.'

'I need a shower,' Bailey said. 'How's the head, mate?'

'Not good.'

'Big bloke like you, still can't keep up.'

The newsreader on the television had moved on to another story.

'Police are still searching for Michael Anderson, the former advisor to Defence Minister Gary Page. Mr Anderson is wanted for questioning over the murder of Sydney woman Catherine Chamberlain.'

'Here we go,' Bailey said. 'What now?'

'In a dramatic development this morning, police now say he is armed and dangerous.'

'*Armed and dangerous*? What on earth are they playing at?'

Bailey picked up his phone and typed a text message to Dexter – brief, and with the usual typos.

Urgent. Cam we meet fpr coffee?

The response arrived within seconds.

Harry's at Woolloomooloo. Let's take a walk.

When?

Now.

Bailey turned to Ronnie. 'I'm going to meet Sharon. I know you like to know where I am.'

'You're on your own, bubba. Things to do.' Ronnie reached into his pocket and pulled out a fresh cigar.

'Yeah, like what?'

'The ambassador,' Ronnie said. 'He needs me.'

He slapped Bailey on the shoulder and left.

CHAPTER 16

Woolloomooloo epitomised the changing soul of Sydney like no other suburb. With its history of war, poverty, migration, economic development and affluence, it also told a story about the shaping of modern Australia.

Bailey had been coming here on and off for decades, most often for drinking sessions that ended with a footpath dinner at a mobile kitchen called Harry's Café de Wheels.

Harry Edwards first parked his caravan café next to Woolloomooloo's naval dockyards in 1938, promising a cheap pie with peas at a time when the Depression was biting hard. It wasn't open long because war beckoned, and Harry headed off to fight the Germans and Italians in the Middle East. When he came home in 1945, he slid open his kitchen door and Harry's Café de Wheels reclaimed the mantle as the favourite late-night takeaway for sailors, cops, journalists, drunken partygoers, criminals and anyone working the nightshift needing a cheap, hearty meal when other restaurants were closed.

With the buzz of his Irish coffee diminishing, Bailey approached the counter. 'Pie and peas, mate. No sauce.' It was the only thing that Bailey ever ordered at Harry's.

Dexter wouldn't be far away, but he was hungry and desperate for something to dull his hangover. He looked down at his stomach, which was pressing slightly on the shirt dangling over his jeans. He really needed to get in shape. Maybe, when all this was done, he'd finally go jogging with Miranda like he'd promised. More quality time with his daughter – how bad could it be?

'Thanks, mate.' Bailey paid the guy behind the counter and took a bite out of his pie. It was good. If exercising meant he could still eat at Harry's, maybe he'd buy himself a pair of trainers. That was still a big maybe.

Woolloomooloo was an upmarket part of town these days, where the salted air blowing off the harbour no longer competed with the smell of urine on the footpath. Like most of the city, the place had undergone major cosmetic surgery, but the developers had somehow preserved its history.

The sense of the past was largely due to the imposing arm of the Finger Wharf. The giant shell was twice as old as Bailey and, on the outside at least, it had retained its honest majesty. Inside, the urbane transformation was immense. Magazine restaurants lined the promenade, each with similar décor and nouveau menus set at the same exorbitant prices. Upstairs were the multimillion-dollar condos owned by celebrities and the cashed-up elite, who paced the planks of the wharf oblivious to those who had walked there before them.

If the wharf's sturdy pylons could speak, they'd describe soldiers farewelling their families for war, lowly paid wharfies loading piles of wool for export, and the arrival of the new Australians – Greeks, Italians and, later, Chinese and Vietnamese – all searching for a better life.

Bailey finished his pie and walked to the corner of the wharf where it would be easy for Dexter to find him.

Whichever way he looked the view was impressive – the matchstick skyscrapers and Sydney Tower, the roof of St Mary's Cathedral, the Art Gallery of New South Wales and the rolling hills of the Botanic Gardens. He could even see the sails of the Opera House and the busiest bridge on the continent. The navy ships moored near Kings Cross were only a few hundred metres away – an imposing reminder that peacetime hadn't come without a fight.

Sydney was familiar to Bailey, but it didn't feel like home. Nowhere did any more.

He looked at his phone. It had been almost thirty minutes since they had exchanged text messages and he was starting to worry.

He sent her another one.

Whre r u?

The fact that Bailey's home had been ransacked meant that someone had taken more than a casual interest in him. He didn't like it. Had he been followed? Had they got to Dexter too? He didn't even know who *they* were.

He studied the people around him; walking along the wharf, across the road and sitting down for breakfast – or brunch, as they liked to call it at this time of the day. No one seemed to care that it was a work day. The place looked like the pages of a gossip magazine brought to life – fake tans, breast enlargements, white jeans and canvas shoes. One old lady with blue hair had a cluster of diamonds around her neck that looked like a bunch of grapes. And everyone was talking, either to the person sitting opposite or on their phone – so busy, so popular; yet so very lonely. At least they seemed that way to Bailey.

Sydney had become a bullshitter's paradise and Bailey didn't like it.

His pocket vibrated. He pulled out his phone – unknown number.

'Hello.'

'You're right about Victor Ho.'

It was Michael Anderson.

'I was wondering when you might call again.'

'Yeah, well, now you can stop wondering. Saw your story online –'

'We shouldn't talk on the phone,' Bailey said. 'Someone could be listening.'

'How d'you know?'

'I just know.'

Click.

'Anderson? Anderson?'

He was gone.

Bailey looked down at the screen on his phone to confirm that the call had ended. It had. But there was a message from Dexter.

Sorry. Be there in 5. Held up. Will explain.

Dexter crossed at the traffic lights just up from Harry's, walking like someone in a hurry, looking over her shoulder every few steps.

She looked stressed and tired when she arrived beside Bailey.

'Are you okay?'

'Not really.'

Bailey took a chance and squeezed her arm. 'Looks like we have a bit to talk about.'

'Yeah, we do. Let's take a walk.'

His natural instinct was to take her arm, only he didn't. He'd lost the right to do that with Dexter. They walked along the wharf in silence.

'It wasn't me,' Dexter said finally.

Bailey didn't know what she was talking about. 'Wasn't you what?'

'Armed and dangerous.' She repeated the line the newsreader had used on television earlier that morning.

'Never thought it was. Reckon it was Davis?'

She shook her head. 'Not directly. It's more likely that that dickhead Rob Lucas has been briefing the media behind my back. And by the media, I obviously don't mean you.'

'Obviously.'

'Davis is into something,' Dexter said. 'Something not right. I'm not sure how Catherine Chamberlain's linked but it's there, somewhere.'

The last time Bailey had mentioned his theories about Davis to Dexter, it hadn't gone down well. But this time he had a source who was incapable of lying – his daughter.

'Davis was a client,' he said. 'I'm sure about that now.'

'How?'

'Miranda saw them together in the city one night.'

'Wait a minute.' Dexter stopped walking and turned so she could see his face. 'Your Miranda?'

'Yeah.'

Bailey wanted Dexter to lead the conversation, ask the questions.

'How on earth does she know Catherine Chamberlain? Did she know what Catherine did in her spare time for cash? Were they friends?'

'Not really. Miranda teaches a law class at university and turns out Catherine was her student. They knew each other, that's about it.'

Dexter walked to the edge of the wharf and stopped next to a luxury catamaran quietly bobbing against its mooring.

She lit a cigarette, took a long drag and blew the smoke across the water. 'Emergencies.'

Bailey couldn't care less about the cigarette. 'I'm sorry.'

'I knew he wasn't a good guy. I was just . . . I was . . .'

'It's okay.'

'It was just . . . I was just so lonely.' She took another drag and gazed past the catamaran towards the eastern tip of the harbour. 'So bloody lonely.'

Bailey didn't know what to say because he knew that she blamed him. Their relationship had failed because of him – the collateral damage of his dysfunction.

She couldn't bring herself to look at him. 'I mean, fuck you – fuck you, Bailey.'

He had to let her get it out. And he deserved it.

'I was so angry at you.' She was talking to the water in between long puffs of the white stick in her hand. 'And I waited. Do you know how long I waited for you, Bailey?'

She let the silence hang, an invitation for him to respond.

'I didn't think to –'

'You didn't think to what? I think you mean that you just didn't think, full stop.'

Bailey stopped trying to explain himself and waited for Dexter to say something.

She took a final drag on her cigarette, which had burnt down almost to the little yellow stump, and tossed it onto the wooden planks of the wharf.

'You didn't think, unless you count thinking about yourself. That's something you were damn good at.'

'I'm here now.'

'What does that even mean?'

'I'm not sure.'

'Well, that's just great!'

'I should never have gone back, don't know why I –'

'Don't bullshit me, Bailey.' She turned back around to face him. 'You know why you went back. You're addicted to it – the rush, the feeling of being important. Being in the place where it's all going down. You've been like that from the moment I met you.'

She turned her back on him, walked a few paces closer to the water's edge.

'A lot has happened since then,' he said.

'Yeah? Why should I listen to you this time?'

'I couldn't come back straight away. Not after Iraq.'

'What do you mean? You'd been in and out of that place for decades. And you've been back here for three fucking years, Bailey!' She looked like she was pleading with him to give her something that would make sense. 'And we'd been there before – the nightmares, the faces that kept you awake. Why couldn't you talk to me?'

'It was different. And I couldn't do it to you, not again. I just couldn't. Had to do it myself –'

'That wasn't your decision to make!'

Yeah, but he'd made it anyway. Big boys didn't cry, especially in front of big girls.

'You want to know? You really want to fucking know what happened to me in that rat hole?'

'Yes! Yes, I do!'

'Excuse me.' A waiter from one of the restaurants on the wharf was standing behind them with a sheepish look on his face. 'Do you mind taking your conversation away from this area? You're interrupting our guests.'

The people in the restaurant had turned their heads away

from their al fresco meals to tune in to the sideshow playing out in front of them.

Bailey eyeballed the waiter. 'Yeah, you can tell the patrons to –'

'Bailey!' Dexter said.

'Okay, mate, we're going.' He grabbed Dexter by the hand and led her away.

By the time they reached the end of the wharf they were alone, apart from the birds and more bobbing boats.

'I was taken.' The way he said the words made them sound like it wasn't a big deal, like it could happen to anyone.

'What?'

'Mad Islamists. They held me for ten months.'

'You, you . . . you were kidnapped?'

'Guess you'd call it that.'

'What happened?'

Bailey looked away, back up the wharf towards Harry's.

'Talk to me – Bailey? I want to know.'

After all this time, she deserved some answers.

'Gerald and I went to Fallujah with an American military unit. The operation went bad. These guys grabbed me, kept me in a cave – did all kinds of shit.'

He touched the skin where three of his fingernails used to be, but he didn't look at them. He didn't want Dexter to see.

'Jesus, Bailey!'

'I will talk about it with you. Can we just not do it now?'

Tears left two neat trails down her cheeks. 'I'm . . . I'm so sorry, John.'

'Anyway, I'm good. Took a while, but I'm almost there – back where I want to be.'

Almost.

'I just never really mastered how to do this.' He was pointing his finger at Dexter and back at himself. 'How to be, you know, us.'

She walked towards him and rested her head on his chest. 'You hurt me, Bailey.'

He put his arms around her.

'I'm done feeling sorry for myself.'

Doctor Jane would have been proud of him. If only she had been here with her notebook.

—

They walked back up the wharf in silence.

'So, what now?' Bailey said when they reached the roadside.

'One step at a time, boyo.'

'Actually, I meant what now with Davis, and Catherine Chamberlain.'

'I know. I was teasing.'

'Well played. So, what now?'

'When's the last time you wore a tuxedo?' Dexter had a mischievous expression on her face.

'Black tie? Gerald's birthday a few years back.'

'Tonight could be a good time to dust it off.'

'What are you playing at?'

'Cocktail party for Davis, the politician in waiting, I've got a plus one.'

'This could be interesting.'

CHAPTER 17

Foreign ambassadors are sent out into the world to sell a positive message about their country to anyone who'll listen. That means going to a lot of parties. So when John Bailey got his hands on the guest list for the launch of David Davis's new political life, he was banking on a very important freeloader being invited.

And he was right.

Chinese Ambassador Li Chen was already in Sydney for the event and, not surprisingly, had managed to squeeze in a lunch down by the water at Circular Quay with some rich Chinese investors he'd been helping to tip their millions into Sydney's surging residential property market.

A bunch of Sydney real estate agents were sitting with them, their glossy brochures spread across the table. One of the guys from *The Journal*'s property section had told Gerald about the gathering – real estate agents always told the papers because it helped them pump up the market – so he'd sent Bailey down for a look.

The ambassador was clicking his fingers at a waiter, pointing to his empty wine glass, when Bailey walked past his table with a beer in his hand. Two seafood platters were set in the middle with oysters, lobsters, dozens of rings of grilled calamari, and chunks of whatever white fish was in season. It smelled good – almost as good as the pie Bailey had just thrown back at Woolloomooloo. Almost.

Bailey found an empty stool by the edge of the water and sat down. The angle of his chair meant that he had a good view of the mostly Chinese men in suits enjoying lunch, as well as the ferries sailing in and out of the quay. Bailey wanted to get a good look at Ambassador Li Chen in action – to see if he was the kind of guy who could be involved in the murder of an innocent girl. That was a journalist's job sometimes – to observe.

Not all diplomats were entertainers, but Ambassador Li was made for it. He was holding court with the type of stories that drew laughter from the rich men's club. Bailey couldn't decide whether he looked more like a B-Grade actor or a used car salesman.

It wasn't long before Li was holding up his empty wine glass again, searching for a waiter. He wasn't having much success. Tired of being ignored, he stood up, slammed his glass on the table and started walking towards the outdoor bar on the other side of the restaurant. By the time he got there he was waving his hands around, remonstrating with the barman and pointing at all the empty glasses.

Bailey kept watching, wondering how the moment might play out, quietly hoping for a security guard to step in and turn it into a diplomatic incident.

Wishful thinking.

The restaurant knew exactly who was dining at that table today and, like most of Sydney, they wanted the Chinese money to keep flowing.

An overweight man in a black leather jacket and loose jeans appeared at the bar and touched the ambassador on the arm, surprising him in a way that caused him to stumble backwards. By the way the man was dressed, Bailey could tell that he wasn't one of the men from the ambassador's table.

Ambassador Li's shoulders slumped and he looked like he was almost being deferential. The other guy had his back to Bailey, making it impossible to see his face. But he could tell that he was important. His left hand was gripped tightly around the arm of the ambassador, creasing his suit coat, and he was leaning forward, speaking right in his face.

The conversation lasted for less than a minute before the fat guy let go of Ambassador Li's arm, patted him on the shoulder, and walked back through the restaurant, away from Bailey. When he joined the pedestrian thoroughfare that cut through the restaurants, he turned briefly to let someone pass. Bailey caught the side of his face – Chinese, round cheeks, black sunglasses, a neat part in his hair. But Bailey wouldn't be able to identify him in a line-up, if it ever came to that.

Bailey looked back at the bar where the ambassador was still standing, straightening his jacket, trying to compose himself. Eventually, he picked two bottles of white wine off the bar and walked towards his lunch table with a forced smile on his face, looking like he'd just seen a ghost.

CHAPTER 18

Iraq, unknown location

Bailey had stopped feeling hungry. It was only water that he craved now.

He was too dehydrated to sweat, despite the intense heat blanketing his body inside his hard metal cocoon. Each breath delivered a sharp pain, his lungs struggling to filter the fumes and dust leaking inside. His head was pounding from the rifle butt they had used to knock him out when they threw him into the car.

They were bouncing along a road somewhere in Iraq and Bailey's skeletal frame was smashing into the hard edges of the boot.

He had been moved so many times since Fallujah that he'd lost all sense of geography. Disorientated by a constant thirst and hunger, he had even lost count of the days.

Trapped in the foetal position, he could barely move. His hands and feet were fastened tightly together with plastic zip ties. He could tell they were plastic because of the way they sliced into his skin.

A warm pool of blood had formed beneath his head. He shifted so that he could at least feel the mess on the floor and get a sense of how much blood he'd lost – a survival instinct for a man who, despite everything, still wanted to live.

Everything mattered now.

The wetness was confined to a small sticky area below his cheek and he could feel a dried patch on his face. The bleeding had stopped. Relief.

Bailey could just make out the sound of male voices over the rattle and hum of the engine – two, maybe three – and they appeared to be having an argument. He wanted to close his eyes, but the fear of not waking up kept him lucid.

Stay awake. Whatever you do, stay awake.

The white strobing moonlight flickered through a crack in the boot. The crunching of the tyres told Bailey they were driving on a dirt road. He hadn't heard any other cars and was feeling more alone with every rotation of the wheels.

The car skidded to a stop. Voices fell silent. Doors opened, then closed. Footsteps slapped the ground outside and around the back.

They were coming for him.

The boot opened. It was a full moon and the stars in the sky offered Bailey a brief moment of beauty in hell. He couldn't see the faces of the three men standing over him, only their shiny thick beards and the white in their eyes.

'Hello, dog!' a man said in Arabic.

'Wait!' A different voice. He stepped in front of the others and pointed his gun at Bailey. Closer. Until he rested the barrel on his temple.

Click.

The pistol wasn't loaded.

Bailey shuddered. The fear in his eyes was what they wanted. His life was cheap. The man with the gun was God.

'Hahahahaha!' The three men danced around the car, hysterical.

Their laughter only lasted a few seconds.

'Imbeciles!' A fourth man had joined them. 'Get him out.'

The men clumsily grabbed Bailey, pulling him from the car and dropping him on the dirt.

'Cut him loose.'

They cut the zip ties from his hands and feet.

'Stand up, Mr Bailey.' The man switched to English.

Bailey recognised the voice, and the hard eyes glowing in the darkness.

'It's been a while, my friend. How are you?'

The posh English accent made the acid in Bailey's stomach churn. He remembered being forced to watch the execution of the US marine. He went to speak, but could only cough, his dry throat preventing the words from forming.

'Here, my friend.' The man handed him a bottle of water. 'Drink.'

Bailey snatched it, fumbling with the lid in a rush to get the liquid inside. He gulped at the bottle, spilling some of the water on his chin and down his neck.

'I know you,' Bailey spluttered.

'You think you know me, Mr Bailey.' The tone in his voice always calm. 'You don't know me.'

He was a murderer.

'From the room.' Bailey took another sip of water. 'The marine. You sadistic –'

'Yes, yes, I remember.' He stepped closer. Bailey could see his face. 'A long time ago now, Mr Bailey. A long time to think. A long time to hate.'

It didn't seem long ago to Bailey. He could see Douglas McKenzie's severed head like it was yesterday. 'Where am I?'

'Do you still hate, Mr Bailey?' the man taunted him. 'Do you know that since the day we were last together eleven thousand Iraqi civilians have died? Collateral damage, they say. Is this what freedom looks like?'

'I'm a fucking journalist, not a marine.' Bailey's gravelly voice sounded more like a growl.

'Yes, yes, Mr Bailey. We've been over this. We know all about you.'

'Where am I?'

'You're in Baghdad.'

'Baghdad? Why am I here?'

The man touched Bailey's chin, lifting his head so their eyes could meet. 'Because your time has come.'

Bailey felt a sudden panic. 'What do you mean?' He didn't want to be the next Douglas McKenzie.

'It's time for you to hear my story.'

'What're you talking about?'

'Soon.' The man turned and started walking away. 'See you soon. It'll be different for you here.'

The man barked an order to the others in Arabic and disappeared into the night.

'I'm talking to you!' Bailey shouted out after him. 'What am I doing here? What am I doing here?'

Bailey felt someone shaking his shoulder. He was lying, sweating and mumbling to himself, on the couch in his overturned townhouse.

'Dad, wake up! Dad?'

Disorientated, he opened his eyes. 'Hey?'

'It's okay, Dad.' She gently stroked his shoulder. 'It's me . . . it's Miranda.'

As Bailey focused his eyes, he could see his daughter's shiny blonde hair dangling across her cheek. 'Sweetheart?'

'That's right, Dad. It's me. It's Miranda.'

Bailey sat up and rubbed his eyes. 'Bugger!' He was angry with himself for having those extra beers down at Circular Quay before stopping by his house. 'We were supposed to meet. I'm sorry. I just closed my eyes for a minute.'

'It's okay, Dad.'

'What time is it?' He looked out the window and could tell it was getting close to dark.

'It's almost five o'clock.'

He held out his hand, Miranda took it and sat down beside him.

'Dad?'

'Yes, sweetheart.'

'What happened here? It looks like you've been robbed.'

'Long story.'

'I feel like you've got a few of those. We need to talk.'

'We do. Sorry . . . sorry for standing you up.'

'You didn't stand me up, Dad. I called your office, they said you hadn't been in all day. Tried your mobile and no answer. So I thought I'd do the old-fashioned thing and pop in. The door was open.'

'Glad you did.' He put his arm around her and kissed her forehead. 'I need a shower, then let's talk.'

'I'll make some coffee.' Miranda walked into the kitchen, stepping over broken bowls and plates, searching through the mess for a kettle and two cups that had survived the break-in.

—

After his shower, Bailey rummaged through the clothes that some prick had spread across the floor of his bedroom until he found a white shirt. The political function with Dexter was a black tie affair and he was determined to look the part. His crumpled dinner suit was there too, somehow still attached to a coat hanger. It would have to do.

He was running low on sleep but the shower had boosted his energy. Cleanly shaven, he was staring at himself in the mirror, struggling to fix his bowtie, when Miranda called out from the door.

'Dad? I've got your coffee. You decent?'

'Yeah.'

'The bat wing, hey?' She was trying not to laugh. 'Need some help?'

'Desperately.'

'I can't remember the last time I saw you clean shaven.'

'Yeah. Simple things were never my strong suit.'

'Where are you off to anyway?'

'Work function.' He didn't want to announce that he was going to a political campaign launch for the police commissioner when he still suspected his house might be bugged.

Miranda looked at her father's face in the mirror, turning the ends of the tie in her hands. His tanned skin, dark brown eyes, the weathered creases of his brow. He smiled at her and the lines spread to his cheeks.

'It's nice to see you smile.'

'What do you mean? I'm always smiling with you.'

'Your eyes, Dad, the happiness in your eyes. I don't see it. Not enough, anyway.'

She finished tying the knot and gently shifted the tips until the tie was straight. She looked up again and noticed her father staring at her, his smile already gone.

'You sounded like you were having a bad dream earlier.'

'Did I?'

'Yes. Have them often?'

'From time to time.'

'Dad?' She paused. 'What happened to you all those years ago?'

He knew it was a question Miranda had been wanting to ask him for years, but he had always found a way to shut it down.

Bailey walked out of the bathroom.

'One day you need to talk to me.' Her voice followed him. 'I want to know. I think I need to know.'

'Okay.' Bailey tapped his hand on the bed. They sat down together.

After his conversation with Dexter at the Finger Wharf, today was confession day. Bailey owed it to his daughter to at least tell her something.

'It was a bad time, Miranda. Beirut, Iraq, the first time. Those were tough years. Nothing like the evil in that place now. So much hate. No solutions, either.'

'I mean *you*, Dad.' She put her hand over his. 'What happened to you?'

'Where do I start?' Bailey was trying not to sound serious. He was worried that sharing too much would drive her away.

'Your messages, phone calls, even letters, they were always random, but there was contact, then it all just stopped. I didn't hear from you for almost a year and when I finally did you spoke to me like you were . . . empty, childlike. Do you even remember?'

'I should never have called you out of the blue like that.'

But he'd needed to hear her voice.

'That's not what I meant. I loved that you called me.'

'Timing wasn't good.' Bailey was speaking without looking at her. 'It was the timing that was a bad idea. I just . . . I just –'

'Just what? Dad?'

'I needed to hear you, hear you speak, hear what you sounded like.'

'What happened? You can talk to me.'

Bailey let out a long breath, contemplating how much he'd share.

'I was kidnapped and tortured.'

Too much.

'What? What do you mean, tortured?' Miranda's voice cracked, her eyes glistening with sorrow.

'Sweetheart, you don't need to hear this stuff.' And he didn't want to tell it. The details were better inside, contained.

'How long did they have you?'

But sitting side by side with his daughter, Bailey didn't have much choice. 'Ten months.'

'*Ten months!*'

'You really don't need to hear about this.' He squeezed her hand. 'It's over, all in the past.'

'C'mon, Dad. I need to know. I think I –'

'No, you don't. Some things are better left. It achieves nothing.'

'Have you spoken to anyone about it?'

'Shrinks? I've had plenty of those. Gerald booked me a gentle genius in London.' The sessions with Genevieve, or whatever her name was, were a disaster. 'Got one here too, Doctor Jane. She's better than the others. Anyway, I've done my talking, unpacking the pain. I'm getting better.'

'What about when you sleep? You were mumbling something about Baghdad on the couch when I got here. Doesn't sound like you've dealt with it to me.'

He wished she would stop. Miranda was the one person he couldn't tell to piss off and she was digging into a place he didn't let anyone go.

'I don't think you ever do, to be honest. You just learn to live with it – and that's what I'm doing. Spending time with you helps, helps a lot. Makes me smile. Even my eyes.'

Bailey squeezed his daughter's hand again, let go, and got up off the bed.

A rainbow lorikeet was sitting on a branch outside his bedroom window. He studied its green wings and the rich red, yellow and blue colours splotched like a child's painting on its feathers. He was looking for something to distract him from the conversation that he had never wanted to have with his daughter.

'Dad?'

'You know, Miranda . . .' But he was here now – in the hole. Humiliated. At least, that's how it felt.

'You know . . .' Bailey's eyes were locked on the lorikeet. He couldn't dare look at her now. He had to keep it in. 'The one thing that kept me going during those months.'

Another long, silent pause.

'It was the sound of your laughter, Miranda. You won't remember because you were so young. We played games together, sometimes in the middle of the night. Neither of us have ever really been good sleepers. I'd do anything to make you laugh – pull faces, hide behind pillows. Silly Daddy.'

'What?'

'Those were some of your first words – *Silly Daddy*.'

At least, that was the phrase he remembered.

If Bailey had turned around he would have seen the tears streaming down his daughter's face. She couldn't remember the games. All she could remember was loving him. Being loved by him. Even when he wasn't there.

'Silly Daddy.' Bailey repeated the words, staring at the splotchy bird through the window. 'I was a silly father, Miranda, missing all those years.'

'Dad?'

The lorikeet flew away.

'Dad?'

With nothing left to distract him, Bailey turned to his daughter. He quickly wiped his eyes. Crying wasn't his thing. He usually found other ways to dim the pain, keep going.

Without saying another word, Miranda walked over to her father by the window and wrapped her arms around him.

The tears came and he let them fall, knowing that she couldn't see. He wasn't humiliated any more. He was relieved. It felt good making up for lost time.

Eventually, he let go and turned away, using his shirtsleeves to dry his cheeks. That was enough honesty for one day, more than he'd ever shared before. Somehow, he knew that his daughter knew it too.

'Thanks, Dad. You know I love you. Whenever you want to talk, I can listen.'

Bailey should have felt weak, but he felt strong.

'Okay, sweetheart.' But he wasn't ready to contemplate going through this again anytime soon. 'I'd better get moving.'

'What's this work function?'

Bailey looked at his watch. Five-thirty. It really was time to go.

'I'll explain in the car. Give me a lift?'

'Sure.'

CHAPTER 19

The sun had already set by the time Bailey and Miranda walked across the broken glass at the front door and outside onto the street. A cool breeze shuffled the first of the autumn leaves along the footpath. Miranda shivered and wrapped a scarf around her neck. The cold weather was finally arriving.

Bailey squeezed into the front seat of his daughter's red two-seater convertible. 'I love that we've got the same taste in cars.'

'Dad, this is a 1971 Classic MG Roadster. The only thing it's got in common with the pile of junk you drive is that it's old!'

'Beauty's in the eye of the driver, my darling.'

'You must have a soft spot for trash.'

It was too cold to take off the soft-top and Bailey's head was touching the roof. 'At least I can fit in my car.'

'Where're we going, by the way?'

'Art gallery, in the gardens.'

Miranda turned the key, the engine faulted and burped, before spluttering to life.

'Sounds a lot like the classic I drive.'

'Just you wait a minute, old man.'

She gently pumped the accelerator until the engine plateaued, settling on a purring rhythm.

'Now, tell me your car hums like that, huh?'

She revved the engine to make her point.

'Similar.'

She punched her father playfully in the shoulder. 'You're shameless!'

Miranda steered the car into the street and tapped the volume button on her radio. The sounds of the Rolling Stones blared from the speakers.

'That's my girl! I managed to teach you something after all.'

'You taught me more than that, but yeah, love the Stones.'

Miranda was swerving through the traffic on Oxford Street like someone in a hurry.

'Next time they're out here, we'll go.'

A Rolling Stones concert with his daughter would be Bailey's perfect night out.

'Eightieth anniversary tour? Sure!'

'Don't say that. You make me feel old. I grew up listening to those boys!'

'You're still growing up listening to those boys!'

'Touché. You also inherited my wit.'

Miranda shoved the car into third gear and roared up the bus lane on William Street.

'Daddy's girl, Mum always said.'

'Especially when you were naughty?'

'Especially then.'

'Your poor mum, the two of us – two of me! She deserves a bloody medal.'

'Sure does.'

'By the way.' Miranda sounded serious. 'Didn't you want to tell me something about the police commissioner?'

They had become so engrossed in the past that Bailey had forgotten all about David Davis. They would be at the gallery in minutes, so he got straight to it. 'You sure he's the bloke you saw with Catherine Chamberlain that night in the city?'

'As can be,' Miranda said, stopping at a traffic light and looking at him. 'I walk up to Catherine to say hello. She didn't look like she was with anyone. As I come up beside her, Davis turns and puts his arm around her shoulder, like they were a couple.'

'Did you speak?'

'Not really. He was drunk and she could see I was confused when he called her Ruby. Then he mumbled something about it being time to hit the hotel.'

'Classy.'

'I could see in her eyes that she didn't want me there.' Miranda was driving again, checking her mirrors and changing lanes as she spoke. 'But she tried to overcome the awkwardness by introducing me as a friend from uni. He looked at me like I'm nothing and said – "Ruby, we're leaving."'

Nothing. The reasons for Bailey to dislike David Davis were growing by the hour.

'Anything else?'

'Not really. I grabbed her hand and squeezed it.' Miranda reached across the gearstick and grabbed her father's hand. 'You know, when you're checking if someone's all right?'

'And?'

'She mouthed the words "I'm okay", then she was gone.'

'Ever talk about it with her afterwards?'

'No, it's her business. I'm just the tutor.'

Miranda steered the car round St Mary's Cathedral and up Art Gallery Road.

'Have you talked about it with anyone else?' Bailey didn't want Miranda getting any closer to this. 'You need to remember. It's important.'

'No, Dad. Just you.'

'Good.'

'What do you think it means?'

'Davis hooking up with a prostitute who winds up being murdered?'

'Yeah.'

'A lot. That's the short answer, anyway.' He looked out the window at a bunch of kids kicking around a footy on the grass. 'Exactly what, I don't know. She may've been told something that put her in danger.'

'Something Davis told her?'

The possibility hadn't occurred to Bailey. Was Davis sharing secrets during pillow talk too? Catherine Chamberlain was an intelligent girl. If she and Michael Anderson were an item, it wasn't out of the question that she might have pieced together something Davis told her and whatever it was that Anderson had shared. But he was speculating.

'Dad?'

'Sorry. You were saying?'

'Do you think Davis told her something that put her in danger?'

'Unlikely.' The less Miranda knew, the better. 'He's the police commissioner, remember?'

'And you have such a high opinion of people in uniform.'

'Okay, got me there. Whatever happens, it's bad for Davis because we can connect him to a murdered prostitute. The cops will be looking back through her clientele. At least, they should be. Unless he's found a way to close that avenue.' Bailey spotted Dexter standing by the side of the road. 'I might get an answer to that question shortly.'

Miranda slowed down out the front of the art gallery and did a 180-degree turn so that Bailey wouldn't need to cross the road.

'Is that Sharon Dexter?'

'Yep.' Bailey hadn't taken his eyes off her since he'd clocked her at the bottom of the art gallery steps.

'So, secret man, there *is* a woman in your life?'

He didn't answer because he honestly didn't know.

Dexter walked up to the car, bent down and smiled through the window at Miranda. 'Hi love. This old boy getting you to chauffeur him around?'

'When he can.' Miranda leaned across her father so she could see Dexter out the passenger window. 'He was too embarrassed to turn up in his old piece of junk.'

'Yeah, yeah,' Bailey said, turning to Dexter. 'Give me a second.'

He kissed his daughter on the cheek, lingering a moment longer to whisper in her ear. 'Don't tell anyone what you told me. If anyone asks you questions about Davis, call me or Gerald, okay?'

Miranda nodded at her father. 'I'm a big girl, Dad. And I got my smarts from you.'

'That's what worries me.'

Bailey climbed out of the car.

'Nice to see you, Sharon.' Miranda called out from behind her father's shoulder. 'Look after him for me!'

'I'll try.'

Miranda waved, shifted into first gear and raced away.

'You look nice, by the way,' Bailey said.

'Steady on,' Dexter said. 'This isn't a date.'

'Can't a bloke deliver a compliment now and then?'

'I guess he can.' She smiled at him, briefly. 'Only, this is work. And frankly, I'm a little on edge.'

'We were right about Davis,' he said.

'Thought you might say that. Where does it lead us?'

'I think it's time I told you about Gary Page and China.'

Dexter nodded her chin in the direction of the crowd gathering at the entrance of the art gallery. 'Can you do it in the two minutes it'll take us to walk up there? Davis is mingling outside and I think he just saw us.'

Bailey linked his elbow in hers and started to escort her slowly to the steps.

'I'll do my best.'

CHAPTER 20

The police commissioner was smiling and shaking hands with the anyones and everyones invited to celebrate the start of his new public life.

Bailey cringed at the sight of David Davis's smiling face as he pretended to be excited to see his guests, when all he wanted was their money. Ideas were important in politics, but nothing was more powerful than a fist full of cash.

Davis understood power better than most. His grandfather, Max Stanley – or Big Max as he was known around town – was the boss of the nation's largest union in the days when workers would bend the arm of big business and break a few bones if it guaranteed the boys a better deal.

Big Max was a hero of working class Australia and, like most union bosses, he had his sights set on Canberra. At the tender age of sixty-seven he was finally preparing to make a run into politics when he dropped dead from a heart attack on a construction site in Parramatta. Big Max had picked a fight with a major developer about work conditions and he'd turned up in his high-vis and hard hat to personally tell the workers to down tools and go home until he'd negotiated them a better pay deal. He hit the dirt before he had even made it to the site manager's donga.

Bailey remembered that day because he'd covered the story for *The Journal*. Big Max's death had sparked a nationwide strike in the building industry. Six days later, and with Big Max six feet under, the workers got their pay rise.

David Davis was no Big Max Stanley. But he'd obviously learned something from his grandfather because he'd made police commissioner of the largest state in Australia at the age of forty-two.

After more than a decade as commissioner, Davis was ready to do something that his grandfather never got to do. He was running for the federal seat of Grayndler, replacing the infamous party stalwart, Doug Smith, who had held the seat for twenty-eight years but had run out of puff and was ready to retire.

Grayndler had been a Labor seat for eighty years and the party held it with a margin of eighteen per cent. Pre-selecting a candidate like Davis, who had a reputation for defending the state against crime, had all but guaranteed it would remain in Labor's hands at the next election.

Big Max would have been proud. From a seat like Grayndler, Davis could make it all the way to the Lodge. That's if he was the squeaky clean candidate the party was banking on. Bailey had his doubts.

—

It was impossible to avoid the man of the hour on their way through the front door. So Bailey and Dexter lined up and prepared to pay homage like the rest of them.

'Lovely you could make it, Sharon.' The words slithered out of Davis's mouth as he stared at her. 'And you've brought a friend with you?'

'Yeah, I have,' Dexter said without flinching. 'David Davis, meet John Bailey.'

The two men shook hands, Davis squeezing tightly in a show of strength that probably paid dividends with the boys. Bailey just found it irritating.

'The journalist?'

'Yeah, that's right.'

'How's life in the fourth estate these days, Mr Bailey?'

'The same.' Bailey made sure to stare him in the eyes. 'Reporting about the bad guys you catch and the ones that get away. But it's rare, of course, that someone slips through the net.'

'Of course.' Davis looked like he was going to continue with their banter, but decided against it. 'Good to meet you. Good luck, mate.'

Mate.

Bailey disliked Davis even more in person.

'We've actually met, *mate*,' Bailey said. 'Long time ago – in the mid-eighties. I broke a few stories about police corruption. We spoke a few times.'

Davis looked around nervously.

'Of course, you were never caught up in those bad old days,' Bailey wedged him. 'The clean ones were the brave ones, right? Different world, policing back then.'

There was a long queue of people waiting to grease the palm of Labor's new man and Davis had noticed some of them paying attention to the conversation.

'Great to have you here, Mr Bailey. Open bar inside. Please enjoy it.'

'Appreciate that!' Bailey could chalk this up as a win. 'More than happy to give it a nudge. Good luck tonight, *mate.*'

He slapped Davis on the shoulder and walked on past.

'What are you playing at?' Dexter whispered when they were out of earshot.

'Sometimes you've got to poke the beast to see if it'll bite.'

'I'd call that a bloody prod, Bailey.'

'Prod? Poke? What's the difference?'

'Oh my God.' Dexter sighed. 'This was a mistake.'

'Don't be like that, Sharon.' Bailey took her by the arm. 'Now where's that bar our boy was talking about?'

They walked inside the gallery and Bailey steered them to a table lined with flutes of champagne beneath Arthur Boyd's eerie painting of a dirt riverbank.

The masterpiece was lost on Sharon.

'You okay?'

Bailey could see that she was distracted, which was under-standable after the bizarre welcome at the door, not to mention Bailey's theories about the defence minister and Davis. It was a lot to take in. An advisor to Gary Page is framed for murdering a prostitute who also counted the police commissioner among her clients. To top it all off, the defence minister had been holding secret meetings with the Chinese Ambassador to Australia.

'This'll help.' Bailey handed her a glass of champagne, devouring half of his own with one gulp.

'French, just like at Gerald's.' He tried to lighten the mood. 'Speak of the devil!'

Bailey finished his drink and grabbed two more glasses of champagne while watching Gerald make his way from the other side of the room.

'Mate.' Bailey handed him a glass.

'Lovely to see you, Sharon.' Gerald kissed her cheek and gave her a one-arm hug.

'Fancy seeing you here.'

'Darling, I've been crashing events like this for decades. It's a little easier now that I'm the editor of the country's biggest newspaper.'

'Calm down there, big shot,' Bailey said. He turned to Dexter. 'I told him. A room full of social climbers and rich dickheads – it wouldn't be the same without Gerald.'

'Watch him,' Gerald said. 'I'm going to mingle, as they say.'

'I'll try,' Dexter said.

'And Bailey?'

'Yeah?'

'Let's talk later.'

Bailey watched his old friend walk into the crowd, nodding and waving as he went. Gerald was good at the bullshit.

There must have been three hundred people inside. Many of them looked like they'd spent their lives hopping from one social event to the next. A gallery opening, charity ball, opening night at the theatre, awards night, socialite wedding. There was always somewhere to go where the drinks and canapés were free and some wanker from the social pages was there, stalking the room, documenting the night for the have-nots who only ever got to read about it the next day.

The political fundraiser was slightly different from other social events because every name on the guest list was expected to bring their chequebook. The only ones getting a free ride were the politicians, who were more used to trading their influence for cash – although, of course, they never admitted it.

Tonight's party was the most important event in town. The people who had turned up in their pretty frocks and black suits thought they were pretty important too. In Sydney, they probably were.

'Is that Matthew Parker over there?' Dexter was pointing at a man partly concealed by the crowd that had gathered around him.

'Yeah. Big name like Davis gets called off the bench, the PM pays a visit. They can be crime fighters together for the cameras.'

'He's a fit looking bastard,' Bailey said, noting the prime minister's barrel chest and chiselled cheekbones.

'Guess so.'

'Must be the surfing, and all those fun runs I see him doing on the television. I always thought a car drove him to the finishing line.'

Bailey was starting to get loose.

'Page will be here too, somewhere. And slow down on the French, will you?' Dexter had noticed him holding another two glasses in his hand.

'Pardon, madam. J'ai très soif.' Bailey winked and took another sip from his flute. 'I think I might have a mingle.'

'Can I come?'

'I was hoping you would.' He held out his arm and she took it.

'Dexter!' They had barely walked another five metres before a group of police called out for her to join them.

'Bring your chequebook, guys?' she said.

'You're kidding, aren't you? Davis can look after himself. We're just here for the free piss!' a short, stocky bloke replied, his colleagues laughing and clinking their glasses at his joke.

'Make the most of it,' Dexter said. 'I don't recall the commissioner putting on a party like this for us!'

'Might leave you to it,' Bailey said in Dexter's ear. 'I've never been popular with the boys in blue.'

'Make sure you come back – and stay out of trouble!'

Bailey walked to the back of the room and climbed the steps to another bar. It had a view over the function space, where he could get a good look at the guests.

'Whisky, mate – two fingers.' Bailey gestured with his hand to the waiter, resting his elbow on the glass-top bar.

'Beer, wine and champagne only on the tab.' The young barman's skin was so tanned it made his teeth shine. He looked bored, like serving drinks was beneath him.

'I'll pay. Single malt, if you've got it.'

Davis was a cheap bastard too.

'Still want a double?'

'Yes, mate, I'll pay for a double.'

'Just checking.'

The glass made a cracking sound when the barman plonked it on the table in front of Bailey. 'Twenty-six bucks.'

'No wonder this gallery looks so nice.' Bailey handed him the money, annoyed that it wouldn't be the last overpriced whisky he'd be buying from the tosser with the tan. He could only do so many glasses of bubbles.

Bailey checked out the room. Half of Matthew Parker's front bench was here. He counted Health, Social Services, Arts, the Attorney-General and the Treasurer. Davis knew how to pull a crowd. Bailey also clocked eight Australian Federal Police officers standing in strategic positions around the room. Their earpieces and bulging jackets made them stand out in the crowd. That was the point.

Ambassador Li Chen was standing close to the stage, a glass of red wine in his hand, having a casual conversation with the foreign affairs minister. Bailey felt like wandering over and asking the ambassador about the death of Victor Ho, if only to gauge his reaction. But it was a little too early to rattle the cage.

He kept looking around, wondering if the mysterious fat guy in the leather jacket would make another appearance. Probably not. By the way he delivered his last message to Ambassador Li down at the quay, he didn't look like the type of bloke who would turn up at a public function.

Eventually, Bailey's eyes settled on the short and stumpy figure of Gary Page in the corner by the entrance. He was deep in conversation with a man with a slicked-back ponytail who looked like a gangster – which wasn't that surprising for a Labor fundraiser. Their conversation looked heated, with Page poking his finger at the man's chest, reinforcing his words.

The two men were interrupted when the lights flickered and the music stopped. Page tapped the man on the cheek with the palm of his hand – a cocky, domineering gesture in anyone's book – and headed for the small stage near the windows. The speeches were about to start.

Page was the master of the stump and tonight was easy because he would be performing before a friendly crowd. He took his place in front of the microphone, the lights on the stage bouncing off his bald head and highlighting the creases in his suit. Page held up his arms in a gesture for quiet, shoulders hunched over like Tricky Dicky.

'I want to welcome you all here tonight.' His amplified voice carried over the uninterested party crashers chatting and downing the free booze. 'But firstly, I should remind anyone taking a shine to the fine art hanging from the walls that there're more cops in this room than you'd see patrolling the harbour on New Year's Eve.'

The crowd roared with laughter – nearly everyone, except for Bailey.

'It's my great pleasure to speak about this man.' Page was pointing at Davis, gesturing for him to join him on stage. 'He's been a great friend and servant to the people of this great state. I could think of no better choice than David Davis to be our candidate for the seat of Grayndler at the next federal election. And let me tell you why . . .'

Bailey had lost interest. He turned to the barman and held up another two fingers to let him know that he was in for the full twenty-six bucks again.

Most of the crowd had moved closer to the stage when the defence minister started speaking, the rest had retreated to the bar with Bailey. Among them was radio host Keith Roberts, who had been encircled by fans paying homage to the sound of his voice. He caught Bailey's eye, waved, and started walking in his direction. He was coming over for a chat. The last time they'd been in the same place together Bailey had thrown a glass of wine over him and used a colourful array of expletives to describe both Roberts' radio program and the man himself. Why on earth would he want to speak to him now?

'That looks like a nice glass of whisky, Mr Bailey. Terrible waste to throw it!'

'How're you, Keith?' Bailey would never apologise to a creep like Roberts, but he was trying to be civil.

'Wonderful, thank you. Top rating program in Sydney, why wouldn't I be? And you? Still the crusading reporter?'

Bailey found the man's hubris irritating. He looked down at his glass. He definitely wasn't going to waste his single malt, not at these prices.

'Not sure we need to go over this old ground again, do you?'

'My dear man, only toying with you. The baggage you must carry around, it must explode from within sometimes. I didn't take it personally.'

Bailey held back from saying what he was thinking. He looked around for a distraction and found one. Anthea and Ian were standing ten metres away, watching Page and Davis do their thing on stage.

He downed his whisky. 'Sorry, mate, another time.'

'Sure, but before you go . . .' Roberts grabbed his arm. 'I've got a question, if I may.'

'Shoot.' Bailey was barely listening.

'I'd love you to come on my show one day to talk about the Middle East. I'd really like to hear your assessment.'

'Yeah, sure.' Bailey didn't know what else to say.

'Great! How's the day after next? Seven o'clock?'

'Call me ten minutes before I'm due on so I can have a shit and shower.'

'Terrific! The war correspondent, John Bailey! On my program! What number should my producers call?'

'This one.' Bailey pulled a pen from his pocket and wrote down ten digits on a napkin. It could have been anyone's number. It certainly wasn't his.

'Excellent. Talk with you then.' Roberts looked happy with himself, folding the napkin and placing it in the pocket of his jacket.

Anthea noticed Bailey wandering in her direction and gave him a look that made him reconsider his approach – he knew that look – but he ignored it.

'Hello darling.' He leaned in and gave his ex-wife a peck on the cheek.

'Ian.' Bailey held out his hand and Ian begrudgingly shook it. He had never liked Bailey and resented being the bloke who had picked up the pieces.

'What're you doing here?'

'Same as you – we're celebrating a change in career for one of the nation's great crime fighters, aren't we?'

'Please.' Anthea squeezed his arm. 'Let's play nice.'

'What do you mean?' The champagne and whisky had gone to his head and his cheeks were flushed.

'Okay, Bailey,' Ian said. 'We get it. I presume you're here in a journalistic capacity? Davis is a good story, correct?'

Correct.

Bailey hated the way Ian often finished his sentences with self-affirmation.

'Sure is, Ian. He is a good story.' And he had always struggled to control himself around Anthea's husband. It was a bloke thing. He'd never like him.

'Interesting to see you here though, Ian,' Bailey said.

'Why's that?' Ian turned his body away from the stage so that he was face to face with Bailey.

'You'd have to be the only merchant banker in Australia that supports the Labor Party.'

Ian went to open his mouth but Anthea stopped him. 'Okay, you two, you can put your dicks away.'

'You're right, Anthea, that could be very embarrassing for Ian.'

Ian's face was going red and Anthea grabbed her husband's arm tightly.

'Hey, is that Sharon Dexter over there?' She changed the subject. 'Didn't I see you walk in together?'

'Yeah, you did.' Bailey was aware he'd outstayed his welcome. 'Better go and see how she's doing.'

He nodded at Ian and bent forward to kiss Anthea goodbye, but instead whispered in her ear. 'Davis is a bad guy. Be careful.'

She gave him a perplexed look – confused at how he could be such an arse, then sincere. The infuriating contradictions of the father of her child.

Bailey sidled past Dexter and signalled to her that he would be back in a minute. He had a burning pressure in his bladder and needed to get to the restroom.

The only people who ventured out into the foyer were those, like Bailey, who had been making the most of the open bar and didn't care about missing any of the speeches inside.

He reached out and leaned with his right hand on the wall in front of him and pissed into the urinal. The lean was an obvious sign that he'd better slow down on the whisky.

There was a tap running behind him. Bailey turned around and could see the man with the ponytail – the one who'd been talking with Page – washing his hands at the marble sinks on the opposite side of the room. He was staring at Bailey through the mirror.

Bailey moved to the sinks to rinse his hands and tried to break the awkward moment. 'Evening.'

'Time for you to go, my friend.' The bloke was glaring at Bailey in the mirror.

'Sorry, do we know each other?' Bailey turned on the faucet and met his gaze, the conversation taking place through the glass.

'No, we don't.'

'My mistake.' He knew that now would be a good time to walk away. But that wasn't John Bailey. 'Friend of Gary Page though, right?'

'I'm not sure if you realise what's going on here, mate.' The bloke turned away from the mirror and stepped closer to Bailey. 'And it can be done one of two ways –'

'Don't tell me you're going to say it's the easy way or the hard way?' The barman with the tan had looked after Bailey a little too well and his whisky glow had given him false courage.

'Nah, you're right. Forget I said anything.' The man winked at Bailey and walked out of the restroom.

Bailey knew this wasn't over. He splashed water on his face and took his time drying his face and hands with a paper towel before straightening his tie in the mirror. Miranda really had done a brilliant job with his bat wing.

He walked outside, bracing himself for trouble.

'G'day boys.'

Three burly men were waiting for him. They could have passed for triplets – shaved heads, tight black t-shirts that showed off their extensive gym work, and more ink on their arms than an entire football team.

'Didn't get invited inside, hey lads? You missed some great speeches, not to mention the open bar.'

'Who the fuck's this guy?' The short guy in the middle was in charge.

'I think I'm the guy you're supposed to escort outside.'

Bailey had an inkling that wasn't all they'd been asked to do.

'Yeah, something like that,' the short guy said.

The two mute brutes grabbed Bailey by the arms while the short talkative one stepped forward and headbutted him in the forehead.

'Fuck!' Bailey would have fallen over had the other two men not been holding him. He refocused his eyes in time to catch a fist crash into his stomach, knocking the wind out of his lungs, making him slump forward, gasping for air.

They steadied him on his feet and escorted him outside, nodding at the security guards on the door to let them know that Bailey, who was too dazed to protest, had had a little too much to drink.

'He's okay. We're looking after him. We'll put him in a taxi round the corner.'

But they didn't put Bailey in a taxi. Instead, they crossed the road and walked him behind a giant oak tree.

'You must've really pissed someone off tonight, mate. Apologies in advance.'

Bailey didn't see the fist that crashed into his temple, nor did he catch the boots that belted into his ribs, stomach and back when he fell to the ground. The beating didn't last long. But he must have sustained another half-dozen punches and kicks before they decided he'd had enough. Their orders must have been to hurt him, not kill him. Small victories.

Bailey looked up to see the three goons walking across the road, back-slapping each other, leaving him lying in a pile of leaves, struggling to catch his breath. He ran his fingers across his ribs and quietly reassured himself that nothing had been broken, then closed his eyes.

CHAPTER 21

Something was poking into Bailey's side, every movement hurt. The smell of freshly mown grass diverted his attention from the pain and reminded him of when he and Mike used to play rugby as boys. The brothers were so close in age that they'd played in teams together, and Bailey had never minded that his little brother was the more talented one. Running out on that field, sharing victories and losses, was enough.

Mike was fast and skilful, which meant that he always played either nine or ten. The playmaking roles. He'd order everyone around on the field and they always listened because he was good. With so many rules, rugby was the closest thing a contact sport came to chess, and Mike always knew where to position his players.

Bailey, on the other hand, was the type of player who only knew how to tackle like a demon and run headfirst into every ruck. He didn't have much talent, just a big heart, and a mission to protect the best player in the team – his little brother.

He wondered what Mike would have thought of him now, lying dishevelled, covered in dirt and leaves on the ground. He probably would have laughed. But Bailey also knew that

Mike would have been disappointed with the way his brother had been hiding from life these past few years. It was why he had been ignoring the gaze of his brother through the clouds, over his shoulder, the sound of his voice in his head. Bailey didn't want to be judged, especially by the best friend he'd ever had.

But something had changed, he didn't need a beating to recognise it. He had spent too long feeling sorry for himself, too long dismissing his second, third and fourth chances in life as rites of passage.

He was lucky to have had a friend like Gerald, who had pulled him out of the Middle East after what had happened in Iraq and sent him to England to be *The Journal*'s Europe correspondent. After all that Bailey had been through, Gerald knew he wasn't ready to come home to Australia. Giving him a new home in London was a good idea and, for a while, it had worked. Bailey was filing regularly, writing about international politics and the ideological love affair between Tony Blair and George W. Bush – two men trying to engineer peace with the barrel of a gun in the post–September 11 world.

Four months after he had been released from captivity in Iraq, Bailey was feeling normal again. He'd moved on from the mad militant in the cave and he was back near the top of his game. Then four young British men with backpacks filled with explosives walked onto three trains and a bus and blew themselves up. Fifty-six people died that day, if you included the bombers, and one of the world's busiest cities was brought to its knees. Less than twenty-four hours after Bailey had written a story about London's successful bid to host the 2012 Olympic Games, he was back in what felt like a warzone.

When Bailey arrived at Edgware Road tube station on the morning of 7 July 2005, the smoke was still billowing from the underground and people were stumbling over each other, their blackened faces in shock at the terror that had killed, maimed and bloodied so many. Later, he stood staring at the bus that had been gutted by the explosion at Tavistock Square, the stains of blood and flesh on the pavement. He talked with some of the hundreds of thousands of Londoners sent home early from work, who had no other option but to walk because the transport system had been paralysed by twisted metal and fear. The people he spoke to in those first hours were resolute that the four Islamic fundamentalists would not change their city. Two weeks later, when another group of young terrorists tried to set off more bombs in London, the people remained defiant.

But the bombs triggered something different in Bailey.

They sent him into a state of confusion and despair. The card that brought down the house. At least, that's how Doctor Jane described it later.

In Bailey's line of work he was used to being alone, just not to feeling lonely. The images of the violent attacks he had covered in Beirut, Iraq, Jerusalem and now London had begun playing like a slideshow of horror in his mind whenever he closed his eyes.

He was drinking himself to sleep. When the bad dreams began to seep into his days, Bailey started opening a bottle at lunchtime. Then breakfast. It had always started with one drink. Just enough to numb the pain. Until just enough was never enough.

Somehow, Bailey had kept filing stories and maintaining the illusion for Gerald and the newspaper's bosses in Sydney that everything was okay with their Europe correspondent. Only it wasn't. The dismantling of John Bailey had begun.

For the next eight years, he bounced around Europe and the Middle East chasing stories, staying busy. He had thought about killing himself so many times that he'd lost count. But he never tried. He couldn't do that to Miranda. Long-distance phone calls to his daughter and work were the only things that prevented him from going over the edge. In between stories, he drank.

The charade finally ended when Gerald found Bailey passed out at six-thirty in the morning in the foyer of his apartment complex in Maida Vale. There was dried vomit on his clothes and he looked and smelled like he had been living on the streets. One of Bailey's neighbours had taped a scathing hand-written note to his chest to remind him that it was the third morning that week that he had failed to make it to his apartment on the second floor. Maida Vale was a nice area and the people who lived in the building didn't appreciate drunks like him spoiling it.

Bailey didn't deny that he was in trouble when Gerald confronted him. There was no point. He was actually relieved that his friend had seen it for himself. Blokes like Bailey didn't talk about this stuff. They just got on with it. A few days later, he quietly packed his bags and boarded a flight to Sydney.

—

Get up, John. Get up!

Bailey could hear Mike's voice and imagine his frowning face staring at him lying in the leaves.

What are you doing?

Bailey opened his eyes and looked up at the clouds, searching for the contours of his little brother's face defined by the moonshine. He desperately wanted to find him, to hear him.

Stop bloody feeling sorry for yourself!

The stubbornness in Bailey had wanted to tell Mike to fuck off, only he knew he was right.

He rolled onto his side, the rustling of the leaves helping him to regain his focus and remind him what had just happened. He looked across the road and saw Gerald standing less than a hundred metres away at the front entrance of the gallery, hand on his forehead, looking out across the grounds of the Botanic Gardens.

Bailey may have lost Mike, but Gerald had his back. His brother born from another. He whistled to get his attention.

Gerald ran across the road and almost tripped on one of the large roots protruding from the ground at the base of the big oak tree.

'Bailey! Are you okay? Are you hurt?' He held out a hand to help him up off the ground.

Bailey could feel the blood trickling from his eyebrow and the sting from the cut on his lip. He had the metallic taste of blood in his mouth.

'I think so.'

'You've got a real knack for pissing people off, you know that?' Gerald steadied him with his arms.

'One of my many gifts.'

'Here.' Gerald handed him his crisp white pocket square.

'Know who did this to you?'

'Associates of that slick looking cretin inside with the pony-tail. My best guess, anyway.' He dabbed away at the cut on his lip.

'Guido Carlos.'

'Why do I know that name?'

'Big property developer,' Gerald said. 'Gives loads of money to political parties – both sides – whoever's winning.'

'Man with principles.'

'If you don't know him. He must've been doing someone else a favour.'

'Page.'

'You sure?'

'Saw them talking together. Page poking him in the chest like he was giving him instructions.'

Gerald brushed a few more leaves from Bailey's shoulders and straightened his tie. 'Been a while since you've had a beating like this in Sydney.'

'Twenty-five years, give or take.' Bailey coughed and spat a mouthful of blood on the grass. 'The boys in blue back then.'

'Sounds about right.'

'Hard to forget,' Bailey said. 'The bad one at least. Wound up in hospital. Detached retina, dislocated shoulder and a few broken ribs. Those guys were bloody brutal. Makes this little touch-up look like a sports massage.'

Bailey brushed the last specks of leaves and grass from the arms of his jacket.

'What're you going to do now?' said Gerald. 'You can't go back inside.'

'I'm going to visit a prostitute.'

'You're what?'

'Give me some credit,' Bailey said. 'A friend of Catherine Chamberlain. I told you about her, remember?'

'Of course.'

'Tell Sharon I got kicked out, would you? And spare her the details.'

'Sure,' Gerald said. 'And, Bailey – be careful.'

The beating had dislodged something in Bailey. 'Meet you at the office later. Reckon I might even have something to write by then.' It had also helped him sober up, clear his head and remind him of the stubborn bastard inside. Bashing a guy like Bailey only hardened his resolve for answers.

'This one has a long way to run yet.' Gerald was sounding like the guarded newspaper editor. 'Don't get ahead of yourself.'

'Can't remember the last time I got ahead of myself,' Bailey said. 'But I've got an itch. I'm going to scratch it.'

CHAPTER 22

It was just after ten o'clock when Bailey wandered into the public bar at The Sheaf and ordered himself a whisky. He and Scarlett had been exchanging a few text messages and he'd sent her another from the taxi, hoping she was still around.

Her reply came through just as Bailey was ordering his second drink.

Be there in ten.

He was onto his third whisky by the time Scarlett walked through the door.

'G'day, old timer.' She sat down on a stool beside him.

'Drink?' Bailey waved to the girl behind the bar to come over.

'Love one,' she said. 'Just knocked off. In desperate need of a cocktail.'

The girl from the bar winked at Scarlett. 'What do you feel like, babe?' She held out her hand and Scarlett took it for a few seconds before letting go.

'Glass of water and a spritz? A naughty one.'

'Do you know everyone who works here?' Bailey said after the girl walked away.

'Told you I'm a local.' Scarlett swung her stool towards him. 'Hey, what the hell happened to your face?'

'Long story. I pissed off someone I shouldn't have.'

'They did a pretty good job on you.'

'Looks worse than it is.'

'Anything for me to worry about?'

'No one knows I've even spoken to you, apart from my editor, Gerald, but he's good at keeping secrets.'

'Okay, reassured, slightly,' she said. 'Gerald? Posh name. Who calls their kid Gerald anyway?'

'I've got no idea.' Bailey liked her frankness. 'And wait for the punchline. His surname's Summers.'

'You're joking! My dad would've barred anyone with the name Gerald Summers from even entering our house!'

She took a sip of her Aperol spritz and let out a long sigh. 'That's good. She sure knows how to make them. Thanks, Chloe!' Scarlett called out across the bar.

'Now, why'd you want to meet?' She put the tip of a napkin into her glass of water and started dabbing at the crusted blood on Bailey's brow.

'Really, I'm okay.' He touched her arm in a way that told her not to bother. He liked that she cared, but he didn't like being the focus of anyone's attention.

'Yeah, yeah.' She pushed his arm out of the way. 'But, sorry, I'm not giving you a choice here. You look terrible. And I'm the one who has to sit next to you.'

'Fair enough.'

He let her clean him up while he pulled out his phone and brought up a picture of David Davis.

'Know him?'

Scarlett had moved on to Bailey's eye and stopped to stare at the image. 'Yeah, he's a regular – a prick too.'

'What else can you tell me?'

'Not much. Didn't have a favourite. Liked to mix it up and, like most men, he was paranoid about discretion.'

'With good reason. Know who he is?'

'Of course I do.' Scarlett stopped dabbing his brow. 'Let me tell you something, Mr Bailey, we know about all of our clients. I do the books with Francesca. We keep tabs on everyone. But privacy is our thing, along with our beauty and class.'

'Indeed.'

'It's no wonder that smirk of yours gets you into trouble, old man.' They were flirting, but like friends. 'Seriously, the clients pay for everything when they come to Petals – and they get it.'

'You're not being so discreet now. Why?' Bailey took another sip of his whisky.

'As I said, David Davis is a prick. You don't want details, but he's not nice to girls.' Her face drooped. 'And there's something else, something I was too afraid to tell you when we first met.'

'Which is?' Bailey put down his glass.

'This guy Davis . . .' Scarlett leaned closer to Bailey, lowering her voice. 'He called in at Petals the other day.'

'You mean he physically paid a visit? Why?' He pushed his whisky glass away. It was time to stop drinking.

'He wanted to see the log of client bookings from one night a week or so ago.' Scarlett was whispering. 'And he had a big argument with Francesca. Made all sorts of threats about shutting us down.'

The revelation raised more questions than answers for Bailey. The only real suspect he knew about was a dead Chinese student. He didn't understand how, or where, Davis fitted in. He was a bastard, but that didn't make him a killer. Having sex with prostitutes wasn't a crime either. But Bailey knew how power corrupted, how it made monsters out of people. After tonight, he couldn't rule anything out. Paranoid about being followed, he decided to switch off his phone.

'Another thing. Some cop, Rob someone, came round today with a warrant and took away the client logs anyway. So I guess Davis got what he wanted.'

'Francesca hadn't given in on the night?'

'Stared him down like a matador.'

He was impressed. But he knew there was still one other suspect, the one everyone was looking for – Michael Anderson. And Bailey still hadn't decided whether or not he could trust him.

'Tell me more about Catherine's relationship with Michael Anderson,' Bailey said.

'What d'you want to know?'

'I don't know – anything, everything.'

'Well, they were both country kids, tough upbringings, single mums. I guess that's one of the things that made them close.'

'What else?'

'I can't tell you much about Michael, but Catherine was a tough cookie. Grew up in Wagga Wagga. Couldn't wait to get out of there. Her mum was a druggie. In the beginning she was paying her way through uni working in bars, cleaning, whatever she could get.'

'How'd she end up working at Petals?'

'She served a drink to Francesca one night in the city and discovered she'd make more in a night than she would in a week doing what she was doing. And that was that. Anyway, her grand plan was to have enough money set aside so that she could quit Petals later this year, especially because things were getting serious with Michael.'

'So you don't think it could have been Anderson who –'

'No way. He's not a killer. Then again, what do I know?'

'A lot more than me.' Bailey slid off his stool, preparing to leave. 'I've got to head off. Thanks for meeting me.'

'You haven't even finished your drink.'

'Work to do. And don't worry, I've finished enough drinks for a lifetime.' Bailey placed a fifty-dollar note on the bar. 'Next one's on me.'

'You're too good, old man.' She took another sip of her drink.

'Stop calling me that. I'll get a complex.'

Bailey was limping slightly as he walked out of the pub. The pain from the beating was kicking in.

CHAPTER 23

Bailey didn't feel safe going home. He'd been bashed, his house had been ransacked and he suspected his home, his phone and probably even his car were all bugged. He needed to find out everything he could about David Davis and Gary Page. The best place to do that was at *The Journal*. And he had promised Gerald he'd meet him there.

'Evening, Mick.' He nodded at the security guy on the front desk.

'Good to see you, Mr Bailey.' Mick had been working at the paper for the past three years. He was a family man who liked the night hours, not just for the penalty rates, but for the after-noons and mornings he got to spend with his kids.

'Must be something going on in the world tonight, hey, Mr Bailey?'

'What do you mean?' He paused at the elevator without hitting the button.

'Mr Summers is upstairs, has a woman with him I didn't recognise and . . .' Mick stopped mid-sentence.

'Don't worry, Mick – Gerald isn't the type.' Bailey wanted to reassure him that he hadn't just breached the boss's privacy. 'I think I know who's with him.'

'Thanks, Mr Bailey. And one more thing.'

'Yep?'

'Someone's been calling for you. Penelope's put a note on your desk.'

'Better get up there.'

Bailey grabbed the note stuck to his computer screen, shoved it in his pocket and walked through the newsroom to Gerald's office. His boss was rocking back in his chair, sipping a glass of whisky and staring out the window.

'Anything out there, old boy?'

Same old joke.

Gerald hadn't heard Bailey walk in and he jolted in his chair.

'Mate!' He spun around and sat upright. 'You okay?'

Bailey touched the cut above his eye. 'A few bumps on the head, couple of sore ribs. Otherwise in pretty good nick.'

Gerald got up and wandered over to the silver platter on the sideboard in the corner of his office. 'Drink?'

'Black coffee for me.' Bailey couldn't remember the last time he'd turned down a whisky. It made him feel strong and in control. 'Got some work to do.'

If Gerald was surprised, he didn't show it. He dropped a capsule into his fancy espresso machine and watched it produce a long black for Bailey, while he poured himself something stronger.

'Mind if I do?' He jiggled the ice in his glass and handed Bailey his mug of coffee.

'Not at all, old boy. Usually the other way round.'

It was approaching midnight and both men were tired.

'Where's Sharon?' Bailey had figured the woman with Gerald was Dexter.

'Bathroom.'

On cue, she walked back into the office.

'Bailey! Bloody hell. Are you all right?'

Bailey turned to Gerald. 'Couldn't help yourself, could you?'

'What can I say? She's a scary woman, and I'm weak.' He held up his arms in surrender.

'Don't be such a tough guy,' Dexter said. 'Getting bashed up by guys working for Guido Carlos is serious. He isn't the type of bloke you mess with.'

'Can't say much about Guido, other than I think he was doing a favour for Page.'

'Are you serious?' Dexter shot Gerald a stern look. 'You didn't tell me that part.' She turned back to Bailey. 'You think Page was behind it?'

'Can't say for sure,' Bailey said.

'How bad is it?' She touched his chin, turning his face from side to side to get a good look at the damage. 'You look like shit.'

'Thanks.' He took a sip of his coffee and noticed the taste of blood still clinging to his gums. 'A few aches. Nothing serious.'

'Your phone's switched off, by the way.'

'Sorry about that.'

'Where've you been?'

'Meeting a contact.'

'Who?'

Bailey shared what Scarlett had told him about David Davis. The revelations sent Dexter into a rage. 'Rob Lucas is as bent as the arseholes we did over in the eighties! I don't know who else Davis may have inside. I'm going to need to play this even closer.'

'What's next?' Gerald said.

'The apartment building,' Bailey said. 'We've got to find those missing minutes on that tape. See if Victor Ho really was there that night.'

Dexter was nodding her head. 'It's about bloody time Mario Monticello made an appearance.'

Bailey could see that Gerald was confused. 'The manager of the apartment building where Catherine Chamberlain was killed.'

'Right.'

'I'm going to the station to find out what else Rob Lucas has been doing behind my back and who else might be involved,' Dexter said.

'Any problems, call me or Gerald here at the office,' Bailey said. 'I'm not going home tonight.'

'I'm a big girl – been doing this a while. You just worry about taking care of yourself.'

'Sharon ...' He stopped her at the door. 'Seriously – be careful.'

Their eyes met in the silence, sharing a moment – a conversation – all of their own.

'As I said, I'm a big girl.'

Dexter walked out of the room.

The two men sat quietly for a few minutes, staring out the window into the night.

'Gerald, look!' Bailey said.

A naked woman was standing with a glass of wine in her hand at the window of her hotel room.

'Told you it happened from time to time.'

She sipped from her glass of wine and then a man, dressed in a white robe, appeared beside her. She put down her glass and stepped towards him, flipping his robe off his shoulders.

'That's a bit more than I'd like to see,' Bailey said.

'Oh dear.'

The man pulled the woman close to him, kissing her neck, before pushing her back onto the bed.

'No wonder you're always happy to put in the extra hours.'

The guy turned off the light.

'Boo.' Bailey sounded like a disappointed fan at a football game. 'At least that's one mystery solved. What're you doing here so late anyway?'

'What do you mean?' Gerald sounded offended. 'I was waiting for you!'

'I'm touched.'

'I've been looking into Page and Davis. How far they go back, past business dealings, etcetera,' Gerald said.

'Find anything?'

'Not yet, but there's something there, has to be.'

Gerald was still talking, but Bailey had become distracted. He remembered the note from Penelope and withdrew the crumpled piece of paper from his pocket. He read it over and over to himself, heart pounding, unsettled about where it might lead him.

'Bailey? Are you still with me?'

Bailey hadn't heard a word since he'd started reading. 'I've got to go.'

'What is it?'

'Anderson.' Bailey handed him the piece of paper. 'He's made contact.'

Gerald read it out loud: 'Call M.A. He's been trying to reach you all afternoon. Room 302. Call 9202 . . .' He stopped reading and pointed to the door. 'Shut that. Let's get him on the phone.'

Gerald pressed the speakerphone option on his landline and started dialling.

They both stood, leaning over the phone on the desk. After three rings, a voice answered.

'Holiday Inn.'

'Room 302, please.' Bailey spoke with a clear, composed voice.

A few more beeps, then a male voice answered. 'Hello.'

'It's John Bailey.'

'Took your time. Let's meet. Thirty minutes. Get a pen.'

Anderson wanted to meet at Black Market in Newtown, a pub that Bailey knew well, always crowded, open late.

'I need to go alone,' Bailey told Gerald after Anderson had hung up. 'I'll come back here afterwards.'

'Be careful.'

It was the second time those words had been uttered in Gerald's office tonight.

CHAPTER 24

People were hopping in and out of taxis on King Street, searching for the next nightspot. The city lockout laws, barring new customers from entering pubs and bars after one o'clock in the morning, had driven people away from the traditional late-night venues around Kings Cross. It meant places on the city's fringes, like Newtown, were heaving most nights of the week. It was an area where students from the two big universities nearby mixed with the suits, out late pretending that it was the weekend, and the inner-west hipsters who had been drinking there for years.

Bailey's taxi dropped him across the road from the pub where he was supposed to meet Anderson. He was still wearing his tuxedo, minus the tie, with the jacket buttoned to hide the dirt and bloodstains from his beating at the art gallery.

There was a long line of people waiting to get inside. Bailey had no choice other than to join the queue and wait for the bouncers to give him the nod. He hadn't lined up to get into a bar since he was a teenager – when he and Mike would go to the Rock Lily at Mona Vale with fake IDs and cans of beer hidden in their bomber jackets. Back then they didn't mind the wait – it was a chance to talk to girls. That was more than thirty years ago and, understandably, Bailey had changed a lot since then.

The line was moving quickly and the bouncers on the door, ushering people inside one by one, didn't seem to mind the haze of marijuana smoke hovering above the crowd.

'Evening, chief.' A cocky bloke, biceps bulging through his shirtsleeves, greeted Bailey at the door. 'Got some ID for me?'

Tired and bruised, Bailey wasn't up for copping shit from a gym junkie. 'What for?'

The bloke slapped Bailey on the shoulder. 'Just fucking with you, buddy. I think your granddaughter's inside. Come to rescue her?'

Knowing he had a cut above his brow and a lip that felt like it was growing by the hour, Bailey resisted digging back. 'You going to let me in, mate?'

'Yes, buddy. You let me know if any of these young hooligans give you a hard time, okay?'

'Stop being a dickhead, Craig.' The other bouncer intervened. 'Just let him in.'

'Thank you,' Bailey said.

'You have fun, big guy.' Craig stepped out of the way and opened the door.

Bailey gave him a look that told him to get lost.

Inside, the music was blaring from a bunch of speakers next to the DJ in the corner. It was so crowded that Bailey was surprised they were still letting more people through the door. The strobing lights bounced off the countless heads bobbing to a beat so loud he could feel the vibrations. The bar was lit up like a city on the horizon and the wait to get a drink was five people deep. Bailey remembered there was a cocktail bar in the gaming lounge upstairs. If Anderson wanted a quiet place to talk, he would most likely be there.

He pushed through the people and walked up a narrow staircase, squeezing past kids walking in the opposite direction, juggling the drinks they'd bought from the upstairs bar to beat the queue.

The cocktail area was more civilised, mainly because people didn't come up here to drink, they came to gamble. The gaming machines were side by side in yet another room where punters could load their machines in peace. It was separated from the bar by a glass door; the owners wouldn't want punters lining up at the bar either – it risked giving them time to contemplate their losses and call it a night.

Bailey hated pokies, but everyone else seemed to love them. Australians just loved gambling – on anything. It was a twenty billion dollar industry where people bet on horses – even fake ones – dogs, football, tennis, rugby and cricket. They even bet on elections. But the most cash went into pokies. Almost every venue had them. It was easy money and the simplest way for publicans to balance the risk of the small margins they banked from booze and food.

Gaming lounges had almost killed live music too. But, unlike the rest of Sydney, the pubs around Newtown hadn't quite given up on musicians and Bailey was relieved to see a bloke playing a piano in the corner. He was in the middle of a jazzed-up version of a Macy Gray track when Bailey entered the room. It might not have been the Stones, at least it was better than the doof-doof dance music blaring downstairs.

He found an empty stool at the bar and ordered himself a single malt. His experiment with late-night coffee was over, for now. He was so tired the warm rush from a glass of golden brown was the only thing that would keep him awake.

'Another one.' He gestured to the girl behind the bar after downing the first.

Just as his second drink arrived, he felt a tap on his back.

Anderson didn't stop to speak. He just glanced over his shoulder to make sure Bailey was following him through the doors of the gaming lounge.

'Got a twenty?' He gestured for Bailey to sit beside him in front of a machine with crowns and jewels splashed all over it. 'I don't have much cash left and I can't use my cards, obviously.'

'No worries.' Bailey handed him two tens.

Anderson straightened the bills and fed them into the machine. The simple act reminded Bailey of feeding documents through a shredder.

'How are you?' Bailey said.

'How do you think?' Anderson was visibly agitated, less in control than he had seemed at Palm Beach two days ago. The stubble on his face was thicker and the red in his eyes suggested that he wasn't sleeping.

'Sorry.' Bailey regretted starting with small talk. 'Wrong question.'

'It seems Page has a useful friend in the force.'

'Was hoping you might be able to tell me something about that.' Bailey probed, not knowing how long Anderson was going to hang around. Things were moving too fast and he couldn't bank on Anderson contacting him again. He needed information. Tonight.

'I know nothing about David Davis, other than that sideshow we saw today. Page obviously thinks he's the squeaky candidate that'll help build the future for the ALP. The middle-aged top cop. He's perfect. Labor's like any business – always future-proofing.'

Bailey was confused. Last time they met Anderson told him about how Gary Page wanted to give China's military greater access to the Port of Darwin and possibly even have some kind of training base in the Northern Territory.

'Davis got anything to do with Page's love affair with China?' Bailey asked.

'I wouldn't rule it out, but the truth is I don't know.'

'What can you tell me?'

Anderson pressed a button on the machine and watched the pictures spin in front of them until they stopped.

'Your turn.'

Bailey did what he was told. Again, the pictures flashed in front of them. An alarm bell blurted from the machine, lights flashing.

'Winner,' Anderson said.

'A lot of noise for fifty cents.'

Anderson tapped the button again, his eyes fixed on the machine. 'Anyway, it's not just what I can tell you – it's what I can give you.'

Bailey raised an eyebrow and looked at him while his finger found the button. 'Go on.'

'Documents.'

Bailey let the word float in the air, hoping Anderson would go on. But he didn't.

'Where are they?'

'In a minute.' Anderson had lost track of whose turn it was and pressed the button again.

'Winner.'

A dollar this time. Bailey was done with the gambling commentary and waited for Anderson to start talking again.

'Page and Ambassador Li have been setting up small companies in China to make materials that a defence force might need.'

Finally Bailey was getting information. 'What type of materials? Hardware?'

'No. Basic stuff.' Anderson pressed the button again. 'Tents, bags, boots, canteens, essentials. Right down to sleeping bags and regulation t-shirts – you get the picture. We're even talking combat uniforms, special materials that have long been made in Australia. In the military, everything's provided. I mean, everything.'

'And?'

'There's always been strict rules about where these goods can be made, but all that's about to change.'

Anderson turned away from the machine so he could gauge Bailey's response.

'Page's been slowly building a case for Australia to start getting better deals for basic stuff, to create an open market. He's tabled a bill before parliament for us to start buying from overseas partners. But he's been clever. It's only for things that won't compromise our security or intelligence.'

Bailey wasn't expecting this story. 'You're telling me that at the heart of all this is that Page is just a greedy crook?'

'That's the only bit I can prove.'

Proof was exactly what Bailey needed. 'What about the documents you keep talking about?'

'Patience. We'll get there. Let me finish.'

'Go on then.'

'The bill before parliament has crossbench support. Page's sold this change in policy as a massive cost saving for the nation and on that front he's right. The GFC is hitting here just as the rest of the world recovers. We haven't implemented any of the recommendations from the policy work that was done on how to replace the massive hole from the mining slowdown. Construction's good for New South Wales, just not anywhere else. The federal budget's stuffed. These guys are desperate to limit spending wherever they can.'

'How big are the savings?'

'Big. Consider this – there are eighty thousand full-time and reservist members of the Australian Defence Force. Every one of them needs a uniform. Boots, socks, sleeping bags, food – you name it, we, the taxpayer, provide it. The numbers are staggering. We're talking about savings of hundreds of millions over the forward estimates.'

They'd stopped playing the machine and Bailey hadn't even touched his second whisky.

'How advanced are Page and Li with their manufacturing operations? And, more importantly, how can they guarantee they'll win the contracts?' These were the questions that Gerald would ask him before publishing the story. Page was a federal minister – they'd need to get every detail right from the start.

'Where else would they get made?' Anderson said defensively. 'The documents prove that Li and Page have prototypes ready to go. This'll be the shortest tender in history. The defence minister's got access to everything, literally, ready to press the go button on Aussie designs in Chinese factories that could be operational within weeks.'

'Still . . . sounds like there's risk involved.' Like any half-decent reporter, Bailey was used to playing devil's advocate.

'Maybe. But the PM wants the stuff to be made in China. He's already said that publicly.'

Bailey couldn't recall hearing Matthew Parker say those words, but he hadn't exactly been on the job these past few years. 'Why's he come out so strong?'

'We've snubbed China in every way possible. The headline act being our bullish support for America's stance on the South China Sea and the defence agreement that'll see more US marines call Darwin home for a few months of the year. Parker needs to give Beijing something. What better olive branch than lucrative contracts to manufacture another country's military gear? And it shows trust – shows we're close.'

'Sounds complicated to me.'

'It is!' Anderson had raised his voice and he looked around, worried he had drawn attention. But every other person in the room seemed to be hypnotised by their machines.

Anderson tapped another button. 'Forget about the prime minister and our relationship with China for a minute.' He lowered his voice. 'Think about this as a couple of crooks using their influence to line their pockets. When these deals are done, Page and Li will see a payday worth tens of millions of dollars . . . minimum.'

'And you told Catherine Chamberlain all about it?'

'Yeah.' Anderson rested his elbow on the machine, closed his eyes and rubbed his forehead with the palm of his hand. 'Stupid. But she was my soul mate. I knew I could trust her. Told her everything – Chinese defence access to the Territory, the scam over contracts. Everything.'

'That was a big gamble.'

Anderson sat upright and stared at Bailey. 'What? Because I ended up getting her killed?'

'I'm sorry, that was insensitive, worded badly.'

'Then what're you trying to say?'

Bailey needed to keep him onside. 'The documents – getting them together, that was a big risk. Did Catherine see them?'

'Of course not. I just can't help thinking her death's linked. It has to be. They need me gone too.' He reached into his jacket pocket and withdrew a fat yellow envelope. 'Everything you need is in here. You need to write this story. It's the best chance I've got to clear my name.'

Bailey wanted to believe everything he was being told, but he wouldn't make a promise he couldn't keep. 'As I said the last time we met, I'll need to find some answers.'

'And I told you I thought you were someone I could trust.' Anderson's desperate eyes were filled with hope. 'I meant it. Don't let me down.'

'I want to get to the bottom of this too, mate.' Bailey stood up and tapped the button on the machine one last time. The pictures stopped spinning, music blared and the word 'jackpot' lit up the screen.

'Well, well, people do actually win money from these things.'

'Appears so.' For a brief moment, Anderson looked like he was happy.

'If the documents support what you're telling me, we've got a story. A big one.' Bailey rested a hand on his shoulder. 'You take the winnings. Sounds like you could do with the cash.'

'Thanks. Nineteen hundred bucks. Might change hotels.'

The girl from the bar arrived at the machine just as Bailey was getting off his stool.

'Your lucky night there, handsome!'

She was already starting her routine for a tip.

'Want it all in cash?'

'That'd be good.'

'Hey, buddy.' Bailey tapped him on the back. 'Get your cash. Don't stick around.'

'That's the plan.'

CHAPTER 25

The lamb was sweating bullets of fat as it turned slowly on the rotisserie in front of the grill. The kebabs they served on King Street were heart attack material, but it was after midnight and Bailey hadn't eaten since his pie at Harry's.

The kebab shop was just across the road from Black Market and Bailey had been seduced by the smell of the roasting meat the moment he walked out of the pub. The Turkish-style wrap was popular late-night fare in Sydney, especially for party people loaded with booze, and shops selling them did big business in places like Newtown.

Bailey pulled back the foil and took a bite. It may not have been healthy but it tasted good.

The line outside Black Market had disappeared and there was only one security guard manning the door. There appeared to be more people leaving than going inside now. Every few minutes, the side door in the alley swung open and small groups of people stumbled outside.

Bailey looked at his watch. It had been fifteen minutes since he'd left and there was still no sign of Anderson. For a bloke on the run, he didn't seem to be in any hurry. Maybe he'd decided to feed some of his winnings back into the machines or, even more reckless, he was getting drunk at the bar with the pretty waitress.

Anyhow, he wasn't Bailey's responsibility, and he'd already handed over his smoking gun – the documents that he thought would bring down Page. Bailey touched the outside of his jacket so that he could feel the envelope stuffed in the inside pocket. He needed to get back to the office and start going through the documents with Gerald.

Bailey put his hand in the air – the universal signal for a taxi – but the car sped past with a group of drunk girls laughing in the back seat. The last third of his kebab was dripping with fat and tahini sauce. He threw it in the bin, doing his best to wipe the juice from his hands with an already sodden napkin.

He looked back across the road just as the side door of Black Market opened again and Anderson staggered into the alley. He appeared drunk, stumbling, being helped by a young Asian woman. Anderson had been sober when Bailey left him in the pokie lounge. Not even Bailey could do a job on himself that quickly.

A car drove up slowly behind Anderson and flashed its lights. The woman stopped walking, which meant that Anderson did too.

Bailey still had his arm out for a taxi and a yellow car pulled alongside.

'Where're you going?' The driver called across the passenger seat. Bailey was too engrossed in what was happening in the alley to answer.

'Buddy? You hail a taxi or not?'

The rear passenger door of the car in the laneway opened and a man climbed out. He grabbed Anderson around the neck from behind and put his hand across his face. Anderson struggled for a moment, then appeared to go limp.

'Hey!' Bailey called out from across the street. 'Hey! Hey! Hey!'

The man turned and caught sight of Bailey waving his hands. It was the fat guy Bailey had seen with the Chinese ambassador at the restaurant down at the quay. Leather jacket, baggy jeans, fat cheeks. The only thing missing was the sunglasses.

'Hey!' Bailey was trying to get the attention of the security guard out the front of Black Market. 'Help! Help! In the alley!'

The guard didn't hear him.

'Do you want a bloody ride or not?' The taxi driver was still parked beside Bailey, getting more impatient by the second. 'Oh, fuck you then, arsehole!'

Bailey stepped in front of the taxi just as the driver was pulling away. The force of the collision propelled Bailey up onto the bonnet, before the driver slammed on the brakes and Bailey was flung onto the road.

'What're you doing?' Bailey yelled as he clambered onto his knees. 'Idiot – you trying to kill me?'

The driver started beeping his horn. 'Get out of the way!'

As Bailey stood up, blocking the traffic, he looked back across at the alley, trying to find Anderson. He just caught the top of his head as it was shoved into the back seat of the car, followed by the woman. The fat guy was standing by the driver's door, staring directly at Bailey. He hesitated, like he was challenging Bailey to cross the street. But before he could the man climbed in the front seat and the car sped off down the road towards the city.

'Get. Out. Of. The. Fucking. Way!' The taxi driver had his head out the window, screaming at Bailey.

'Okay, mate. Okay, mate.' Bailey waved his hand at the bloke, trying to get him to calm down.

He touched his coat pocket to make sure the documents were inside. They weren't. The envelope was sitting on the street beside him. It must have fallen loose from his pocket when the car hit him. He bent over, picked it off the road and slipped it back into his jacket.

Bailey turned to the driver, who was still beeping his horn.

'Any chance of a ride to the city?'

'Fuck off.'

—

It only took Bailey a few more minutes to find a ride back to *The Journal*. On the way, he called Dexter. It was late but she answered.

'How'd you go?' She sounded like she was still working.

'Anderson's been taken.'

'What'd you mean – taken?'

'A big fat Chinese guy picked him off the street. Looked like he'd drugged him. Then he threw him in a car and took off.'

'Are you sure?'

'The whole bloody thing happened in front of me.'

'Where? How long ago?'

'Newtown, outside that pub, Black Market, five minutes ago. The car was a black Toyota; Camry, I think. New-ish. Heading north. The licence plate was CV something – didn't catch it all. A one in there, maybe a six too. Sorry. And I couldn't see the driver, but there was a young Asian woman with them. That's all I've got.'

'Okay, thanks,' Dexter said. 'And Bailey?'

'Yeah?'

'Don't get any stupid ideas. Leave this one to me.'

'Since when have I had a stupid idea?'

Dexter laughed briefly. 'We've got traffic cameras all over the city. I'll find him.'

'Hurry.'

CHAPTER 26

The documents were laid out on Gerald's desk. The night sub and two young online reporters were the only staff left on the newsroom floor. Gerald and the rejuvenated figure of John Bailey were working feverishly behind the closed door of the editor's office, piecing together the shady dealings of Gary Page and Ambassador Li Chen.

'Another one.' Bailey pointed to a picture of an Australian army uniform. 'Made by a textile business in Wangaratta with high-tech materials. Four hundred people work at that factory. Contract's worth seven million dollars a year. Shifting it to Page's Chinese factory would cut the manufacturing costs to three million dollars – less than half the price!'

'Strong stuff.' Gerald pushed his glasses to the tip of his nose, rubbed his eyes. 'Somehow your boy Anderson's got his hands on Page's personal files but we're a long way from printing this, mate. Needs a few checks and balances.'

Bailey ignored Gerald's sensible interjection. 'Look!' He was tapping his finger on a page that was stapled to the back of the Wangaratta contract. 'Manufacturing instructions right down to the bloody makeup of the cotton and plastics in the fibres.'

Bailey took off his jacket, exposing his white shirt stained with dirt, grass and dried blood from the beating he'd copped beneath the big oak tree. But he didn't care. He hadn't even noticed the jacket's torn sleeve from the incident on the road with the irate taxi driver.

'I can count sixteen different companies, all made to look like existing Chinese businesses. Not one of them has the name Gary Page or Li Chen on it.'

'Then who owns them?'

'Signatories are most likely members of Li's family, or maybe politicians looking to boost their bank balances.'

'My point is –'

'Hang on, mate,' Bailey said. 'It's not hard to find a corrupt official in Beijing. Like grains of sand on a beach. They reckon there's a hundred bloody billionaires in the Chinese Congress.'

He was on a roll and wasn't prepared to stop.

'Here's the clincher.' Bailey waved more sheets of paper in front of Gerald. 'Sands Enterprises. These are private company statements for an umbrella group listed in the Virgin Islands. Crosscheck the names of those Chinese companies and you'll see – every single one of them is listed on these sheets of paper. And guess who the two directors of Sands Enterprises are?'

'Gary Page and Li Chen.'

'I'd call that a smoking gun, wouldn't you?' Bailey said.

'No wonder Michael Anderson was in hiding.'

'Let's hope he's still alive.'

'There's not much we can do, mate,' Gerald said. 'Like Sharon said, she'll find him. Let's focus on the things we can control. Anderson's best chance may be us getting this stuff out in the open.'

'Yeah, maybe.'

Bailey turned his attention back to the documents on the table.

'Here's a company that makes tents.' He held up another sheet of paper. 'There's one that makes boots.' He held up another.

They went on like this for the next few hours – working out, one at a time, how each company linked back to Li and Page.

'Hell, there's even a company that makes cups, plates, bowls and cutlery!' Bailey said. 'If the military needs it, these guys are ready to make it.'

'Bailey,' Gerald said. 'Bailey, it's early in the –'

'Page and Li only need a handful of these companies to get the nod and they'll get a mighty payday! They're ready to hit the go button on nearly everything that the army might put up for tender.'

'Bailey!'

Bailey looked up, startled, from the papers on the desk. 'Yeah? Sorry. This is a lot to absorb. What's the time?'

'That's what I've been trying to tell you.' Gerald rubbed his eyes again. 'It's four-thirty. I think we should get some sleep. We'll need legal poring all over this in a few hours, so save yourself.'

'Yeah, sleep.' Bailey felt a pang of tiredness. 'Been a big night. A big day.'

Gerald pointed to one of two leather sofas in his office. 'You take that one.'

Bailey followed his instructions and lay back on the sofa, wincing with pain until he found a good position that put less pressure on his ribs. Maybe he had broken one or two after all.

Gerald looked across at Bailey, who'd already closed his eyes. 'You okay, mate?'

'Yeah, old boy. Just a few bruises.' Strangely, the bruises made him feel better about himself, more alive.

'Remind me, how much is the Australian Defence Force budget?'

'Roughly? Thirty-five billion dollars a year.'

War reporters always knew how much was spent on the blood and the brave.

Gerald's head slumped back on the padded arm of the sofa. 'What on earth have we got ourselves into?'

'Been a while, Gerald – you and me, in the trenches.'

They were both talking with their eyes closed, like kid brothers sharing a room.

'That's what I'm worried about. Now stop talking and go to sleep.'

'Cuddle?' Bailey couldn't resist.

'You're incorrigible.'

'I love it when you use big words.'

CHAPTER 27

Sydney, Friday

The newsroom was already buzzing when Penelope walked out of the elevator on the fourteenth floor, with the booming voice of Rachel Symonds, the chief of staff on the assignments desk, barking orders at reporters to hit the phones or get moving to the scene of whatever story was unfolding somewhere in Sydney.

The digital team was busily monitoring the morning television and radio programs, sending tweets and posting content to social media. The news business never stopped these days. It was only the big name journalists who came in late, if they came in at all.

Penelope gently knocked on the editor's door.

No answer.

She quietly opened a crack and peered inside. Bailey and Gerald were both snoring on the two leather sofas and the room stank of sweat and alcohol.

The telephone on Gerald's desk started ringing and Penelope hurried across the room to answer it.

'Gerald Summers' office,' she whispered.

'It's Mick . . . got this woman on the phone again. Says it's urgent . . . she can speak to either Mr Summers or Mr Bailey. Are they there?'

'Yeah . . . they're here.' Penelope stared at the two men, sound asleep, contemplating which one she'd wake. 'Hang on.'

She gently tapped Bailey's foot. 'Bailey, Bailey.' When that didn't work, she bent over and poked her finger at his chest. 'Bailey!'

'Aaaaahhhh!' He was startled awake by the pain in his ribs.

'I'm sorry,' Penelope said, 'are you hurt?'

Bailey remembered the art gallery, the meeting with Anderson, the documents and falling asleep on the lounge. Big night. He had a rotten taste from the fatty kebab on his tongue.

'Bailey? Are you okay?'

He opened his eyes. 'It's okay, Pen. What's up?'

'There's a woman on the phone, the second time she's called. Says it's urgent.'

Bailey was struggling to sit upright. The beating in the Botanic Gardens had done more damage than he'd thought, or maybe it was the taxi driver.

He twisted his body off the sofa, limped across the room and picked up the phone. 'Yep.'

'Bailey, it's me.'

Dexter.

The worry in her voice was like a shot in the arm. 'Are you okay?'

'I'm at a warehouse in Alexandria. Michael Anderson's dead. You'd better get here. It's not pretty.'

Dexter had been a cop for a long time. She'd experienced a lot, seen a lot. Bailey could tell that she was rattled.

'I'm coming.'

He was wide awake now, jotting down the address while Penelope booked him a taxi.

Bailey shook Gerald's shoulder until his friend opened his eyes.

'Anderson's dead.'

'What?' Gerald sat up, wiping the drool from the corner of his mouth.

'Dexter called. He was found in Alexandria. I'm going there now. You stay here. Somebody needs to mind the documents.'

Bailey picked his crumpled dinner jacket up off the floor and slipped his arms through the sleeves, wincing again at the sharp pain in his ribs.

'I'll get legal in here.' Gerald was already up off the sofa, staring at the pages scattered across his desk. 'Get moving.'

Mick was still on the front desk when Bailey walked out of the elevator.

'Long night for you, Mr Bailey.'

'You too, mate.'

'It's not over yet. Mr Summers wants me upstairs as soon as Kevin gets here. He wants me to guard his office or something. Penelope just called.' For someone who had been up all night, Mick sounded excited. 'You guys must be on to something big?'

'Something like that.' Bailey didn't have time to chat. 'Thanks, Mick. That's my taxi out front, better run.'

Bailey climbed in the car out front of *The Journal* office, trying not to think about the scene that awaited him in Alexandria. His head was pounding, his ribs ached, his elbow felt like it'd been whacked with a sledgehammer, and his throat was crying out for water. But nothing compared to the guilt that was burning a hole in his gut as the taxi edged closer to the warehouse where Michael Anderson's lifeless body had been found.

Bailey had been out of the game for almost three years. The mere possibility that he might have led the killers to Anderson made him question his fitness for the job.

He had always protected his sources.

—

Dexter was standing out front, smoking a cigarette, when Bailey arrived. A police car and her unmarked Holden were the only two vehicles on the scene.

'What's up with him?' Bailey pointed to the bloke emptying his guts in the bushes by the door of the warehouse.

'First on the scene. He was okay until a few minutes ago.' Dexter didn't look too good, either. 'It's confronting in there.'

The guilt was gnawing at Bailey but he was going inside, no matter what. 'How long have I got?'

Dexter wasn't going to try to talk him out of it. 'Five minutes. Then this place will be crawling with forensics and television crews. The morning shows love this shit.'

They walked past the cop at the door. He was standing upright and wiping his mouth. Embarrassed by the mess he'd made in the bushes, he avoided eye contact with Dexter and didn't even ask about the man she was escorting into the crime scene.

'Someone heard screams coming from inside at around five o'clock this morning.' Dexter led Bailey through the door. 'Unidentified call to triple zero. My guess is they wanted us to find him.'

'What makes you say that?'

'You'll see.'

A dim light filtered through the windows along the ceiling of the warehouse. Bailey squinted, trying to adjust his eyes. The space looked like it hadn't been rented for years – smashed windows, damaged walls, damp and mouldy, with cracks in the concrete floor exposing the dirt underneath.

Graffiti was all over the place, barely legible messages, mostly about inequality and injustice, voices of the ballooning masses living below the poverty line. They were the forgotten souls of a beautiful city, who spoke with a can of paint on a wall that no one would see. The only other sign that people had once lived there were the dusty old beds and linen scattered in the corner. The warehouse was so decrepit that even the homeless had abandoned it.

'Over there.' Dexter pointed to a chair in the corner. 'I'll wait here.'

Anderson was sitting upright. From behind he looked peaceful. But as Bailey got closer he could see a pool of liquid on the floor. By the smell and colour, he guessed it was a mixture of piss and blood. Anderson was facing the wall, his hands and legs tied to the chair.

'Remember, we don't have long.' Dexter's warning carried across the room.

But Bailey hardly heard her, his senses dimmed by the horror before him. He walked around the chair and caught a glimpse of Anderson's face.

'What the fuck?' He gagged, lifting the back of his hand to his nose, anything to shield himself from the violence.

Anderson's fingernails had been torn out and were scattered on the floor. Not just the nails, chunks of skin had been ripped off in the force of the action. Two of his fingers were missing and were sitting, bloodied and mangled, in the mess on the concrete. A rag had been stuffed into his mouth to silence his screams.

His shirt was torn open, his pants crumpled around his ankles. A car battery was on the floor beside him, cables connected to his genitals and the nipples on his chest. His face had been beaten to the point where his eyes were so swollen they almost concealed the lifeless pupils staring into nothing.

There was a neat hole in Anderson's forehead – the bullet had been saved for the end. And, at the end, Anderson must have welcomed it.

Bailey shuddered, trying to imagine what had happened. Whoever had done this didn't just want Michael Anderson dead – they had wanted him to talk.

He must have talked.

No one could have withstood the horror that had unfolded here. And now his torturer knew about the documents that could bring down Gary Page and Li Chen, and cause a major scandal for Matthew Parker's government.

Acid was burning in the back of Bailey's throat, a physical response to the burden of blame.

'I did this.'

The empty warehouse was an echo chamber.

'What'd you say?' Dexter was standing more than three metres away.

Bailey turned around. 'I should have been more careful, should have got him to turn himself in.'

He shook his head, angry and helpless.

They didn't have much time.

'What'd he tell you?' Bailey could tell Dexter was relieved he was walking back towards her so she wouldn't have to look at Anderson's tortured corpse up close again.

'He gave me documents, incriminating stuff about Gary Page and the Chinese ambassador setting up dodgy offshore companies for defence contracts.'

'How's that work?'

'Not now.' Bailey looked around to see if the killer, or killers, had left anything else behind.

'Bailey?'

'We've been through the documents back at the paper. They look legit. Lawyers are looking at them with Gerald now. Page and Li are nothing but two-bit crooks.'

Dexter nodded her chin at Anderson's body strapped to the chair. 'Now they know what you have on them.'

'Must have been tailing me.'

'It's possible.' Dexter was always honest. 'But maybe they were going to find him anyway. This was professional. Whoever did this knew what they were doing.'

'Either way, I was the link, the one talking to –'

'There's more – and you're not going to like it.'

She handed Bailey a blood-splattered folder.

'What's this?'

'Open it,' she said. 'Someone's trying to frame you.'

'What? Why?'

'Shut you up, discredit you. How the hell should I know?'

Bailey took the file. Inside were photographs of him walking down a hallway. He flipped the page and there were others of him out the front of an apartment building. All the pictures had a time and date at the top. They looked like stills taken from a security camera.

Bailey's shock turned to anger. 'Is this where I think it is?'

'Yeah. Catherine Chamberlain's apartment building. The date and time puts you at the scene during the missing minutes on the tapes, round the time we think she was murdered.'

'Clever, maybe too clever.' He tapped the photograph. 'They're the clothes I was wearing that first day when I saw you inside the apartment.'

'Clothes? A jury wouldn't buy that,' Dexter said. 'And let's be honest here – you're still wearing your suit from last night.'

'Yeah, fashion has always been my undoing. Where'd you find them?'

'Where d'you think? Sitting on that poor bastard's lap.'

Planted evidence was never going to be difficult to find.

'What do we do with it?' Bailey knew exactly what he wanted to do with the photographs, but it was Dexter's call.

'Destroy them.'

'The bloke outside?'

'I'll take the chance. He's all over the place. An elephant could have walked in here and he wouldn't remember.'

They both knew that the photographs wouldn't matter as long as they found the missing minutes on the security footage at Catherine Chamberlain's apartment building. The photographs were just a warning. At least, Bailey hoped they were.

'Bloody Mario whatever-his-name-is. Where the bloody hell is he?' Bailey said.

'Don't worry. He has to turn up sooner or later.'

'If this all turns to shit, can you be the one to put the cuffs on me?' He lifted his arms, wrists together.

'Don't.' Dexter wasn't smiling. 'Anyhow, it won't come to that.'

She was interrupted by the screeching of car tyres in the street. Car doors clicked open and closed, the sound of voices carried through the door.

'You need to go – now!'

The voices were getting louder. Bailey looked around the room for another way out.

'Over there!' She pointed at a hole in the wall, the back door for the squatters who had once called this warehouse home.

'Thanks.' Bailey started walking. 'Call Gerald if you need me. I've ditched my phone – too much of a risk.'

He bent down, grimacing at the pain in his ribs, and climbed through the wall. He poked his head back through the hole and saw David Davis emerge through the door.

'That who I think it is?' Bailey heard him ask her.

Dexter nodded and escorted him towards the chair in the corner. 'He's dead.'

'What else did you find?' Davis said.

'Nothing.' She was forthright – strong – giving nothing away. If Davis was somehow involved, she needed to be. 'But we're still looking.'

'Look harder.'

Bailey stepped away from the building and stuffed the photographs into his trousers. He wasn't worried about damaging them. Within minutes they'd be smouldering in a rubbish bin by the side of the road.

CHAPTER 28

'Still here, mate?'

Mick was standing outside Gerald's office when Bailey got back.

'I'll stay as long as I'm needed.'

Bailey gave him a friendly slap on the shoulder and walked through the door. Ronnie Johnson was perched on the edge of Gerald's desk, sucking on the end of his cigar, thumbing through the documents that had cost Michael Anderson his life.

'We're sharing already?' Bailey directed his question at Gerald without acknowledging the CIA agent sitting in front of him.

'Not even a hello, bubba?'

'Seriously.' Bailey's steely gaze was locked on Gerald. 'What's going on?'

'I called Ronnie and told him to come in. We're in over our heads with this, Bailey. I needed a second opinion.'

'Isn't that what she's for?' Bailey pointed at the woman sitting on the sofa he'd woken up on that morning.

'And hello to you, Bailey. Nice to see you, as always.' Marjorie Atkins had been a legal associate at *The Journal* for thirty-five years. 'You've got something big here. Wouldn't say you're in over your head, but it's going to take a massive pair of balls to publish it.'

'It's lucky that our Gerald is so very well endowed, Marj.' Bailey had a deadpan look on his face. He wasn't joking.

Marjorie had worked closely with Bailey on his police corruption stories many years ago. She was tough and he liked her. But after what he'd just witnessed in that warehouse in Alexandria, he wasn't up for compromises.

'So, your advice is to print it?'

'The evidence in your possession is certainly compelling,' she said.

'But?' There was always a but with Marjorie.

'However, these are documents that've been provided to us on the word of one man. A man who, I might add, is now dead.'

'What's the call?'

'For God's sake, Bailey, let her finish,' Gerald said.

Marjorie was used to Bailey's impatience with due process. 'I've already got my team looking at Sands Enterprises in the Virgin Islands. If that company checks out, then I would say your risk is only moderate.'

'Moderate?'

'You know me, Bailey. I won't ever tell you to print something. That's the decision of the editor. There's still a considerable risk involved, I'd say. You're dealing with the defence minister, for starters, and you'll be alleging serious leaks from inside both the Treasury and the DOD so, even if you're right, you could be wrong.'

Legal speak for we're screwed either way, thought Bailey. But he wasn't about to say it out loud. He wanted to roll the dice.

'It's a risk we should take.'

'What Marjorie is saying is that they'll fight us to the end,' Gerald said.

Bailey's temper was flaring. Everyone could see, but he didn't care. 'So what?'

'Which means it'll cost.' Gerald ignored him. 'The difference is that these guys can do it with taxpayer dollars, something that hasn't bothered them in the past.'

'So, what the fuck do we do?' Bailey said. 'Ronnie? Got anything you'd like to contribute? Or are you just along for the ride?'

'Settle down, Bailey.' Gerald tried again to ease the tension that had enveloped the room. 'No one is saying we can't print anything, not yet.'

'Actually, bubba,' Ronnie said, 'I've got a lot.'

'And?'

Ronnie got up, closed the door and returned his cigar to the corner of his mouth.

'The information I'm about to tell you remains in this room.' He took a moment to meet the eyes of all of those listening.

'Enough with the bullshit, Ronnie. We know the drill. Secret squirrels. Just get it out.'

Ronnie waited until there was quiet.

'Anderson had been working for us.'

'What the fuck!' Bailey erupted. 'After all the promises of playing it straight and sharing information, you drop this on us. You're unbelievable!'

'He's right, Ronnie.' Gerald was back in Bailey's corner. 'This is hard to take, even from you.'

'Well, if Bailey hadn't started getting taxis everywhere maybe we wouldn't have missed the rendezvous with Anderson last night and the poor bastard would still be alive!'

'Don't you dare pin that on me!' Bailey stepped towards Ronnie, fist clenched, his rage compounded by the fact that Ronnie had still been using surveillance on him.

'Boys, boys, boys!' Marjorie could yell louder than any of them. 'We're adults, aren't we?'

The door to Gerald's office creaked open.

'Everything okay in here, Mr Summers?' It was Mick.

'Yes, mate. An animated conversation, that's all.'

'Of course, sir. Just checking.' Mick closed the door.

'Let's hear what Mr Johnson would like to share with us,' Marjorie said.

Bailey stepped back from Ronnie's towering frame – which was sensible, when he thought about it – and walked over to the window.

'Okay,' Bailey said. 'Let's hear it.'

Ronnie wasn't in a hurry. He strolled to the coffee machine in the corner of Gerald's office, slipped a capsule inside and let it do its work.

'When you're ready, mate,' Bailey said.

Ronnie took a sip of his long black and nodded at Gerald, acknowledging the taste.

'The lawyer needs to go.'

'Marjorie stays.' Gerald looked like he was about to explode. 'Now, tell us what you know or get the fuck out of my office.'

'Okay, bubba, your way then. I'm too old for the game anyway.'

'We all are.'

At least they could agree on something.

'Let me start by saying my people brought me into this charade late in the piece. Anderson was never our priority. Ambassador Li Chen was our focus – who he was meeting, what information he was passing back to Beijing. The twenty-first century is all about China. The booming economy that's helping us all. But, really, we're in the dark about their real intentions. All we know is they don't like anyone getting involved in their domestic affairs.'

'Thanks for the lesson in geopolitics.' Bailey was glaring at him. 'Get on with it.'

'We've got a country of 1.3 billion people and we know next to nothing about them. They're building military bases out of sand in the South China Sea, putting missile batteries on beaches, landing fighter planes on runways – all in disputed waters, on islands that didn't even exist two years ago.'

For Ronnie, the context was important and he was becoming more animated as he went.

'Some might dismiss these concerns as squabbles about rocks in the ocean. We don't. Beijing has identified more than two hundred reefs and rocky outcrops that can be converted into islands – and why do we care?'

Ronnie let the question hang in the air like a school teacher.

'The answer? Simple economics. This is the busiest shipping route in the world. More than seven trillion dollars in cargo passes through this passage every year – and we think Beijing is making a play to control it.'

Bailey was getting a little tired of the lecture. 'How's this relevant? And, if it is, what the fuck are you guys doing about it?'

'You mean what are *we* doing about it.' Ronnie looked like he was enjoying himself.

'We, you, us, them – seriously?' Bailey said. 'I hope this riddle has an ending.'

'The Pentagon starts waving military strategies across the president's desk about bolstering our presence in Asia. Someone raises the idea about a permanent military base in Australia to complement our bases in places like Japan and Korea. Australia's one of our closest allies in the region, we do training exercises together already – it makes sense.

'But the president wants to go further. It's like the military's this new toy he gets to play with, so our two countries start discussing the idea of naval patrols in the South China Sea – sending warships weaving in and out of a twelve nautical mile area that China claims as sovereign territory. Flyovers too. Even war games eventually. We can finally put those Joint Strike Fighters we've been building for you in the air and see how the Chinese react.

'The Philippines, Malaysia, Vietnam, Brunei – they're all up for it because they've got claims in the disputed waters too. And China's Nine Dash Line cuts straight across all of them. It's the size of bloody Mexico so it's little wonder everyone's so pissed. Plans are drawn up and the Pentagon starts shifting assets and we're getting ready to move. And then something strange happens.'

Finally, Ronnie looked like he was getting to the point.

'The same ideas being exchanged between Washington and Canberra are turning up in wire taps in Beijing, information fed via Ambassador Li Chen – and he wasn't getting it from our side. It was clear you had a leak. So we tool up on Li – I'm talking 24-hour surveillance. We're following him everywhere, to every meeting. When someone shakes his hand we have someone watching. We've got ears on his office, his car, the front gate at his residence. If this guy farts, we hear it. If he –'

'We get the picture,' Gerald said.

'It was while we were paying close attention to the people around Li that we stumbled across young Victor Ho.'

'The dead student?' Bailey said.

'Some kind of gofer. Li passed stuff to him, he passed stuff to Li. Other than that, young Victor spent most of his time at Sydney University.'

Ronnie stopped talking and walked over to the sofa where Marjorie Atkins was sitting, feverishly scribbling on a notepad. 'Don't do that.' He took the pencil out of her hand.

'Please, tell me this monologue's going to give us more than what we already know,' Bailey said.

'Almost there, bubba.' Ronnie winked at Bailey. 'We start noticing some late night and early morning meetings – unscheduled, random, like walking along rivers or in the type of parks people avoid when the sun goes down. Li's careful – we never get close enough to listen in. But we did catch on to who he was meeting –'

'Gary Page.' Bailey said it for him.

'That's right. Then we put a watch on your defence minister to see if we could get anything from his end.'

'And?' Marjorie was so absorbed in the story she'd slid to the edge of her seat.

'Nothing. The guy's careful. He knows what he's doing, knows the risks. Which leads us to Michael Anderson.'

'Why'd you choose him?' Bailey asked.

'Two reasons, neither of them compelling. The first was that even though he always travelled with Page, he didn't attend every event on the minister's calendar. That gave us windows. Secondly, we'd observed a couple of big arguments between them. Tension is always something to exploit.

'Getting him on board took time. At first, he told us to go away, he got scared and mentioned words like treason. He's right – even spying for an ally is still spying. You can get in a lot of trouble.'

'Hence why we've been telling you to piss off for so many years.' Bailey was calming down.

'Yes, bubba. I got that message from you loud and clear,' Ronnie said. 'Then one day one of our guys gets a random call from a public phone – Anderson wants to meet. We set it up and he spills his theories about Page's views on China, as good as confirming for us that Page was the leak.'

'And just what does the CIA do with this kind of information?' Marjorie said.

'Nice try. What I will tell you is that it usually gets fed back through channels and then misguided people like Page suddenly have a good reason to retire, absolving them of all influence. Civilised, mostly – this isn't the Cold War in the seventies.'

Ronnie slipped his unlit cigar inside the pocket in his jacket and took another sip of his coffee.

'What'd you do?' Gerald said. 'We can all see that Page still has a job.'

'Nothing.' Ronnie looked like he knew he'd disappointed them. 'We want the Chinese to know we're muscling up on this side of the world. It didn't matter that they knew about the possibility of war games in the South China Sea. Sure, it's provocative, but that stuff's always a showcase.'

'That's a funny game you've been playing all these years,' Bailey said.

'I don't think any of us really understand the method, as long as we're winning.'

'And are you?' Gerald asked.

Ronnie shrugged his big shoulders. 'Not so easy to measure, any more. Anyway, it all changed at that very first meeting with Anderson because he was already on to the scheme about defence contracts that Page had been concocting with Li Chen but he never gave us any paperwork. Not like this.' Ronnie tapped his finger on the pile of documents on Gerald's desk.

'Why not?' Gerald said. 'He was your guy, and he obviously wanted to expose Page.'

'He got spooked. One of our agents put too much pressure on him. He stopped trusting us, said we couldn't protect him, so he walked.'

'And now he's dead,' Bailey said.

'We tried to help him, bubba.'

'Did we?' Bailey was staring out the window, almost as if talking to himself.

'Want my advice on what you guys can get away with?' Ronnie was always up for giving free and frank advice. 'Write about the defence contracts – at least you can prove that part. The leaking is a whole other story. It happens more than you'd think.'

'Thanks for the tip, and thanks for being straight with us,' Gerald said.

'See ya, boys.' Ronnie gave Bailey a friendly slap on the shoulder and put his cigar back in his mouth. 'Good to meet you, Marjorie.'

The three of them waited for Ronnie to close the door behind him before discussing a game plan.

'We've got work to do.' Gerald seemed to know exactly what he wanted them to do. 'We're going to write this thing.'

'What about the spying allegations?' Marjorie asked.

'All of it,' Gerald said. 'Starting with Michael Anderson's murder.'

'That's my boy.'

Finally Bailey had something to smile about.

CHAPTER 29

Gerald was softly snoring on the sofa while Bailey was putting the finishing touches on the story. It was eight o'clock in the evening and they'd been writing all day – firstly, an article about the gruesome murder of Michael Anderson in a warehouse in Alexandria. Suspect and motive unclear. That story had already been uploaded. The second was even bigger – one long exposé that could bring down a defence minister and possibly the government of Matthew Parker.

Bailey and Gerald hadn't left the office all day. Neither had Marjorie Atkins. She loved being needed on the big stories, especially the ones that reinforced the role of the fourth estate. Stories with consequence. She'd been doing it for decades, never growing tired of it.

'Bailey, look at this!' Marjorie had been reading through the documents one last time to make sure they hadn't missed anything.

'What is it?' He was exhausted and apprehensive about yet another rewrite.

'I can't believe I missed it.' She was shaking her head, holding a piece of paper in her hand. 'We've been wondering about David Davis? Well, here's the link. Money. Guess who deposited fifty grand into an Australian bank account with the receipt notation: "Davis – Grayndler Campaign"?'

Bailey walked over to Marjorie and took the piece of paper from her hand. It was an expenditure list.

'Sands Enterprises.' Bailey read it aloud. 'Marj, you're bloody amazing!'

'It's dated three months ago. Looks like Davis's plan to go into politics has been in the works for a while. Now we've got him tied to Page.'

Bailey screwed up a piece of scrap paper and threw it at Gerald. 'Hey! Sleepy head!'

The paper hit Gerald on his chin. He sat up, startled. 'Bloody hell, Bailey, what is it?'

'It seems Sands Enterprises has made a not so little donation to the soon to be local Member for Grayndler.'

'Davis?' Gerald rubbed his eyes and put on his glasses.

Bailey didn't bother to hide his delight. 'Mr Squeaky Clean, the man of the hour, not so squeaky. I reckon this might give Page a little leverage, don't you?'

'Hang on a minute.' Gerald put up his hands to give his brain a few extra seconds to catch up. 'You think Page is putting pressure on Davis over the Chamberlain case?'

Bailey had never floundered with his special dislike for corrupt cops. This one had the added bonus of being the bloke who'd slept with his ex.

'That's exactly what I'm suggesting.'

'We can't print it, Bailey – we just can't.' Gerald was shaking his head. 'We still don't know the identity of her murderer. The only thing we can write is that he's received money from a company that we can link to corruption.'

Marjorie cleared her throat on the other side of the room. 'And, I might add, Mr Davis may well argue that he knew nothing about what the directors of Sands Enterprises had been up to. Also, we haven't linked the Australian account to Davis yet.'

'At best, it's a smear.'

'All right, then,' Bailey said. 'Let's smear! Questionable political donations – the public loves this shit!'

'Bailey. Think rationally here.'

'Okay, I get it.' Bailey wasn't going to fight a losing battle. 'But my feeling is we're just scratching the surface on this.'

'No one will argue with you there, mate,' Gerald said.

Bailey decided to change the subject. 'Nancy dropped these off while you were sleeping.' He tossed Gerald one of two clean shirts hanging on the back of the door.

'If you don't mind me saying, both of you could do with a shower,' Marjorie said.

'We're used to each other's stink.' Gerald plucked a can of deodorant from a drawer in his desk and threw it to Bailey. 'Shower in a can?'

'Thanks.' Bailey took off the stained white shirt he'd been wearing for almost two days, sprayed his underarms, then slipped his hands into the sleeves of one of Gerald's freshly preened shirts.

'Nice.' Bailey was admiring the cotton. 'I'm keeping this.'

'It's yours. At least you'll look respectable one day a week.'

Gerald's phone rang.

'I said no calls. Oh, I'm sorry, sweetheart. Hang on – I'll get him for you.' Gerald sheepishly handed the receiver to Bailey. 'It's Miranda.'

'Dad!'

Bailey sat up. Something was wrong.

'Are you okay?'

'I think . . . I think someone's following me.'

'What?' Bailey was trying to stay calm.

'I noticed him in the bar near court. I was having a few drinks after work. When I left, he did too. He's been walking about fifty metres behind me for the last six blocks.'

The image of Anderson's mangled corpse flashed through Bailey's mind. His heart was racing. Anderson could have told them anything.

The documents.

If Bailey was the new target, anyone close to him could be a target too. They'd get to him any way they could. From what Bailey had seen, they were capable of anything.

Anything.

'Where are you? Exactly where are you?' He was speaking quickly. 'It's important that I know your exact location.'

'Dad, what's going on?'

'Your location, Miranda. I need to know exactly where you are.'

Gerald rested his hand on Bailey's shoulder, but he shrugged it away aggressively.

'Miranda?' Bailey said again.

'Sorry, I was looking for a street sign to be sure. I've just turned off George onto King Street.'

She was only four blocks away.

'I'm going to put you onto Gerald and I want you to stay on the phone and keep talking to him, okay? I am coming down to meet you.'

He handed the receiver to Gerald. 'Don't let her hang up.'

Bailey limped out of the office and was at the elevator within seconds. He kept hitting the button, knowing that it wouldn't make the doors open any quicker.

Tap, tap, tap.

He had to do something to make himself feel like he was doing all that he could to get to Miranda. He had to protect his daughter. Nothing else mattered.

Within a minute he was running past Penelope, through the foyer and out onto Sussex Street. The city was mostly bright lights bouncing off black windows. Apart from the steady stream of cars in the post peak-hour traffic, the streets were quiet, footpaths almost empty. Few people worked late on a Friday night and most of the popular bars were on the other side of town.

Bailey headed north on Sussex Street until he hit King. He turned the corner and could see Miranda running, heels in one hand, the other holding her phone to her ear.

'Dad!' She caught sight of him up the street.

Bailey clocked a car with tinted windows slowing behind her. It was the same black Camry that he'd seen in Newtown – licence plate CVC 163 – the one that had sped off with Michael Anderson and his killer inside.

The car drew alongside Miranda, the rear door opened.

'Run! Miranda! Run!' Bailey was forty metres away now.

It was all happening in slow motion.

The door was wide open. Miranda didn't see it – she had her eyes fixed on her father, his hand still in the air from when he'd yelled her name seconds before, sprinting towards her.

The car windows were so dark Bailey couldn't see inside.

'Run! Run!' She wasn't a confident city lawyer any more, she was Bailey's little girl, three feet high, innocent and vulnerable, running towards her silly daddy, wanting him to protect her.

In an instant it was over.

The car door slammed shut and the driver sped off up King Street.

Miranda had been running downhill and she almost tripped into her father's arms, dropping her shoes and phone onto the footpath.

'What's going on?' She was struggling to catch her breath.

Bailey was puffing so hard he couldn't speak. As he held his daughter tightly, he noticed a police car on the other side of the street. The cop must have spooked whoever was in the Camry. Right place, right time, for once.

The policeman opened his window. 'Everything okay there, miss?'

'Yes, thank you.' Miranda stepped back so the cop could see that she wasn't in any danger. 'This is my father.'

Bailey was bent over, resting his hands on his knees. He couldn't remember the last time he'd run that far. The stale air in his lungs was burning a hole in his chest. Each breath triggered a piercing pain from his already damaged rib cage.

He gave a thumbs up signal to the policeman. 'We're all good here, thanks, officer.'

'Okay, then, you both take care.' The policeman closed his window and weaved his car back into the traffic on King Street.

Bailey's eyes followed the car until it disappeared on the crest of the hill two blocks away. He scanned the footpath, first the left, then the right side of the street. There were hardly any pedestrians. A group of young foul-mouthed kids were staggering together – the end of a long session, or fuelling up for a big night out. There were a few business types, a woman walking a tiny dog and a couple holding hands on the other side of the street, heading downhill towards the water and, most probably, a dinner reservation at Cockle Bay.

One person stood out – a young man loitering in the shadows on the corner of the next block, staring in their direction. It was probably nobody.

Bailey wanted to be sure. 'Hey!' he called in his direction. 'Hey, hey, mate!'

The man disappeared around the corner.

'That him?' he asked Miranda.

'Him who?' Miranda was too startled to focus.

'That bloke on the corner.'

'I'm not sure. I didn't see – and Dad?' They were standing under a street lamp and something else was clearly bothering her. 'What happened to your face?'

'Long story. Let's get inside.'

Gerald pulled Miranda into his arms when she walked through the door of his office. 'Bet you're glad that's over.'

'A bit rattled is all.' Miranda's cheeks were flushed.

'Get a good look at him?' Gerald said.

'Not really. Just enough to know that I'd seen him in the bar earlier. Young Asian bloke.'

'You're safe here.'

'I could do with a drink.' Miranda looked hopefully at Gerald.

'Like father, like daughter,' Bailey said. 'Don't keep her waiting, Gerald.'

'Two Baileys? Good God!' Gerald said. 'Whisky okay, Miranda?'

'The other Bailey would like one too, thank you, old boy.'

'You need to call Dexter – something about finding the manager of Catherine Chamberlain's apartment building,' Gerald said.

'What's all this about?' Miranda said to anyone willing to provide the answer.

Bailey withdrew Detective Sharon Dexter's card from his wallet and punched her number into the phone on Gerald's desk.

The conversation lasted about five seconds. He didn't have time for that drink any more.

He turned to his daughter. 'Gerald will fill you in, sweetheart. I've got to go out.'

Dexter had found Mario Monticello. He was prepared to show her every piece of security footage he had from the night of Chamberlain's murder.

Bailey looked at his watch. It was almost eight-thirty. 'Are we publishing tonight?'

'Midnight.' Gerald sounded resolute.

'I won't be long. Don't click the button till I'm back.'

'Be careful, Bailey.'

'I'm going to meet a cop. What could go wrong?' Bailey slapped Gerald on the arm. 'Miranda, I want you to stay here. I'm not sure it's safe to go home tonight.'

'Okay, Dad.'

Bailey walked out the door and bumped straight into Mick, who was standing guard outside again. He was a big man and it was like hitting a brick wall.

'Mate, do you ever go home?'

'Got a few hours' sleep, Mr Bailey. Had dinner with my boys, tucked them in. That's all I needed.'

Bailey felt better knowing Mick was watching over his daughter too.

CHAPTER 30

It was getting late but the day wasn't done with Bailey yet.

There was no sign of the black Camry or the man who'd been following Miranda when he walked onto the street outside *The Journal*. He paced around the block – twice – before hailing his taxi, just to be sure.

Bailey rested his head against the car window and stared out into the night, resisting closing his eyes because he didn't want to risk giving in to his exhaustion.

The car was moving slowly in the traffic up William Street. He was keeping himself alert by studying the people strolling along the footpath, their clothes and faces, all dressed up with places to go. He could hear groups of friends talking loudly, teasing each other, excited about the start of the weekend, the chance to get drunk and to forget about life for a while.

Couples, new and old, hand in hand, some arguing, some smiling, others simply in a hurry to get to someplace other than work. It made Bailey think about Dexter, what it might be like to hold her hand and walk down this street. There was still time, maybe.

It also distracted him from the fact that someone was trying to frame him for murder. He didn't need to close his eyes to see Michael Anderson's bloodied face staring back at him. That image would stay with him forever. His puffy eyes, mashed cheekbones and that bullet hole reprieve from the pain. The torment of torture – willing it to stop, even if it meant dying. Bailey was one of the few people who could describe what that felt like.

The taxi was getting close to the famous Coca-Cola sign at Kings Cross. Bailey picked a twenty-dollar note from his wallet and tapped the driver on the shoulder.

'Drop me anywhere out of the tunnel, mate.'

He wanted to walk the final few hundred metres. Not just for the fresh air – he wanted to check if anyone was on his tail.

Dexter was standing out the front of Catherine Chamberlain's apartment complex with an old man, partially obscured by the puffs of smoke from his pipe.

'Detective Dexter.'

'Mr Bailey.'

The formalities sounded odd.

'Long time since I've seen someone smoking one of those.' Bailey turned on his charm and extended his hand to the manager of the apartment building. 'John Bailey.'

'Mario Monticello.' They shook hands. 'You've got a good grip, Mr Bailey!'

Mario had a thick Italian accent that gave rhythm to his words. He must have been only five feet tall, but the way he spoke and the beam of his smile gave him presence.

'I love the pipe,' he said. 'Bad habit I got from you Australians when I came over in 1956!'

Mario drew back and let the smoke puff out the corners of his lips. He tipped the rest of the simmering leaves into the gutter and waved for them to follow him inside.

'Mario has been visiting his daughter in Melbourne,' Dexter said.

'Lygon Street – best pizza in Australia. I love my daughter, but I really only go for the pizza.'

'Mario doesn't have any other copies of the tapes he gave Constable Rob Lucas a few days ago,' Dexter said. 'He was as surprised as we were about the black hole at around eleven o'clock.'

Bailey responded with a worried glance, wondering why they were here.

'Terrible, terrible thing that has happened to this girl. I want to help, any way I can.'

'Mario says there's another camera angle – one he didn't think we'd need,' Dexter said.

'Oh, right,' Bailey said.

'This is not a good angle.' Mario led them into the foyer. 'It was the temporary entry to the building when I had the main entrance refurbished. The stupid builders took so bloody long I got paranoid and put another camera there so I could see who's coming and going.'

Bailey was staring at the ceiling, trying to find it.

Mario nudged him with his elbow. 'Up there.' He pointed at the fire exit in the corner. 'It points the other way, you see, so it won't catch anyone coming in, only going out. I have been meaning to get rid of it but my system is too easy – record, change tape, record – so I never bothered.'

'Let's take a look at it, hey Mario?' Dexter said.

'Of course, of course. Follow me.'

Dexter and Bailey followed him down the hallway to his office. The door would only open halfway because of the piles of boxes stacked around the room. He cleared the top of a small filing cabinet and gestured for them to sit.

'I do filing the old-fashioned way.'

Mario disappeared behind a pile of boxes and began shifting them into an uneasy tower next to his desk. He seemed to be clearing a path so he could get to a large cupboard in the corner.

'Here we go,' he said, opening the door. Inside, dozens of VHS tapes were stacked inside in piles. Each one was neatly marked with a camera number and day of the month.

'You see? System works!' Mario said. 'I keep tapes for one month, then record over them again. We want camera nine from exactly one week ago, no?'

'That's right.' Dexter seemed relieved that Mario could make sense of the chaos in his office.

He moved another box on his desk to clear a space in front of an old television with a built-in tape deck. Next, he used his hand to sweep the thick layer of dust from the screen.

Mario held up a tape with the word 'sixteen' scribbled in thick black writing on the label. 'Sixteen?'

'Sixteenth of the month,' Dexter said. 'Good system.'

'Here we go!' He inserted the tape and the machine flickered to life.

Mario handed Dexter the remote control. 'You do it.'

Bailey watched as Dexter spooled the recording, the numbers ticking over in the corner of the screen. Mario was right – even at high speed they could see that no one used the fire exit. Dexter hit play when they were close to eleven o'clock.

'What's on the other side of that door?' Bailey said.

'Not much – a pathway alongside the building. No one uses it.'

The little time code at the top of the screen showed two minutes past eleven when a sturdy figure wearing a large coat and a baseball cap appeared in the foyer. From this angle they could clearly see the top of his head, not much else, and his body was side on. He turned around and took a step towards the main entrance, all the while keeping his head down.

'We're not going to see his face.' The pessimist in Bailey called it early.

'C'mon, c'mon, c'mon.' Dexter was talking to the screen. 'Look up, damn it. Look up!'

Having surveyed the area around him, the man walked towards the camera and the fire exit, without once raising his head. The recording only captured a clear image of a baseball cap with the insignia of the New York Yankees. They couldn't even make out the colour of his jacket because the pictures were in black and white. He walked directly underneath the camera and disappeared.

'So, he comes into the foyer through the main entrance and then leaves through the fire exit?' Bailey said.

'Wait!' Dexter said. The clock on the screen showed that it had been approximately three minutes since the man first appeared. 'The black hole lasted for fifteen minutes.'

Bailey kept his eyes on the screen.

After a few more minutes, the man reappeared, unsteady on his feet, like he'd been pushed backwards by something. Or someone.

'That door is a bit hard to get open,' Mario said. 'It needs a bit of muscle.'

Bailey and Dexter were glued to the screen.

The man in the cap was trying to regain his balance when a second person stepped into the frame. The man grabbed the new guy by the jacket, trying to steady himself. The force of the action spun both men around and the camera caught the sides of their faces. Dexter hit the pause button.

The room fell silent as everyone took a moment to process what they were looking at.

'Holy shit!' She grabbed Bailey's arm. 'It's Davis! And –'

'He's just let Victor Ho in the building.'

'No wonder he was pressuring me to let this thing go.'

'I'd say that there is a pretty good reason.'

Dexter stood up and pointed at the screen. 'I want to see what's on the other side of that door.'

'Let's go.'

'Give me a minute.' Dexter turned to Mario. 'I'm taking it there are no other copies of this?'

'These tapes are an expensive business,' Mario said.

'Meet you down there.' Bailey walked out the door.

—

Bailey pushed down hard on the long metal beam that stretched across the fire exit door, kicking the bottom of the wood that had swelled with the humidity. He couldn't get it open. By the time Dexter joined him he was ramming the door with his shoulder.

'You need a little more muscle there?'

'Damn thing won't budge!'

'That's because you need to push down and pull.' She was trying not to smile. 'It's an old fire door – opens inwards rather than out.'

'Now you're an expert on doors?' Bailey bashed the door again with his shoulder.

'No, really. Give me a go.' She nudged him out of the way and followed her own instructions. After a stern pull, it opened.

'Lucky guess.'

'God, you're stubborn.'

Bailey stepped out onto a narrow dirt pathway covered in leaves and branches. 'Some fire escape. Wouldn't want to be in a hurry to –'

Bailey heard Dexter gasp behind him. He turned around to see a gloved hand covering her mouth, a flash of electricity slam into her neck and Dexter slump to the ground.

He lunged at her attacker, only to be clobbered in the head by something hard, then he too hit the deck.

Reeling from the crack on his head, Bailey tried to grab his assailant's leg, but was pushed back. A foot stamped heavily on his chest, knocking the oxygen from his lungs and paralysing his torso on the ground. His already damaged rib cage sent a piercing pain through his body.

It was almost pitch black, with the thick canopy of trees hiding the moon and the stars. All Bailey could see was a pair of white eyes staring at him through a black mask.

Then a flash from the taser as it discharged fifty thousand volts into his neck.

CHAPTER 31

Baghdad, January 2005

Someone ripped the blindfold off his head and untied the rope that had been binding his hands tightly behind his back.

'Sit.'

A hand landed on Bailey's shoulder, pulling him backwards until he fell unsteadily into a chair.

'How do you feel?'

He rubbed his eyes, trying to focus on the man sitting opposite, get a handle on where they had brought him.

'Where am I?'

'Baghdad.'

They were in a large room, surrounded by empty tables and chairs. It looked like some sort of restaurant.

'How long have I been here?'

'Here in Baghdad? Or as our special guest?'

Bailey recognised the posh accent. It belonged to the violent bastard from the cave.

'An answer to both would be good.' The shackles might have been off, but he needed to keep his head. 'If you wouldn't mind.'

The man was staring at Bailey like they were old friends.

'Well, Mr Bailey, I think you could guess from your long drive here that you have only been in Baghdad for a few days. But it has been ten months since my men first met you in Fallujah.' He pointed to the small huddle of men sitting near them.

Bailey wanted to punch him in the face. 'You mean slammed a rifle butt into my head and kidnapped me.'

The man shifted in his chair and rested his elbows on the table between them.

'There wasn't much we could do about that, I'm afraid. I do regret some of the other acts of violence. My men can get carried away when they meet someone from the occupying nations.'

Bailey looked down at his two bent fingers, the red flesh where three of his fingernails used to be. 'As I keep saying, I'm a journalist.'

His captor leaned forward, closer to Bailey. 'And that is exactly why we are sitting here in this café together.'

'Is that where we are, a café? It's hard to know when you arrive blindfolded.' If Bailey was going to die, he didn't want the final scene of his life to be one where he broke bread with a murderer.

'This is a public place and you are close to your freedom.'

Freedom.

After ten months in captivity, Bailey didn't know what to believe.

'Bullshit.'

It was just another trick, another torture technique, to punish an invading *kaffir*.

'My name is Mustafa al-Baghdadi and you, John Bailey, are going to tell my story.'

'What?' Bailey wanted to believe him, but it didn't make sense.

Mustafa slid a pen and notebook across the table. 'Pick it up.'

'I don't have much choice here, do I?' He stared at the pen, a remnant from his stolen life.

'I was hoping that you would see this more as an opportunity, considering what has happened to so many of your allies in uniform.'

That was Mustafa's way of saying – live or die. If it was the price of freedom, Bailey would do it. They were just words.

Bailey began with his name. 'Mustafa, the chosen one, from Baghdad?'

Mustafa didn't seem surprised by Bailey's understanding of Arabic. 'These are names given to me by others.'

Olives, bread and tea were placed on the table by a woman wearing a niqab.

Bailey didn't snatch at the food like he'd done during the days, not long ago, when he'd felt close to starvation. Since arriving in Baghdad, he'd been given regular meals, showers, clean clothes, even a mattress to sleep on. Still, he wasn't going to turn down fresh food. He quietly munched on a piece of bread while listening to Mustafa.

'I was born and raised in the suburb of al-A'miriyah which, as you probably know, being a learned man, is an affluent Sunni neighbourhood.

'My father was an influential man, a holy man, who knew Saddam but was never his friend. When the United States drove the National Guard back across the Kuwaiti border, we all sat here and waited for the international community to do more. Saddam was a bad man. Leaving him in power hurt us all.'

'So, you wanted regime change back in '91?' Bailey, the journalist, was re-emerging.

'Many promises were made to Sunni leaders, like my father, here in Baghdad. Promises that were made by the CIA. Promises that Saddam found out about, that he used to purge his enemies, even those who were not.'

'Like your father?'

Mustafa had vengeful eyes. 'Like my father, my mother and my three older brothers.'

'Killed by Saddam?'

'One night they came for all of us. I was a young boy, I had my hiding places. I was the coward who watched them all get dragged away.'

Mustafa picked an olive from the bowl, turned it in his fingers and put it in his mouth.

'I never saw them again,' he said. 'Kill the father and the sons must go too. Saddam's paranoia – you must always eliminate the threat of revenge.'

Mustafa clicked his fingers and gestured for the woman to return to pour the tea.

Bailey watched the brown liquid flow from the pot into their cups. It reminded him of the water that spilled into his mouth and nose when that filthy rag was stuck to his face. Simulated drowning, or waterboarding. A torture technique sanctioned by the White House and enthusiastically copied by its enemies.

Bailey looked up and caught one of Mustafa's guards staring at him, smirking, reading his mind. He shuddered at the sound of the tea catching in the cup. The man's smirk became a smile, and Bailey saw he was missing half his front teeth. Bailey remembered – he was the bastard who had poured the bucket on him when he was lying on his back, strapped to a table, head dangling over the end, shaking violently with each splash of water.

He had lost count of the number of times they slapped that wet rag on his face. It was the most terrifying thing they did to him. Worse than the pliers that ripped out his fingernails, the hammer blows to his fingers, the cigarettes butted on his back. Nothing compared to being pushed to the brink of drowning over and over and over again.

Waterboarding was supposed to be about extracting information, only nobody asked Bailey a question. Not one.

The woman finished pouring the tea without saying a word.

Mustafa watched her walk away before resuming his story. 'I went to London to live with a wealthy uncle who'd escaped Saddam's purges. He sent me to good schools, university too.'

Bailey looked away from the guy with the bad teeth in the corner and scribbled notes on the paper in front of him. The skin where his fingernails used to be was still raw and it was painful to write.

'Sounds like a good life, a lot to give up.' Bailey could see that Mustafa hadn't always been an Islamic extremist. He wanted to know how he got here.

'September 11 changed everything – not just for me, for all Muslims,' Mustafa said. 'Suddenly, we're all terrorists! Even those who had embraced another culture and – Allah forgive me – turned their back on Islam.'

'In favour of a western life of sin?' Bailey challenged him. 'I've heard these arguments.'

'Mr Bailey, don't test my patience. Remember, you are my guest.'

Bailey flipped a page on the notepad and grabbed himself an olive. 'Go on, then.'

'When the United States and its war on terror extended to Iraq, I watched on television as the bodies of my country-men were sacrificed for a freedom that would never come. My country is a complicated one – only Islam can make sense of it.'

'What did you do?'

'I found sanctuary in returning to the mosque. In Finsbury Park, I found guidance from wiser men who reconnected me with the struggle, our holy war.'

Bailey knew all about the North London mosque. It was a place where young British men had been radicalised and recruited to fight for Al Qaeda. Richard Reid, the petty criminal who tried to blow up an American Airlines plane with bombs packed in his shoes, was one of them.

'Months after the Americans tore down Saddam's statue in Baghdad, I returned home.'

'And changed your name to the chosen one from Baghdad?'

'As I said, it was others who gave me these names.'

Bailey moved on, wanting to understand how monsters were made. 'What did you do?'

'I'm a doctor. Did I not mention?'

'A doctor?'

'These were my studies and the skills I brought back with me. At first, I helped in hospitals but soon my focus shifted to the brave martyrs who were fighting against both the Shias, who were being armed by Iran, and the stupid Americans who, by then, were firing their weapons at anyone.'

'Doctor turned jihadist?' Bailey said aloud the words he was scribbling on the notepad.

'If you had witnessed the slaughter of the innocents, like I have, then you, too, would look for another way.'

Bailey had seen it. He'd spent more than fifteen years seeing it. He didn't like the comparison. 'This isn't about me.'

'Collateral damage – the words of the occupiers,' Mustafa said. 'In any other place, you'd call it murder.'

'Your bombs kill civilians too.'

'The struggle has its price.'

'And you think the people of Iraq agree with you?'

'I have many followers, Mr Bailey,' Mustafa said. 'None have I asked to follow me.'

They were distracted by a commotion at the entrance of the café. Mustafa looked over at his men by the door and waved his hand to invite the new arrivals to join them.

Bailey's pen dropped to the floor.

Ronnie Johnson was walking across the room with two Iraqis Bailey didn't recognise. He was carrying a small leather sports bag, which he dumped on the table in front of Mustafa.

'It's all there.' Ronnie didn't even look at Bailey. 'I'm taking him, Mustafa – now.'

'Mr Johnson, I was hoping you might join us for a cup of tea?'

Bailey stared at his old friend, waiting for some type of recognition. He had been in captivity for ten months and, sensing his freedom, could feel the emotion building inside.

'Get up, Bailey.' Ronnie still didn't look at him.

Bailey pushed back his chair and did as he was told.

'Please.' Mustafa tried to intervene. 'Sit back down. We're not finished –'

'Yeah, you are.'

Ronnie walked around the table and grabbed Bailey by the arm with his big right hand. 'We're going, bubba.'

Bubba.

Finally, a word that connected Bailey to a world he thought he would never see again.

Two of Mustafa's men stepped towards the table, blocking their way out.

'We're leaving.' Ronnie pulled a grenade out of his pocket, dangling it by the pin. 'Before this gets messy.'

'Don't forget my story, John Bailey. It will be worth telling someday. Maybe it'll be part of your story?'

Mustafa unzipped the bag. Inside Bailey could see thick wads of American bank bills – Benjamin Franklins, all of them.

'You can count it later,' Ronnie said.

Mustafa motioned for his men to step out of the way.

Bailey was trying to calculate the cash in his head. It was a lot. 'What the fuck is that?'

Ronnie put the grenade back in his pocket and nudged Bailey to get him walking. 'Don't turn around.' With a firm grip on Bailey's bony arm, he led him to the door and outside.

Blinded by sunlight and the sudden realisation that it was over, Bailey tripped and fell on the dirt.

'We need to get out of here, bubba. It's a dangerous neighbourhood.'

Bailey put his hand in the dirt to balance himself, but Ronnie still had hold of his arm and steadied him to his feet.

'I'm sorry. I just . . . I just –'

'Later, bubba,' Ronnie said. 'Plenty of time for that. Right now, we need to go.'

They piled into an old hatchback. Ronnie and Bailey ducked their heads between their knees in the rear passenger seat.

Their driver carefully steered the car through the outer suburbs of Baghdad, trying not to arouse suspicion. The warring militia groups had people everywhere.

Ten minutes elapsed before it was safe for Ronnie and Bailey to sit up.

'Mustafa al-Baghdadi,' Bailey said. 'Who's he to you?'

'If we're ever going to end this fucking war, these are the people we need to deal with.'

'Nobody won today.'

Bailey thought about the cash and wanted to throw up.

'It's not about winning any more, bubba. At least you're alive.'

CHAPTER 32

Sydney, Friday

A chemical smell was stinging Bailey's nostrils and burning his eyes. He blinked to flush out the fumes and clear the white glow clouding his vision. It didn't work. The pungent liquid used to wake him had been smeared across his upper lip and nose. It was like steam rising through his eyes. He was powerless to wipe it away. His hands were tied to a wooden chair, along with his ankles.

Bailey could hear the faint hum of traffic outside and a loose sheet of corrugated iron on the roof flapping in the wind. Another distinctive noise was coming from the shadows in front of him – garbled rushes of air. They were the sounds of a fat man breathing.

'You're a restless sleeper, John Bailey.'

He was speaking slowly, with an accent clipping the end of his words.

Bailey was too disorientated to acknowledge the man sitting opposite. He blinked again, this time shaking his head and holding his eyes tightly closed for a few seconds, trying to encourage his tear ducts to open and let the salty water clear the gunk from his eyes.

'We don't have much time.'

The moisture was building, easing the burning sensation from the chemicals, clearing Bailey's eyes. He was sitting in almost total darkness, were it not for the soft glow of the night sky slipping into the room. The man was talking to him from an adjacent chair, his face disguised by the dark.

'Where am I?' Bailey said.

The man leaned forward, the moonlight bouncing off the round contours of his face. Bailey knew him. It was the fat guy he first saw with Li Chen at the quay, then again outside the pub in Newtown. The guy who kidnapped Anderson.

'I know you,' Bailey said. 'Who are you?'

'You should be less concerned about who I am and a little more worried about what I'm going to do to you.'

'And what's that?'

'I'm going to hurt you,' he said. 'And then I am going to keep hurting you until you tell me everything you know about Gary Page and Ambassador Li Chen.'

Bailey knew fear better than most. He also knew how this was supposed to play out. He avoided his kidnapper's stare and studied his surroundings, desperate to find something that would give him hope. The concrete floor was stained and covered with dust. Graffiti was splashed across old brick walls. At least half of the windows that Bailey could see were either cracked or smashed.

He knew this room.

In the corner, about ten metres away, sat an empty chair, police tape cordoning off the area around it.

'You murdered Michael Anderson.' Bailey wasn't sure whether to be frightened or angry. 'And you did it here.'

He wanted to know why his kidnapper would bring him to the scene of Anderson's horrific death. 'Why?'

'This is the most secure place in Sydney, John Bailey,' he said. 'The police have blocked off its surrounds and the forensics team will not be back until the morning.'

Bailey felt a sudden rush of rage, remembering the bloodied, tortured corpse he had found here only hours ago. 'You're a fucking animal!'

'You Australians have such foul mouths.'

'Who *are* you?' If Bailey was going to die, he at least wanted to know the identity of his killer.

'I will be asking the questions, John Bailey.'

The man got up and walked over to a small table. It was so close that Bailey could have reached out and touched it, were his hands not tied to the arms of the chair.

The man was busy untying a sheet of leather. Bailey noticed smoke rising from a smouldering pile of plastic. He could see an old VHS tape with the word 'sixteen' written on the label. The film had been ripped out and set on fire. It was Mario Monticello's tape. The evidence against David Davis and Victor Ho. Destroyed.

Dexter.

'The woman with me. Where is she now?'

'Don't worry about that. It's not your concern.'

Bailey remembered the flash of light and Dexter falling to the ground. After that – nothing. 'What did you do to her?'

The man unrolled the leather and spread it across the table. There must have been a dozen pockets, each with a metal instrument inside. It looked like a carpenter's toolkit. Only, it wasn't.

Anderson's killer ran his fingers across the pockets while he decided which lethal tool to call on first. Bailey knew how these things worked. It had to be something that would inflict pain, while not detracting from the task at hand. Extracting information. And Bailey would be a tough assignment, he'd make sure of it.

'Let's start with this one, shall we?' He held up a small hammer. 'One of my favourites. It will fracture, or at least crack, a bone. The pain will be sudden, and it will be excruciating. But I think it'll be a suitable way to begin our conversation, don't you?'

'Are you going to talk like this the entire time?'

'Funny.'

'No, I mean it.' The only weapon Bailey had was his mouth. 'Since you're a talker, tell me – does this shit make you hard?'

The man ignored the insult and smashed his elbow into Bailey's cheek and started trying to force a rag into his mouth.

'For when you scream.'

He rammed the cloth so far inside Bailey's mouth that it touched the back of his throat, making him gag.

'Because you will scream.'

He brought the hammer crashing down on the thumb of Bailey's right hand. Bailey bit into the rag to distract his mind from the pain. He felt dizzy, his chin slumping to his chest.

'No, no. Head up. Head up.' He grabbed Bailey by the chin and lifted his head. 'We're just getting started.'

Bailey could feel the warmth of his torturer's rank breath each time he whispered into his ear.

'Now, let's begin.' He pulled the cloth from Bailey's mouth. 'What did Mr Anderson tell you?'

The initial shock from the pain was waning and Bailey was regaining his composure. The sharp pain in his thumb was becoming a dull throb.

'What did Anderson tell *you*, is my question.' The old defiance in Bailey was overpowering his common sense.

The man ignored the question and calmly walked over to the table and slipped a metal object over his knuckles. The sound of footsteps and metal chinking together warned Bailey about what was to come. Within seconds, a fist crashed into his cheek, likely fracturing the bone, causing his head to snap to the side and his body to jolt with the force of the blow.

'I love nothing more than wearing knuckledusters, you know,' the man said. 'You can feel the vibration of the metal rings on your fingers when they bounce off the face of a fool like you, someone stupid enough not to give me what I want.'

'There's . . . there's . . .' Bailey was trying to catch his breath. 'There's a special place in hell reserved for people like you.'

'Let me be clear about the rules again, Mr Bailey.'

'There are rules? I thought that —'

This time he caught Bailey on the jaw, splitting his lip and splashing blood across his tongue.

'As I was saying . . .'

Bailey could see that he was getting under the man's skin.

'The rules are simple. I ask questions, you provide me with answers. There'll be pain – I won't deny this – but the extent of this pain is entirely up to you.'

Bailey chose pain.

'So, you're Li Chen's hatchet man? The boy he deploys to clean up the mess when his greedy schemes go wrong?'

Another fist smashed into Bailey's stomach, knocking the wind from his lungs, sending him into a coughing fit. Saliva and blood splashed on his legs and the concrete floor.

'Answer my questions!' He buried his fist into Bailey's gut again, leaving him winded and gasping for air. 'Too much talking!'

'Got ya,' Bailey said, smiling a blood-soaked smile.

The man turned his back on him, his heavy breathing the only sound punctuating the silence.

'I wonder if this was how you addressed your kidnappers in Iraq?'

'Don't pretend you know me, fat boy.'

'Can't you see what's happening here? There's no way out for you, John Bailey. In China we talk about the *chi* – the energy in the blood. It's the force of life and nature, about influence and momentum. That force is working against you. You're as stupid as the rest of them. The sleeping dragon is waking up but nobody wants to know.'

'What're you talking about, you lunatic? It doesn't matter

what I tell you. Li Chen is done. Exposed. Page too. The game is up. There'll be no payday.'

'I'm not interested in any payday. I play a different game, Mr Bailey. But finally it appears that we're getting somewhere.'

He walked back to the table and picked up something that looked like a pair of pliers.

'Now, tell me what you know about this game. Or better still, open your mouth. You can answer my question in a moment.'

He grabbed Bailey's neck and bashed his battered cheek with his elbow, trying to force open his mouth.

Bailey felt the cold metal arm of the pliers rest on his lip, so he clenched his jaw as hard as he could to stop it from getting inside and doing its work. He was shaking his head from side to side, until an elbow crashed into his cheekbone again. And again. And again.

Weakened and disorientated by the pain, Bailey was struggling to stay lucid. The pliers entered his mouth, searching for a tooth.

Torture. Pain. Fear. Bailey had been here before.

His mind turned to Miranda. The lawyer, all grown up. His little girl with the cheeky smile. All that he needed to do was close his eyes and she was there in the darkness, numbing the pain. He could even hear her laughter. *Silly Daddy*. Just like in Iraq.

Year after year, Bailey had waved goodbye to her at airports so he could follow his dreams. His obsessions. John Bailey the war reporter. The Middle East correspondent. The Europe correspondent.

It didn't matter what this guy did to him.

Nothing hurt more than the pain of knowing he had left Miranda behind to tell other people's stories, forgetting that the most important story in his life was hers. Theirs.

Miranda had a life of her own. Despite everything, she had let him back in. He had missed too many years. He couldn't miss any more.

He would survive. He had to. He had done it before.

Bailey's head was swinging from side to side. The pliers found a tooth, shredding and cracking it while the fat man yanked and pulled, trying to wrench it from Bailey's mouth.

The pain was incredible, sharp and ferocious. Bailey was delirious.

Focus, he told himself. Miranda – your reason to live. Second chances.

A second chance with Dexter too.

It had been too many years but his memories were her memories too. She would listen to him. Really listen. Lift him up out of his lows. Their love was real, despite the way he had cast it aside to watch the American cavalry roll into Baghdad and tear down that statue of Saddam.

His captor was bashing away at his mouth in search of another tooth. Bailey groaned and tried to clench his jaw. It was useless. He was trapped in this warehouse murder scene.

His mind wandered again, scanning images of better days. Sharon Dexter's naked body on the bed beside him. The days they'd sleep in until lunchtime, not because they were tired but because there couldn't possibly be anything better to do.

Their lovemaking was the one thing that took Bailey away from the violent things he'd seen. He was cupping her breast in one hand now, the other sliding down between her legs. He loved the sounds she made when they were innocent together. He wanted to hear them again.

He had to make it out of here alive.

Dexter and Miranda. John Bailey's two reasons to live.

Pop!

A peculiar sound brought Bailey back into the room with his torturer. The metal pliers slipped from his mouth and clanged on the ground.

Bailey looked up at the face of the man before him, the menace in his eyes replaced by confusion. He shuffled backwards, unsteady on his feet. He reached behind him, touching his shoulder blade, bringing his hand back around, staring at fingertips stained with blood. Bewildered by an attack he didn't see coming.

Pop!

The sound echoed again from the back of the room. The fat man fell forward onto one knee, close to where Bailey's ankles were bound to the chair. He reached for the table, trying to keep himself from falling, desperately clutching at the metal objects, searching for a weapon.

Pop! Pop! Pop!

This time the bullets hit his chest. Three splotches of red. He tumbled forward, his head crashing into the table, turning it onto its side, scattering the leather sheet, the torture apparatus and the ruined VHS tape on the floor.

Bailey's eyes moved from his kidnapper's groaning body on the concrete to the far corner of the room. Ronnie Johnson was bent down on one knee, his gun steadily pointed at the lonely figure on the ground.

'Bailey!' Ronnie got to his feet. 'Is he armed?'

Bailey spat a glob of blood and broken teeth on the ground. 'I think he's dead.'

Ronnie had climbed in through the same flap in the wall that Bailey had used to leave the warehouse earlier that day.

He jogged the short distance to Bailey and checked on the near-lifeless body on the ground. He put his hand inside the man's jacket and pulled out his gun, tossing it on the ground out of reach, just in case.

Ronnie withdrew a knife from his pocket and cut through Bailey's restraints.

'Are you okay, bubba?' Ronnie inspected his friend's face, disfigured – temporarily, at least – by violence.

'The sick bastard was enjoying that.' Bailey spat more shards of tooth on the floor.

'It's okay, bubba.' Ronnie grabbed him under the arm with one of his giant catcher's mitt hands, pulling him to his feet. 'It's over.'

When Bailey was steady, Ronnie walked back to the body on the ground, flipping it over so that the man was face up.

'Son of a bitch.'

Bailey noticed the surprised look on Ronnie's face. 'Know him?'

There was still life in the fat man's eyes. He was trying to say something.

Ronnie knelt down so he could hear.

'You win ...' Blood spluttered from his lips. 'You win, you . . . you lose.'

'What?' Ronnie slapped his face for more. 'What are you saying!'

The man's eyes stared into nothing, his head falling lifelessly to the side. Dead.

'What did he say?'

'You win, you lose.'

'You know him?' Bailey asked.

'Bo Leung, one of China's most senior intelligence agents. Haven't heard peep from him outside the Republic for years. I came across his handiwork in Africa, and Hong Kong before the handover, among other places. He was a violent lunatic capable of anything.'

'I can testify to that.'

'Bubba.' Ronnie put a hand on his shoulder. 'You're pretty banged up. We'd better get you to a hospital.'

'Later. We need to get back to Gerald.' It even hurt to speak but Bailey wasn't resting until this was over. 'What's the time? I've got no idea how long I've been here. Prick knocked me out.'

Ronnie looked at his watch. 'Almost eleven.'

'Fuck! Give me your phone,' Bailey said. 'Dexter was with me. We were attacked back at the apartment.'

'She's fine, Bailey.'

'How do you know?'

There was another noise in the corner. Bailey watched Detective Sharon Dexter climb through the hole in the wall.

'Sharon!' Bailey kept staring at her until she was standing beside him.

She put her arms around him, causing him to shudder with pain, then stepped back, gently touching his bloodied and bruised face, the dent in his cheek, the cuts on his lips.

'What the hell did he do to you?' She looked around at the overturned table and the kit of tools scattered across the floor.

'Forget about it. It's over.' Bailey was never one to look back and he wasn't about to start now. He rested his chin on her shoulder and closed his eyes, exhausted, but with a reason to live. It felt good. After what he had been through, he needed a moment to reset.

'I hate to interrupt, bubba,' Ronnie said, 'but I just shot a guy, which means we really need to go.'

Bailey let go of Dexter.

'Yeah, we do,' she said. 'I can't be seen here either.'

Dexter bent over and picked up Mario Monticello's security tape from the floor. The film had been reduced to a sticky pile of plastic.

'Destroyed,' Bailey said.

'Don't worry about that now. We've got to get out of here.'

'How'd you guys find me, anyway?' Bailey said.

'I followed you to the apartment building. Found Dexter unconscious beside the building while I was trying to find a way inside.'

'And then you thought you'd do a routine check on the crime scene?'

'Not quite, bubba.' Ronnie reached out and touched Bailey's jacket underneath his collar, picking off a small round object, about half the size of a button.

'You're joking.'

'Sorry, bubba. I know how you hate being ignored.'

'When?' Bailey asked.

'Back in Gerald's office. A friendly pat on the shoulder, not hard to do.'

'Well done, genius.' Bailey attempted a smile. 'But what the fuck took you so long?'

'Sorry. Got here as fast as I could.'

Bailey stopped at the door. 'That's twice, Ronnie.'

'Who's counting, bubba?'

Neither of them was any good at the emotional stuff. 'Thanks. Thought I was gone this time.'

'Don't mention it.'

Ronnie slapped him on the shoulder, forgetting about the bruises.

'Aaaaghh! I take that back – you're an idiot.'

Bailey waited for Dexter to tear down the police tape blocking the door and then followed her through it. He was limping, grimacing with each step.

'C'mon, we need to get moving,' she said.

The lights to Ronnie's car flashed – unlocked.

'You get in the front,' Dexter said to Bailey.

'What happened to chivalry?' Bailey tried to make a joke while carefully lowering himself into the seat. The pain was coming from so many parts of his body that every movement hurt.

'Plenty of time for that later.'

'I'm gonna light this.' Ronnie picked his cigar off the dashboard. 'Hope you don't mind.'

'I'm actually relieved to see you finally smoke one of those things.' Bailey winced again. The cut in his lip had started to dry and any facial movement was causing it to crack.

'We need to get you to a hospital,' Dexter said.

'Bumps and bruises. I'll be okay.'

'Bullshit. We're going.'

'Later. Trust me, I will go, but later. We've still got work to do to put this to bed.'

Bailey didn't want to turn around to face Dexter. His eyes wouldn't hide the pain. His head and jaw were aching. His cheekbone was fractured. His right thumb was broken. He might even have a few broken ribs from the beating outside the art gallery. But he couldn't go to hospital, not now. Not after a man had just tried to kill him because of the story he was writing.

'Hey Ronnie?'

'Yeah?'

Ronnie wound down his window and blew some smoke outside.

'That guy back there –'

'Bo Leung. What about him?'

'What's he doing here?'

'Cleaning up. That's my guess anyway. A guy like him doesn't turn up for no reason. Last we heard, he'd taken a desk job in the Ministry of State Security.'

'What was he doing?' Bailey wanted to know everything about the man who'd almost killed him.

'Cybercrime. Everyone thinks Russia's the big player. They're not. The Chinese mastered it a long time ago – stealing company blueprints for knock-off designs. Hell, they built half their economy on it. But this fella took it to a whole new level.'

'What d'you mean?'

'We think Bo was the guy in charge of their secret military hacking unit, run out of a rundown apartment block on the outskirts of Shanghai. We've never got close enough, never got inside. But we know what they do.'

'Which is?'

'Attack foreign government computer systems – bring them down, damage them, steal whatever they can.'

'It still doesn't explain why he's here.'

'I don't know what to tell you, bubba. There could be something else at play, something we don't know about.'

'This is all very interesting,' Dexter said from the back seat. 'But we really need to get Bailey to a hospital.'

'Not yet,' Bailey said. 'I will go, I promise. First, I've got to get back to *The Journal* to finish writing this story. Too many people have lost their lives. We've got to publish and put an end to it.'

'Okay, then.' Dexter knew there was no point arguing with him. 'You're a stubborn man, John Bailey. I'm giving you three hours. If we're not on the way by then, I'm calling an ambulance. Got it?'

Bailey held up his mashed right thumb, without turning around.

'Got it.'

CHAPTER 33

'What the . . .' Gerald's jaw dropped when he caught sight of Bailey at the door.

Miranda saw him too. 'Oh my God, Dad. What happened?'

Bailey limped into Gerald's office with Dexter and Ronnie steadying him.

'Been a long night, sweetheart.' He reached out and took Miranda in his arms, ignoring the pain triggered by the contact. It was the longest hug he'd had with his daughter in a long time. Or ever. Bailey's reason to live. The pain was worth it.

'I'm fine. Just a few bumps and bruises,' he said.

'Bumps and bruises!' The look on his daughter's face told Bailey more than he needed to know about his injuries. Miranda touched his bloodstained cheek, which was already turning blue. 'We need to get you to a hospital.'

'You should listen to your daughter, Bailey.' Marjorie was sitting with a pile of documents on her lap on the sofa. 'You look like crap.'

'Later. Gerald and I've got work to do. Unfinished business.'

'I've been trying, honey.' Dexter touched Miranda on the arm. 'We'll get him to a doctor as soon as this is done.'

'Are you going to tell me who did this to you, Dad?'

'Bad guys, sweetheart.' At least he wasn't lying. And there wasn't any point telling her about Bo Leung's torture kit. Anyhow, as painful as it was, what had happened to Bailey in the warehouse wasn't part of the story.

'You need to do better than that, Dad.'

'Couple of thugs working for a corrupt politician, I think. They're trying to throw us off the scent, intimidate us.'

Even absent parents could justify a white lie to their children.

'Okay, Dad.' Miranda backed off. 'As soon as you're done here, we're taking you to a hospital, whether you like it or not.'

'I'll make sure of it,' Dexter said.

'Couldn't imagine better escorts than you two,' Bailey said. 'And Miranda, meet my old friend, Ronnie Johnson. He's an American spy, a real one.'

'Your old man's a comedian.' Ronnie chuckled uncomfortably. 'Your dad and I knew each other in the Middle East. He's told me all about you. Nice to finally meet you.'

'You too.' Miranda's hand disappeared inside Ronnie's big mitt. 'You're the bloke from Bondi the other day!'

'Told you she's sharp, Ronnie.'

Bailey was eager to change the subject. He sidled up beside Gerald and pointed to the documents spread out on his desk. 'What's happening here?'

Gerald leaned in. 'You okay?' After almost thirty years of friendship, he could clearly tell when Bailey was bullshitting. But he wasn't about to make a scene.

'Fallujah . . . Mark II.' Bailey realised how ridiculous the words sounded.

Gerald placed his hand on the back of Bailey's neck and pulled him close. With glazed eyes, he studied the face of a man he'd seen banged up too many times before.

'For the last time, mate.'

'Yeah, banking on it.'

Bailey slowly lowered himself onto a leather sofa in between Miranda and Dexter. He wasn't going to hospital until they'd published the story, which meant they needed to get back to work.

Gerald walked back around his desk to his computer screen. 'I think we're good to go with this, right, Marjorie?' He had spent the past few hours working on Bailey's draft.

'Yeah. Sands Enterprises checks out. Li Chen and Gary Page are the sole two directors. We've also got a copy of Page's reform bill that will open the door to overseas contracts. And guess what?' Marjorie said. 'The bill's due before parliament next week. Anderson also had the paperwork to show how the Chinese companies operated, so we've got the designs Page lifted from Treasury and Defence.'

Marjorie tapped her finger on the pile of documents on Gerald's desk. 'The usual legal risks aside, this is about as solid as we'll get it.'

'Do I get a look?' Ronnie was standing on the other side of the room, pouring himself a glass of whisky from Gerald's silver drinks platter.

'Sorry, Ronnie. You're welcome to stick around but you're a passenger now. And help yourself.'

'Get me one, would you?' If anyone needed a drink, it was Bailey.

'Sure, bubba. Two swollen fingers coming up.'

'Did you learn anything from the manager of the apartment building? Mario whatever-his-name-was?' Gerald remembered the reason Bailey had left his office in the first place.

Dexter looked at Ronnie and Bailey. Both nodded for her to be the one to break the news about the involvement of the New South Wales Police Commissioner.

'We have evidence that makes David Davis at least an accomplice in Catherine Chamberlain's murder.'

'What?' Gerald was shocked. 'How?'

'You mean, we *had* the evidence,' Bailey said.

'Check your email,' Dexter said to Gerald.

Bailey was looking at Dexter, confused, while Gerald fidgeted with the mouse, searching his inbox.

The room went silent, with everyone waiting for him to open the file.

'Good God!'

Bailey tried to get up off the sofa, groaning from the pain of the struggle. It took three goes, but with a little push from Marjorie, he was up. He hobbled over to join Gerald at the other side of the desk. 'What is it?'

Gerald was watching his computer screen, shaking his head. 'Bloody genius.'

'What the hell?' Bailey couldn't believe he was staring at the faces of David Davis and Victor Ho, the same footage he'd watched earlier that night.

'Well, that settles that.' Ronnie had joined them behind the computer.

'It's the security camera footage from the night she was killed, straight from the monitor in Mario Monticello's office,' Dexter said. 'Davis was the one who let Victor Ho into the building. All time coded. It checks out.'

Marjorie had a question. 'Yeah, but –'

'Wait for it.' Dexter knew what she was about to ask – the lawyer wanted proof that the recording was genuine. 'Meet the manager of Catherine Chamberlain's apartment building.'

With the footage still running, Dexter had zoomed out the camera on her phone to record Mario standing beside the monitor with a bewildered look on his face.

'And what's your name please, sir.' They could hear Dexter's voice on the recording.

'My name is Mario Monticello, the manager at 72 Leopold Street, Rushcutters Bay. Okay, darling, are we done?'

The recording stopped on a freeze-frame of Mario giving a thumbs up to the camera.

'Got him,' Gerald said.

'Brilliant, Detective Dexter,' Marjorie said.

Gerald turned to Dexter. 'How hard can we go?'

Dexter knew precisely what they could print. 'The New South Wales Police Commissioner is expected to be taken in for questioning today about his involvement in the murder of a woman in Rushcutters Bay.'

'He was also a client,' Bailey reminded Gerald. 'And I think this gives us leeway on that fifty-thousand-dollar donation from Sands Enterprises for Davis's campaign?'

'It does,' Marjorie said. 'Use it.'

'You'd better organise another print run,' Bailey said. 'We're going to need the first five pages.'

'Online first.'

'Of course, old boy,' Bailey said. 'But won't those headlines look good in print?'

'Yeah, they sure will, Bailey.'

'Penelope!' Gerald yelled at the closed door of his office. 'Are you still out there?'

The door clicked open and Penelope's head appeared, sleepy-eyed.

'I'm emailing you something. Make two copies on separate thumb drives and then drop the video on the server. It shows two murder suspects in the Catherine Chamberlain case. Andy on the online desk can help you. Nobody publishes without checking with me.'

'No worries.' Penelope disappeared again.

Dexter turned to Bailey. 'I've got to go.'

'Where?'

'Davis,' she said. 'I want to be the one to bring him in.'

'Be careful.' He held her hand, then watched her walk out of the room.

'We've got some work to do, old boy.' Bailey pushed a chair up against the other side of Gerald's desk and examined the state of his hands. 'It's lucky I'm a two-finger typist.'

'I might as well hang around.' Miranda curled her legs on the sofa. 'It's not often I get to see my old man at work.'

Gerald grabbed her a blanket. 'Sleep here tonight. We'll all walk out into the sunlight together once the ink is dry, and we've ignited a political firestorm.'

Miranda accepted the blanket and spread it over her legs. As much as she loved the idea of watching her father at work, the only reason she was sleeping on the couch was so she could take him to hospital when the story was done.

'I'm staying too.' Ronnie lay back on the other sofa and closed his eyes with a fresh unlit cigar wedged in the corner of his mouth. 'Wake me when you're done, bubba. I love a good story.'

'I guess I'll just make do with this armchair.' Marjorie was sticking around too. Bailey knew she would want to read over the final draft. Thorough, as always.

'That's a full house.' Gerald rocked back in his leather armchair, twirled around and stared out into the night.

For the next few hours, the only sound in the room was the gentle tapping on Bailey's keyboard.

CHAPTER 34

'Mr Summers.' Penelope was at the door again.

'I'm sorry to interrupt, but . . .' She seemed unsure how to tell them. 'You've got some, errrr, visitors.'

Ronnie had already sat up at the sound of Penelope's voice.

Gerald looked at Bailey, still tapping away at his computer, and then at his watch. It was three o'clock in the morning.

'Know who they are?'

'Well, yes.' Penelope looked confused. 'It's . . . they are . . .'

'C'mon, Pen, it's the middle of the bloody night.' Gerald was tired and not in the mood for coaxing.

'Mr Summers, it's the . . . the prime minister.'

'What?'

Bailey had never met Matthew Parker, but he knew that prime ministers almost never visited the office of a newspaper editor. And they certainly didn't do it in the middle of the night.

Penelope was awaiting her instructions. 'What shall I do?'

'What do you mean? Bloody well let him in!' Gerald said.

'Yes, yes, I did that. They're down the corridor and –' Penelope paused at the sound of footsteps slapping the carpet in the hallway, growing louder by the second. Like horses at the track, there was a pack of them, and right now the pack was charging towards Gerald's office.

'Prime Minister –' Penelope tried to introduce Matthew Parker at the door, but he brushed past her and walked straight in.

The prime minister wasn't alone. Parker's long-time chief of staff, Felicity Coleman, and the head of the Australian Security and Intelligence Organisation, Richard Allen, followed their boss into the room. Each with a scowling face to rival the other's. Three plain-clothed federal police officers stopped at the door, waiting outside.

The abrupt entry of Parker and his entourage had been orchestrated to interrupt and intimidate the tired, bewildered eyes staring back at them.

'Gerald.' The prime minister held out his hand and Gerald shook it.

Bailey looked up from his keyboard, a white glow of light shining on his face. Matthew Parker was smaller than he'd imagined, although there was no mistaking his presence in the room. He was a powerful man who carried himself like he had the keys to the country. In truth, after three election victories and having guided Australia through the global recession, he had a firmer grip on power than any prime minister for decades. He was proving untouchable for the Opposition, and political journalists often joked that he was coated with Teflon.

Parker seemed content being arrogant, as long as the public believed he was still the same working class union organiser who never stopped fighting for the little people as he rose through the rank and file of the Labor Party. He was also the guy who wasn't afraid of making enemies on the left when he borrowed ideas from the other side of politics.

His popularity was boosted by the fact that he seemed to grow better looking with age. He was a fitness fanatic with a permanent tan, probably from all the days he spent running and riding his longboard at the beach. Bailey had always wondered whether he had cheated his years with a bottle of hair dye. Up close, he was handsome; everything looked natural. Bailey was disappointed. Parker had been prime minister for eight years and it hadn't aged him at all. At least, not like Tony Blair, who had entered Downing Street a youthful agent of change, only to leave a grey, weathered old man battling to defend his legacy.

'It's three o'clock in the fucking morning. Who are all these people?' Felicity Coleman had a reputation for being blunt and aggressive.

Gerald was unmoved. Bailey knew his old friend was accustomed to dealing with political animals, even the feral ones. He knew when and how to bark back.

'May I ask, to what do we owe the pleasure of your company at this ungodly hour of the morning?'

'Don't fuck with us, Gerald.' Coleman understood power and she was wielding it like an axe.

'Felicity, please,' Parker intervened. 'Let's try to keep this civil, shall we?'

'Thank you, Prime Minister.' Gerald smiled at the prime minister's chief of staff.

'Firstly, I'd like to know who our audience is here tonight, if you don't mind, Gerald?' The evenness in Parker's voice suggested he'd prepared a speech and was ready to deliver it.

Gerald pointed his finger around the room, introducing everyone, one by one. 'Our lawyer, Marjorie Atkins. This is Ronnie Johnson from the US ambassador's security detail.'

Ronnie's job description invited a snigger from ASIO chief Richard Allen.

Gerald saved Bailey for last. 'And this is –'

'John Bailey.' Parker finished the introduction for Gerald. 'Celebrated war correspondent and contemporary drunk.'

'Hard to argue with that,' Bailey said.

'But it seems you have come out of retirement, John?' Parker had made a habit of addressing people by their first name. It gave him an instant level of superiority.

'Could say that. Nothing like a good story about corruption in the halls of power to get you going.'

Gerald frowned at Bailey. He should have known better than to provoke the prime minister.

'Well …' Parker took a moment to meet the eyes of everyone in the room. 'This little story of yours is precisely why we're here.'

'And just how are –'

'Who's that?' Coleman was pointing at Miranda, softly snoring on the couch.

'That's my daughter,' Bailey said. 'She stays.'

'Of course. We'll talk quietly.' Parker's confidence now looked like sleaze.

'And by the way, this meeting never happened,' Coleman said. 'Or we walk out the door.'

'Fine,' Gerald said.

Richard Allen stepped forward and handed Gerald a yellow file with ASIO's classified stamp on the cover. He opened it. Bailey managed to catch a glance. The first thing he saw was a picture of Defence Minister Gary Page shaking hands with China's Ambassador, Li Chen. The image was grainy. It looked like it had been taken from a distance in a park somewhere at night.

'We've been watching Li and Page for a while now,' Allen said.

'Spying on your own?' Ronnie had joined Gerald on his side of the desk and was looking over the newspaper editor's shoulder while he thumbed through the file.

'Don't start that shit, Ronnie,' Allen said. 'There's a reason you're here.'

'Yeah.' Ronnie winked at him. 'The weather.'

'You two know each other?' Coleman said.

'Ronnie Johnson isn't a bloody security guard on the ambassador's detail as he might try to tell us. He's US intelligence. CIA.'

'Retired,' Ronnie said, smiling.

'Don't believe him.' Allen clearly didn't like the presence of a foreign spook – even a friendly one – in his patch. 'You guys never leave.'

'You've got some good stuff here. Solid work.' Ronnie was eyeing the documents, knowing he was irritating Allen. 'And now you're sharing. Appreciated.'

'I wish the same could be said for you guys.'

'That always depends on who we're watching, doesn't it, Dick?' Ronnie looked like he was enjoying himself.

'Gentlemen, please.' The prime minister was growing tired of the charade. 'Let's keep this as pleasant as possible, shall we? Because ultimately we're all on the same team. Aren't we?'

'You tell us,' Bailey said. He hadn't moved from his seat in front of the computer.

'You look like you've had a very rough night, John.'

First name again.

'Bar fight, Bailey?' Coleman asked.

'Yeah, something like that.' Bailey ignored the insult. He was more interested in skimming over the documents that Gerald was handing him, page by page, across the table. The dossier was virtually identical to the one that Anderson had given him in Newtown.

'If you had this stuff on Page, why's he still in his job?'

'We've been building our case,' Allen said.

'Seems risky, considering the bill about defence contracts is due before parliament next week.' Bailey wasn't intimidated by the three figures standing over him. He wanted them to know that the ship had sailed on Page.

'We know what we're doing.' Small beads of sweat were forming on Richard Allen's forehead and he dabbed at them with a handkerchief from his pocket. He was wafer thin and stank of cigarettes. Like many military and intelligence types, his work was his life.

'I mean, it's a risky move, considering two people are dead and we can connect both to Gary Page.' Bailey wasn't afraid of firing shots, testing the audience.

'And that's exactly what we're here to discuss,' Parker said.

The prime minister was smiling again and his over-confidence was gnawing at Bailey.

'What Mr Parker's saying is that you can't print that.' Coleman, the attack dog, was used to finishing her boss's sentences and delivering the bad news. They'd been running this routine ever since Parker was appointed the opposition's foreign affairs spokesperson more than a decade ago. She was a savvy political operator – tall, attractive, with big sculpted hair and a figure that struggled to maintain its halcyon days, not that she seemed to care.

'I can publish whatever I like.' Gerald may have been one of the most polite newspaper editors *The Journal* had ever employed, but he was a fierce defender of the role of the fourth estate.

'No, you can't –'

'Gerald,' Parker interrupted his chief of staff. 'I'm hoping we can come to an agreement here, because –'

'There won't be any agreements,' Bailey said.

'Because,' Parker continued, 'I'm sorry to say but this has become an issue of national security.'

Ronnie coughed, like he was trying to contain a chuckle.

'You guys are fucking desperate,' Bailey said.

'Bailey, please.' Gerald clearly wanted to handle this his own way. 'Go on, Prime Minister. Explain to me why the behaviour of a corrupt minister in your cabinet is now a threat to national security.'

'I was hoping you might be more reasonable, Gerald. If your story alleges that Gary Page is somehow connected to the murders of both Catherine Chamberlain and Michael Anderson, it'll threaten to compromise all of our dealings in the sensitive area of defence.'

'What the prime minister is saying,' Richard Allen chimed in. 'What he's saying is that Australia is balancing many difficult and often strategically important relationships. This type of scandal could undermine those relationships.'

'Thanks for the lesson in international diplomacy.' Bailey was too tired, sore and bruised to entertain this nonsense. 'But it sounds more like bureaucratic speak for, "Please don't make my government look bad".'

Gerald swivelled his chair, turning his back on Parker and his entourage, contemplating his next move. Whatever the decision, there was no way back. Publishing a story like this would put his job on the line.

Bailey followed his eyes out the window, at the bright lights bouncing off the glass of the concrete jungle, the hotel windows, wondering if an awkward moment was about to slice through the tension in the room.

'Spot anything?' Bailey said.

'Not tonight. There's still time.'

'What the hell are you two talking about?' Coleman wasn't used to being defied.

Gerald extended his hand across his desk. The prime minister ignored it, staring into the editor's eyes, waiting for his answer.

'I think we're done here,' Gerald said.

'You're making a big mistake.' It was the closest that Parker had come to losing his cool.

'We're running with the story.'

Gerald's hand had been suspended in the air for more than twenty seconds before he eventually let it flop by his side.

'Fucking arseholes.' Coleman was less restrained. 'You'll regret this!'

'Penelope?' Gerald raised his voice to the closed door of his office.

'Yes, Mr Summers.'

'The prime minister's ready to leave.'

Matthew Parker and his entourage filed out the door without saying another word.

'I hope you know what you're doing.' Marjorie had watched the entire exchange without making a sound.

'You'll be fine, bubba. Get your story out, or these guys will beat you to it.' Ronnie had been on both sides, so he knew about fall guys and when they fell.

'Yeah,' Bailey said. 'What could go wrong?'

Gerald stared blankly at the door until the pack of stomping feet stopped echoing down the hall and they heard the faint sound of the elevator doors opening and closing. The editor had made his decision. He didn't need any more advice.

'Bailey,' Gerald said.

'Yes, old boy?' For a guy who had barely slept in three days, Bailey was chipper.

'Notice he didn't mention Davis?'

'Yeah. What d'you think it means?'

'Let's publish and find out. It's time we put this thing to bed.'

CHAPTER 35

Sydney, Saturday

'Bailey . . .'

Bailey was almost sound asleep, lying flat on the floor. He didn't move.

'Bailey . . . Bailey . . . Bailey!' The woman's voice was getting louder each time she said his name.

It was almost five o'clock in the morning and Marjorie and Gerald hadn't noticed Andrea Jacobs from the online desk standing at the door, trying to get Bailey's attention. They were reading over the final stories that were about to hit the printers and go on the website.

'Bailey!' Andrea almost yelled, this time. 'You awake?'

'Yeah?' Bailey answered, barely moving, eyes closed. There was no point opening them, yet. It could be a dream.

'Bailey!' Andrea tapped his foot with her shoe.

'*Yes* . . . I said!'

He had been lying as still as possible to avoid the bolts of pain that reverberated throughout his body every time he moved.

'The phone on your desk keeps ringing. I answered it.

Some guy called Marty, says he's a friend of Scarlett's? I tried to take a message, but –'

Bailey held up his hand. 'Stop talking for a second, would you?'

'Just give him a moment, please, Andrea,' Gerald said.

Scarlett. Scarlett. Scarlett.

The name was bouncing around in Bailey's brain.

Scarlett!

Scarlett knew things that could get her killed and Bailey suddenly felt sick at the thought of her body turning up somewhere in Sydney. Another Michael Anderson.

Bo Leung might be dead, but there was at least one other potential killer out there – he wore a police uniform and held the most powerful law enforcement position in the state. Scarlett was Catherine Chamberlain's friend. But for Police Commissioner David Davis she was a liability, another loose end to be silenced. Dexter might not have arrested him yet. Bailey had involved Scarlett in his search for answers, his chase. Her blood would be on his hands. More blood that he'd never be able to wash off.

'Scarlett . . . Scarlett's on the phone?'

'Not Scarlett, Bailey.' Andrea had to start over. 'Some bloke called Marty. He's on the phone now. Says he's a friend –'

'He's on the phone now?'

Bailey was struggling to get his body to respond to his need to get up.

'Yes, as I've said, on your desk.' Andrea walked out of the room, clearly frustrated.

Bailey rolled onto his front. He was in bad shape and needed to do it slowly. Elbows on the carpet, one hand, then one knee.

'Bubba, are you all right?' Ronnie got to him first. He bent down, grabbed him under the armpit, and pulled him to his feet.

'Bubba?'

Bailey ignored him and limped out the door, headed for his desk. He got there, eventually. Ronnie and Gerald were standing beside him when he picked up the phone.

'No. Stay where you are.' Bailey said into the receiver. 'I'm on my way.'

Bailey emptied his lungs in one long, painful breath. 'She's alive.'

'Who is she, bubba?'

Bailey hadn't mentioned Scarlett by name to either of them. He hadn't needed to.

'Friend of Catherine Chamberlain's, worked with her at Petals. I need to meet her – now.'

'Take Ronnie with you.'

'I'll keep my distance, bubba. You look like shit, no offence, and you really should be in a hospital.'

'I wish people would stop saying that.'

'Seriously, Bailey. You're not going alone,' Gerald said.

There was no point arguing; Bailey was too tired and in too much pain. Part of him was also scared, rattled by the steady, violent hand of Bo Leung. Having Ronnie with him was a good idea, although he'd never admit it.

'Fine, but I need to talk to her alone.'

'No problem. Where is she now?'

'In a bar three blocks from here. She was going to come here, but I told her to stay put.' Bailey didn't like the idea of Scarlett being followed on the street like Miranda.

They were headed south on Sussex Street towards a small bar called The Fox Hole, Ronnie trailing fifty paces behind Bailey. The bar had been closed for hours. Marty said he would be waiting at the side door on Erskine Street. He had kept his promise.

'John Bailey?' Marty was a short, stocky man with a shaved head, beard and tattoos. He could easily have been mistaken for the bouncer.

'Marty?'

'Yeah.'

The two men shook hands and Bailey winced as Marty unwittingly squeezed the thumb that Bo had bashed with a hammer.

'Looks like you've had a rough night.' Even in the dim glow of the streetlights, Marty had obviously noticed the cuts and bruises on Bailey's face.

'Could say that,' Bailey said. 'Can we go inside?'

'Wait.' Marty stared at Bailey. 'Scarlett says you're a good guy, but I've never seen her so afraid. Please tell me I don't need to worry about anything here.'

'Not from me, Marty.'

Bailey wasn't sure about the rest. He didn't know if he had been seen talking to Scarlett during their meetings in Double Bay. At least Bo Leung was dead. One killer out of the way.

'Not good enough, mate.'

'I'm a reporter,' Bailey said. 'In less than two hours we're publishing a story that's going to piss off a lot of people. As soon as the story's out, Scarlett will be safe, no matter what.'

'Okay, let's go.' Marty was placated, at least for a while. 'She's downstairs. Bar's closed.'

'That's a shame.'

Bailey hobbled down the dark stairwell, each step a struggle that delivered a different shot of pain. At the bottom was a wall decorated with a large speckled mural of a crowded beach, with people carrying surfboards, sunbathing, frolicking in the water, playing volleyball on the sand. Beaches like these were only a short drive from where he was standing, but after the night Bailey had just had, the scene splashed on that wall was like a foreign country.

Scarlett was sitting alone on a stool in the corner of the bar.

'She wants to talk to you in private.' Marty turned and walked back up the staircase.

It was dark inside and the room smelled like a cocktail of disinfectant, air freshener and beer. Bailey was trying not to limp, keen to hide his injuries from Scarlett.

He noticed two steaming cups of coffee on the bar.

'Got anything stronger?'

'Sure.' She reached over the bar, grabbed a schooner glass and shoved it under the beer tap so the cool yellow liquid could gather in the glass.

'Marty was too tight to unlock the cabinet.'

'I'll forgive him.'

Bailey took a long sip. The beer relaxed his muscles as it slipped down his throat, diverting his senses from the pain. A moment to enjoy after being thrust through the gates of hell.

'I don't think he likes me,' Bailey said.

'Don't take it personally. He's just being protective.'

'Boyfriend?'

'Something like that.'

'Well, I hope he takes care of you. You deserve –'

'Jesus! Mr Bailey, you look like shit.' Scarlett noticed his mashed thumb on the schooner glass and the cuts and bruises on his face. 'What is it with you?'

'You should see the other guy.'

'You weren't lying when you said you were good at pissing people off!'

She reached out and touched his bulging cheekbone, the dark shades on his skin.

'Seriously, I think you need to get that looked at.'

'Pissing people off is one of my gifts. And don't worry, I'm okay, but it's five o'clock in the morning. What're we doing here?'

'I've been trying to call your mobile since yesterday,' she said. 'Got to be honest, I'm pretty bloody scared.'

'This thing's nearly done, Scarlett. We've got it. We know who killed Catherine. My editor and lawyer are both going over it right now. We're about to publish, then it's over.'

Scarlett was shaking her head. 'That's just the thing, Mr Bailey. I don't know that it will be over.'

'What d'you mean?'

'What Michael told me,' she said. 'I think there's something else, something other than what happened to Catherine.'

'You've been speaking to Michael?' Bailey put down the coaster that he'd been turning in his hands. 'The recently deceased Michael Anderson?'

'Yeah.'

It seemed so long ago that Bailey had written about the discovery of Michael Anderson's body in a warehouse in Alexandria. Scarlett had never mentioned that she'd had contact with him.

'You met with him recently?'

'Two nights ago. He said he was going to see you.'

More guilt.

'What'd he want?'

'He gave me something.' Scarlett was rummaging through her handbag.

Bailey had no idea where this was going, what else Anderson knew.

Scarlett pulled out a sealed envelope and handed it to Bailey. Inside was an old photograph, the size of a postcard. It showed three young men standing shoulder to shoulder in bright orange jackets in front of a chessboard.

'Did he tell you what it was?' Bailey's eyes were locked on the picture.

'All he said was that he stole it from the study in the defence minister's home.'

'Why'd he give it to you?'

'He said. He ...' Scarlett was struggling to hold back her tears. She grabbed a tissue from her bag and blew her nose. 'He said it was his insurance policy, something that would keep him alive, no matter what.'

Bailey reached across the table and held her hand.

'What else did he say, Scarlett?'

'He told me to give it to you, but only if something happened to him.'

'Scarlett,' Bailey was still holding her hand. 'I need to ask you a couple of questions, really important ones. Okay?'

'What's going on, Mr Bailey?'

'Did you look at the photograph and have you told anyone else about it?'

Scarlett blew her nose. 'I didn't look at it. The envelope was sealed. He told me not to open it. I haven't told anyone, except for you.'

'That's good, Scarlett.'

'What happens now?'

'Marty's a good guy, right? You trust him?'

Scarlett laughed at Marty through her sobs. He was sitting at the bottom of the staircase on the other side of the room, watching them. 'Yeah, he's a good one.'

'That's good, because I need you two to stay here. Don't let anyone in and don't leave until you see my story appear on *The Journal*'s website, okay?'

'Marty's flat's upstairs. We'll go there.'

'I need to go now. I don't know what this photo means, only that it could change everything.'

'How?'

'That's what I'm going to find out.'

Bailey slipped the photograph into his jacket pocket. He took a long swig of his beer, slid off his chair and placed the nearly empty glass on the table.

Scarlett stopped Bailey before he turned to walk away. 'You take care, old man.' She pulled him in and gave him a peck on the cheek.

Bailey reached out and grabbed the glass. He hated not finishing a drink.

'You too, Scarlett.'

He thanked Marty for the beer and limped up the staircase faster than he had travelled down.

He didn't notice Ronnie waiting for him outside on the street. 'How'd you go, bubba?'

Bailey spun around, startled, and annoyed at having triggered another rush of pain in his ribs. 'Do you always have to sneak up on people, Ronnie?'

'Yeah, bubba,' Ronnie said. 'Part of the training.'

'Well, stop it. It's starting to piss me off.' Bailey could feel the days catching up with him. 'We need to get back to the paper.'

CHAPTER 36

Dexter

Detective Sharon Dexter loved watching the morning arrive at Maroubra Beach. It was the one thing she missed about the place. The orange glow of the sun, the clean air and the sounds of the waves dumping water on the sand. The cloudless days were her favourite, when the stars and the moon lingered hours after the sky turned blue.

Today was a blue sky day.

Dexter had parked her car at the northern end of the beach. It was the best spot to take in the sunrise and watch the surfers. She knew the sands here better than any other beach in Sydney because for two years she had shared them with the married man who presumably was still sleeping in the apartment building behind her. She touched the cool metal of the cuffs hanging from her belt, imagined wrapping them around his wrists. Taking him down. The water was building in her eyes, reminding her that she was human. The thought of having shared a bed with a man who had helped carry out a murder was almost too much.

Dexter had been staring at the ocean for more than twenty minutes before she called for a squad car to meet her outside the home of Police Commissioner David Davis. Humiliated for ever having loved him, she knew that she had to be the one to bring him in. It was tearing at her insides, but she wouldn't hide from it. She thought about her father, the principled publican who had raised his daughter alone, with a broken heart. The Dexter name was built of stern stuff and Bruce Dexter would have told her to do what was right.

A police car pulled up and two young uniformed officers stepped out, a man and a woman. Dexter had been sitting on the bonnet of her car and she slid off to meet them.

'Detective.' The young woman closed the door, checking her belt and vest were holding tight. 'I'm Constable Lucy Craven and this is Constable Hamid Khan.'

It was the end of the night shift and they both looked tired.

'Detective Sharon Dexter.'

'Got the call out for back-up. What's going on?' Constable Craven said.

'I'm about to arrest someone for murder.' Dexter didn't flinch, she was ready. 'You guys okay with that?'

'Better than handing out speeding tickets,' Constable Khan said. 'What case?'

'Prostitute was murdered in Rushcutters Bay a couple of weeks back. Bloke across the road was spotted on security cameras. Just got our hands on the vision – we need to move.' Dexter was careful about how much she told them.

'Warrant?' Constable Khan said.

'Yeah.' Dexter held up an envelope. 'Justice Watson wasn't happy with the early morning call but he obliged.'

In fact, Justice Watson had been floored by Detective Dexter's request when she woke him. He had only agreed to sign the warrant after Dexter threatened to leak to the media his reluctance to do so. The list of public figures that Bailey was taking down was already a long one; Dexter knew he'd be happy to make room for another.

'Who's the guy we're arresting?' Constable Craven asked.

'One of the girl's clients.' Dexter had been rehearsing what she would tell them because she didn't want Davis's name hitting media outlets, scooping Bailey.

'What'd you want us to do?'

'You,' Dexter pointed to Constable Craven, 'come with me.'

After the trouble she'd been having with Rob Lucas, she wanted a female at her back, someone who would never be invited to join the boys' club.

'Constable Khan,' Dexter said, 'you wait down here. Watch who goes in and out.'

He looked disappointed. 'Sure.'

Constable Craven followed Dexter across the road to the main entrance of the apartment building.

'Sea Breeze.' The young cop read the sign on the wall. 'Nice building. This bloke must have cash.'

Dexter could have told her that he had a beautiful apartment too.

She withdrew the key that Davis had once given her and

opened the door to the foyer. 'Been watching him for a week. Had a key cut,' she lied.

They caught the elevator to the seventh floor. Dexter's heart was pounding.

'You okay?' Constable Craven had noticed the change.

'Yeah, thanks. Been a long night.'

They walked down the corridor and Dexter raised her index finger to her lips.

'Wait out here,' she whispered. 'I'll knock and go in alone. I need to talk to him for a minute before we take him in.'

Constable Craven nodded. It was Detective Dexter's case. She was happy to follow orders.

Dexter hesitated when she reached the door to Davis's apartment. After a few deep breaths, she was ready. It had to be done. It was the right thing to do.

Knock. Knock. Knock.

The sound of footsteps could be heard inside. The door clicked open.

'Sharon.' Davis was swaying slightly in the doorway. He didn't look surprised to see her. Dressed in a white shirt and trousers, his feet were bare and he looked like he hadn't slept.

'Who's that?' He pointed at Constable Craven, her head leaning to one side, trying to see the man talking at the door.

'She's here if I need any help.' Dexter had her game face on.

'You won't. Come in, let's talk.' He said it like it was an order.

Dexter watched Davis walk back inside, then turned to Constable Craven.

'What the fuck?' The young constable mouthed the words to Dexter.

Dexter gestured with her hand for her to stay put, then threw the key to the front door onto the carpet near Craven's feet – just to be sure – and closed the door behind her.

The apartment looked the same – neat, few decorations and furnishings, which Dexter had always found cold. The paintings on the walls were the type of bright, airy canvases you'd expect to find hanging in hotels. But she'd always loved the large open-plan setting, cleverly designed around the magnificent view of the Tasman. The dining table, lounge area, even the stone-top kitchen, were all positioned so you could eat, relax, entertain and cook while looking at the water.

Davis sat down in the shiny leather armchair by the window and stared out at his three million dollar view. A half-empty bottle of Jack Daniel's was sitting on a coffee table beside him. He poured himself another.

'Know why I'm here?' Dexter said.

'Sit down.' Davis pointed at the chair opposite and returned to watching the waves. He wasn't taking orders. He was giving them.

'Beautiful sunrise. Really got lucky with this joint, huh, Sharon? You remember those mornings when we'd wake to that light, take an early walk on the sand?' He was slurring his words.

'Yeah, I remember.'

'We were good together.'

'Imagine your wife thought the same thing about the two of you.' Dexter needed to be careful, she couldn't let this get personal.

'That was complicated, Sharon. You knew that. Finances, houses, kids.' Davis sighed and took another sip of his whiskey. 'I really let those kids down.'

'I'll ask you again, David. Do you know why I'm here?'

He turned and looked at her. 'I'm not who you think I am.'

'Then who are you, David? Tell me.'

He finished his drink and poured himself another without bothering to offer one to Dexter.

'He had me, Sharon.' Davis was mumbling, staring at the sea. 'Had me over a fucking barrel.'

'Who had you, David?'

'Don't you fucking play games with me!' His aggression shocked them both. He leaned forward and rubbed his eyes, visibly exhausted, shaking like a meth addict on the way down. He emptied his drink in one gulp this time, slamming the glass on the table, putting his head in his hands.

Dexter stared at the shattered man before her, wondering why his life – his children, his job and the accolades that flowed – had never been enough.

'David?' She was trying to speak with an even, calm voice. 'Who had you over a barrel, David?'

Dexter wanted a name.

He sat upright slowly. He poured himself another Jack Daniel's, took a long swig and sighed again.

'Gary fucking Page.' He was speaking slowly, taking long pauses. 'Wouldn't have to do it myself. Just help this Victor bloke get in, get out, get rid of any traces.'

'You're taking about Victor Ho –'

'Yeah . . . Victor fucking Ho.' He picked up his glass again.

'David, we're talking murder here. Victor went upstairs and –'

'Stop fucking judging me!' Davis turned to Dexter, almost snarling.

She needed to stop pushing, stop interrupting. Let him talk.

Dexter followed Davis's gaze down to the sand. The first surfers of the day were stretching by the water and starting to paddle out to the break. There was a beautiful left-hander peeling around the headland and the boys in their wetsuits were in a hurry to catch some waves before the crowds arrived.

'I should have learned how to surf. What a waste.'

'David, I need you to tell me everything. I need you to tell me about Gary Page.'

'You won't get him.' He was more measured this time. 'He's smarter than you and me. Prick called me two hours ago. Told me it's over.'

'What's over?'

'He had me exactly where he wanted. The power pressed on my neck, pushing me into the water. Don't drown, don't drown.' Davis was waving his hands around crazily, like he was trapped in some awful pantomime. 'Do what he says. It'll all go away!'

'What will go away?'

'The pictures. He's got pictures of me with that fucking slut Ruby Chambers – Chamberlain, whatever she called herself. Enterprising little bitch, that one. There are pictures of me with two, three women. You can judge me all you like. It doesn't matter. Not now, anyway. Page's right, it's over. There's no way back.'

'I'm not judging you. I just want to know what happened.'

Davis was shaking, rocking gently in his chair.

'That bitch who runs Petals, Francesca someone, she collects stuff on clients, high profile ones like me.' Davis's head was back in his hands, talking to the floor. 'Page found out about the pictures, got hold of them.'

Dexter felt torn. Sickened, but at the same time wanting to comfort him, pull him back from the edge. She needed to keep him talking. The most information you ever get from a criminal is on the day you take them in. That was today. Dexter knew it. Davis knew it too.

'What'd he say? What was he going to do with them?'

'What d'you think!' He sat up again, head swaying. 'Give them to that shit tabloid *The Mail*. Said he'd even send them to my daughters!'

'Why would he do that?'

'Page and I were close, you know, as close as you can get to a bloke like him. He'd tapped me for Grayndler – Grayndler, Sharon! That's a lifetime membership to parliament, right there. Even told me he'd find the cash to fund the campaign.'

He stopped talking again, staring at the water, like he was contemplating opportunities lost.

'Then this fucking prostitute opens her big mouth to me one day.' He took another sip from his drink, his third since Dexter arrived.

'What'd she say?'

'She tells me a story, a story about what some idiot in Page's office had told her one night when he was paying her to bite a pillow.'

Dexter ignored the crude description. 'And?'

'She reckoned Page was in a conspiracy with China's ambassador to rig defence contracts, make themselves rich. No detail. Just put it out there to me like it could really be happening. As if she fucking knew!'

'Why would she tell you that?'

'Why do you think, Sharon? I'm the fucking police commissioner! Said she was scared for him, looking for advice. Maybe she thought I could help, I don't know.'

Davis threw his hands in the air, laughing like a madman.

'What'd you do?'

'Didn't think anything of it! It was so far-fetched, especially out of the mouth of a stupid bloody hooker.'

Davis was finding new words to insult Catherine Chamberlain, the dead woman who was reaching up from her grave, taking him down. Dexter owed it to her to make him pay for his crimes. She wanted a confession.

'But you told Page?'

'One night, we're having a few drinks, discussing the timing of my entry into politics. I made a joke about it,' Davis said.

'And?'

'He hit the fucking roof! I'd never seen him so mad. I told him, surely it's bullshit. He said, of course it's bullshit! But he couldn't have people saying crap like that around town.'

Davis grabbed the bottle of Jack from the table, flipping the lid onto the floor. This time he took a long swig straight from the bottle.

'He couldn't leave it alone. I thought he'd just sack him!'

'And by "him" you're talking about Michael Anderson?'

'Don't get fucking cute with me, Sharon.'

'What'd Page do?'

'Two days later we meet again. Hands me an envelope with pictures of me inside and tells me the Grayndler plan is off the table until I've fixed his problem. The pictures are nothing but an incentive to get it done, he says. Then we'd move on as planned.'

Dexter sensed she was losing him. 'David, we can –'

'I thought I understood power, how to wield it, build it, hold it.' Davis was gritting his teeth, making a fist with his hand.

'David –'

'Page is on another level.' He was speaking to no one, like Dexter wasn't in the room any more. 'To really have power, you need to dehumanise yourself, make the end justify the means. I'm just not built like that. I thought I was, that money was power . . .'

Davis took another swig from the bottle.

'No, no, no.' He was shaking his head. 'To be amoral, unforgiving, to take something that's not yours . . . to kill . . . kill someone –'

'David –'

'To steer the bus into the crowd and frame someone else for driving it, take what's not yours, never blink, let nothing get in your way, whatever it takes, get it done – that's power!'

Davis turned to Dexter, making a fist again. 'That's power!'

He was scaring her. 'If you're willing to testify, we could strike a deal. The courts would go easy on you –'

'Are you out of your fucking mind?'

'David, I'm sorry. I'm sorry about what's happened to you, but two innocent people are dead and –'

'Stop talking!'

Dexter froze. There was nothing she could say that would calm him down.

'I'm sorry. I'm sorry,' he said softly. 'I'm not a bad man, Sharon. You know that, don't you?'

'I know, David. It's okay, it's okay. I know.'

He kept shaking his head. 'I didn't know, I didn't know –'

'It always seems like there's no coming back, David.' She tried again to bring him back to reality, the point where he would accept his fate, let her take him in. 'We can work something out –'

'What, Sharon? What can we work out? There's no deal here. No deal that won't involve prison. You know what they do to guys like me in prison?'

Dexter heard a noise at the door and turned to see the face of Constable Craven peering inside. When she turned back around, Davis was rummaging through a drawer in the coffee table. He pulled out a gun.

'No, David. No!'

'I wasn't lying to you when I said this was over.'

Davis held the gun to his temple and pulled the trigger.

The bullet went straight through his head and smashed through the window. His body slumped forward in his chair, the gun clanging on the tiles. Pieces of skull, blood and glass splashed all over the room – the floor, table, armchair, and across Dexter's face.

'Detective! Detective! Are you okay?'

Constable Craven was calling out from the other side of the room, while at the same time wrestling with the radio on her belt to call for an ambulance.

Dexter could barely hear her. She could barely hear anything over the ringing in her ears from the gunshot.

A gentle breeze was flicking gusts of cool air through the shattered glass and onto her face. She listened to the ringing, staring where the glass used to be, searching for something to reassure her that life would go on.

She found it. First, the horizon, then the waves.

The surfers were frantically paddling towards a line-up of large creases rolling towards them. A run of ripples was bearing down, each wave growing taller, threatening to break beyond their position in the water.

One of the surfers made it to the first wave just before it broke, turning on the crest in time to get his reward. A rush of powerful strokes and he was on his feet, guiding his surfboard across the face with his back to a wall that rose high above his head. He boldly cut into the water with the edge of his board, turning up and down the face, before bending his knees, tucking low, and disappearing – for a few seconds, at least – inside a sheeting barrel.

It was beautiful.

Dexter followed his ride all the way to the shore where, in one casual movement, he gracefully flicked his board over the back of the wave and dived into the white, churning water, having tamed something wild. Eventually, his head poked up. He collected his board and began paddling back out towards the break, ready to do it all over again.

CHAPTER 37

They closed the doors of the taxi out the front of *The Journal.* Bailey was in no condition to have walked the four blocks from The Fox Hole and they were in a hurry.

Mick was back manning the front desk when Bailey hobbled through the foyer with Ronnie by his side.

'How're you holding up, Mr Bailey?'

'Taken a few, landed a few,' Bailey said. 'Tell Gerald to clear out his office. We're heading up.'

'Will do.'

Marjorie, Penelope and Miranda were standing in the newsroom's tiny kitchenette, sipping from their cups of tea, when Bailey and Ronnie walked out of the elevator.

'Copy's good, mate! Gerald flicked the switch about twenty minutes ago!' Marjorie called out.

'Dad! Dad!' Miranda put down her cup and hurried across the newsroom floor to cut them off. 'I think it's time we got you to a hospital, don't you?'

'Give me a minute, sweetheart.' Bailey didn't stop for her. 'One more loose end.'

'A minute is all I'm giving you. I mean it!'

The two men walked into the editor's office. Gerald was sitting, alone, in his big chair facing the building across the street. He still liked to stare out the window, despite having lost his view across the water. It helped him to think. Right now, he was reflecting.

'We set the country on fire today, boys.' He had heard them come in but didn't turn around. 'The other papers are already quoting us online. Morning radio shows love it, social's gone ballistic, just waiting for the TV channels to catch up.' Gerald pointed to the big flatscreen on the wall in his office playing one of the morning chat shows.

There was nothing a newspaper editor liked more than breaking a news story that captured an entire nation's attention.

'Yeah, about that, we need to talk.'

'The girl tell you anything we didn't already know?'

'Not what she told me.' Bailey was rummaging through his coat pocket while Ronnie closed the door behind them. 'It's what she gave me.'

He tossed the photograph onto Gerald's desk. His boss turned around after hearing it land on the wood.

'What've you got there, bubba?'

Ronnie walked to the other side of the desk beside Gerald. Bailey had refused to show the photo to Ronnie until they were all back in the office together.

There were three men in the picture, each wearing the same uniform.

'They're wearing Princeton jackets,' Ronnie said.

'How d'you know?' Bailey said.

'You knew I was Ivy League, right?' Ronnie grabbed a half-chewed cigar from his coat pocket and shoved it in the corner of his mouth.

'Seriously?' Bailey wasn't in the mood.

'I've worked with enough Ivy League types in the bureau to know the insignia. And there isn't another college in the world pretentious enough to give its students bright orange jackets.'

'Princeton chess team of 1979.' Gerald pointed to the placard beside the chessboard in the photograph.

'A chess team has five players,' Gerald said.

'Yeah, well, these guys obviously liked each other enough to get their own photo. That's Matthew Parker and Gary Page.' Bailey tapped the heads of the young Australian students. 'Third guy's Bo Leung, the bastard who worked me over in the warehouse.'

'Son of a bitch – you're right,' Ronnie said.

'What does it mean?' Gerald said.

'Turn it over.'

Gerald flipped the photograph on his desk and Ronnie's cigar slipped out of his mouth and dropped to the floor.

'White dragons and chess.' Ronnie read out the words scribbled on the back of the photograph. 'Son of a bitch!'

'What?' Bailey said.

'Can't be.' Ronnie was shaking his head. 'This can't be right.'

'Can't be what, Ronnie?' Bailey said. 'It's been a long bloody few days, mate. I'm not up for the runaround from you this morning. In fact, I dare you to even –'

'Bubba.' Ronnie held up his hand. 'Give me a minute.'

'What for?'

Ronnie stared at the photograph in silence.

'You want a minute for what?'

Ronnie picked up his cigar, slipped it back into his mouth and stepped away from the desk towards the window. 'We heard Victor Ho mention the words "white dragon" in an exchange with another student at the university. He said something about ensuring that nothing could compromise Operation White Dragon. Nobody knew what that meant.'

'An operation?' Gerald said. 'What operation?'

'Our guess – the scam over defence contracts had threatened to undermine something else, something bigger.'

'What? Chinese students like Victor Ho helped run some kind of intelligence operation?' Gerald said.

'Goddamn it,' Ronnie said under his breath. 'Bo Leung's devoted his life to State Security. He must have recruited Parker and Page at Princeton. Or, at least, they started a friendship that turned into something else later.'

'Do you realise what you're saying?' Bailey said.

'Operation White Dragon is Parker, Page and China's top spy, Bo Leung,' Ronnie said what all three were thinking.

'Former top spy,' Bailey said. 'You made sure of that.'

'Does that mean it's over?' Gerald asked.

'You win, you lose.' Bailey repeated Bo Leung's dying words on the floor of the warehouse.

'We win, we lose,' Ronnie said. 'There were two moles inside the Australian Government. One of them got greedy. The other's the most powerful person in the country – the prime minister – and we've got nothing to prove it.'

'What about the photograph?' Gerald said.

Ronnie was shaking his head. 'It's just that – a photograph! Three Princeton students from the chess team. Bo Leung's a mirage. The Chinese will have a cover for his identity even before his body's repatriated.'

'What on earth have we walked into?' Bailey asked the question, knowing Ronnie didn't have the answer.

'With Bo Leung dead, the Chinese will know that we know.'

'And that's why Parker was here,' Bailey said.

'Oh my God!' Gerald was looking at his television, reading the breaking news flashing across the bottom of the screen.

NEW SOUTH WALES TOP COP DAVID DAVIS FOUND DEAD IN HIS MAROUBRA APARTMENT.

The television was showing footage of an ambulance and police cars blocking the street outside an apartment building. The pictures were from earlier in the morning, Bailey could tell by the sunlight. A body covered in a sheet was being wheeled on a stretcher towards the open doors of an ambulance. They could see Dexter in the background speaking to a small group of police officers before she walked out of the picture. Gerald turned up the volume and the newsreader declared that there were no suspicious circumstances, the media's coded language for suicide.

The men had been mesmerised by the breaking news on the television and they missed the gentle knocking on the door.

'Mr Summers?' Penelope's face appeared through a crack.

'Yes?'

She walked over and handed Gerald two pieces of paper, both still warm from the printer. 'The prime minister's released a statement about Gary Page. And there's one from the Chinese Embassy too.'

He took the paper from her hand and started reading.

'And Mr Summers?' Penelope said. 'Detective Dexter's downstairs. Shall I show her up?'

'Yes, yes,' Bailey answered for Gerald, who was distracted by the statements.

'Slimy bastard,' Gerald said. 'Parker's temporarily stood Page down and launched an investigation. He's even suggesting Page could be innocent.'

'What the fuck?'

'You know how this runs, Bailey,' Gerald said. 'It says here that Page's being investigated for leaking classified information about defence materials. Their statement stresses that we're talking about design specs for boots, tents, clothing, cups and saucers.'

'What about Li Chen?'

Ronnie turned the page. 'Only one line. "The ambassador's been recalled while the investigation takes place." He's probably already on a plane.'

'Why'd we bother?' Bailey thumped the desk with his good hand. 'This is bullshit.'

'Don't worry, bubba. Parker's desperate. You've got Page. He can't hide from this. And my guess is that we'll never see Li Chen again.'

'And Parker?' Bailey said.

'Yeah.' Ronnie bit down hard on his cigar. 'That's a whole new ball game now, bubba.'

They were interrupted by another gentle tap on the door. Penelope opened it and Dexter, pale, her eyes bloodshot, stepped inside. Without saying a word, she walked over to Bailey and buried her head in his chest.

He put his arms around her. 'It's over,' he said. But he knew it was a lie. The kind you tell when you know someone is at rock bottom and can't handle any more truth.

Truth.

The truth? It wasn't over. Davis might be dead, along with the psychotic Chinese agent who had tried to kill Bailey. Ambassador Li was gone. But there was every chance that Page would beat any investigation. Politicians always found a way. Unless they were caught with a bag of cash, gun in hand, or with their pants around their ankles, they always made it back because they had other politicians to protect them. Who was Bailey kidding? He knew officials who'd sold out their families in order to keep their chair at the table. Keep a hold on power. Michael Anderson and Catherine Chamberlain had died for nothing. And so had David Davis. Collateral damage. All of them.

'Dad!' Miranda was standing beside Bailey, trying to get his attention. 'It's time. We're taking you to hospital.'

'Listen to your daughter.' Dexter let go of him. 'She's smarter than you, remember?'

'Okay, okay.' His adrenalin had gone, replaced by exhaustion and pain. Everyone could see it.

They turned back to the television and listened to the newsreader finish her report about Gary Page.

'Let's call it a day, shall we?' Gerald went to switch off the screen.

'Wait!' Bailey grabbed the remote control from his hand and turned up the volume.

The newsreader had moved on to a story about a series of suicide bombings in Iraq, carried out by a new terrorist group claiming to be behind a Sunni insurgency that had already taken control of the city of Mosul.

'. . . and this morning we can show you the face of the insurgency that has led to more than a thousand deaths in three weeks,' the newsreader said. 'His name is Mustafa al-Baghdadi, the self-proclaimed leader of Islamic Nation, a group that has declared war on the government in Baghdad.'

A grainy photograph of Mustafa al-Baghdadi appeared on the screen. He looked older than Bailey remembered, but with the same piercing eyes.

'Turn it off, bubba.' Ronnie touched Bailey on the shoulder.

'Wish I could.'

Bailey turned away from the screen and limped out of the room with his daughter and Dexter by his side.

CHAPTER 38

Bailey woke to the sound of laughter, familiar voices speaking over each other, sharing stories and occasionally mentioning his name.

He tried to open his eyes to see the faces behind the sounds, but his eyelids were weak and heavy – stuck together by a long sleep. It took a few goes before he got them apart.

At first, all he could see was the white ceiling, white walls, and silhouettes of people standing around his bed.

'How, how long . . .' He was struggling to get the words out, his throat was so croaky and dry. 'How long have I been out?'

He might as well have been talking to himself.

'Hey, anyone?'

Bailey started to identify the people in the room one by one.

Miranda was there. So was her mother, Anthea. Bailey could hear Penelope too. And Gerald, the lone male voice, laughing just the same.

'Is anyone going to bloody answer me?'

'Dad!' Miranda noticed her father trying to sit up. 'He's awake!'

Bailey stretched his eyes wide open, so the air could clear the final fog of sleep.

Miranda's face was the first to appear above him. 'How're you feeling, Dad?'

'Like I've been hit by a bus. How long have I been out?'

'About eighteen hours,' she said.

Anthea, Penelope and Gerald filed along the sides of his bed.

'And this one hasn't left your bedside, mate.' Gerald put his arm around Miranda, his soft smile making him look awkward.

'Nice of Nancy to let you pop in too, old boy,' Bailey said. 'After the past few days I thought you'd be in the naughty corner and –'

'Hello, John.' Nancy appeared from behind Gerald.

'Nancy,' Bailey said. 'Lovely to see you. Thanks for coming.'

'Look at all these people who care about you.' Anthea was trying hard not to laugh at her ex-husband's uncanny ability to offend.

Other than Ronnie, who wasn't the visiting type, the only person missing was Dexter.

'So, the main man's awake.' A young bloke with designer stubble, who looked more like a student than a doctor, appeared at the end of the bed. 'Mr Bailey, can I call you John?'

'Just call me Bailey, everyone else does.'

'Okay, Bailey, I'm Doctor Andrews. You can call me Peter. How're you feeling?'

'Ready to get out of here, thanks Peter.' Bailey didn't like hospitals.

'I'd like to keep you in for another night, I'm afraid.'

'Nah, I think I'm good, thanks.' Bailey also didn't like taking orders from Generation Y.

Miranda pressed his arm. 'Dad, can you just let him speak?'

'Thanks . . . uummm?'

'Miranda.'

'Thanks, Miranda.' He smiled at her.

'Hey, Peter.' Bailey was irked by the attention the doctor was giving his daughter. 'Over here, mate. What's the verdict?'

'Not great, I'm afraid.' Peter's focus was back on Bailey. 'Three broken ribs, a fractured thumb and cheekbone, significant bruising in your right arm, abdomen and liver. You were quite badly dehydrated and . . .' He looked confused. 'You seem to be missing three fingernails from your right hand. How did –'

'But nothing too serious, then?'

'Well, if you look at each injury in isolation, you could say that. But I'd say you're in pretty bad shape. You need to –'

'Go home?'

The charade continued for another few minutes before Anthea intervened. 'John, Peter would like you to stay for another night, so that's what you're doing. Okay?'

Bailey gave up and nodded, defeated.

Gerald was trying not to laugh as he watched the doctor fumbling with Bailey's patient chart. 'Yeah, mate, young Peter here knows a lot more than you about this stuff.'

'Thank you, Gerald,' Bailey said.

'Okay, then,' Peter said. 'Now we've got that sorted, Mr Bailey – Bailey – the nurses will look after you tonight. I'll be back to check in on you tomorrow. All being well, you'll be able to go home.'

'Thanks, Doc.' Bailey scowled grumpily. 'I'd like you all to piss off now. Thanks for visiting.'

'You're such a bore.' Anthea kissed him on the forehead and left.

'Yeah, Dad. Behave yourself.' Miranda gave Bailey a hug and followed her mother out the door.

Penelope patted him on the leg. 'You rest up, Bailey.'

'Don't rush back to work, mate.' Gerald and Nancy were the last to leave.

Bailey closed his eyes. He was exhausted. Maybe the doctor was right. A little more rest and he'd be good to go.

—

When Bailey woke again it was night time. The clock beside his bed told him it was ten o'clock. The nurse had let him sleep but she had left a tray with a tired casserole, stale-looking bread roll and a yoghurt for his dinner.

He sat up, already feeling better – stronger – than when the doctor had seen him earlier in the day. But he was desperate to get to the toilet to relieve his bladder.

There was a needle stuck in his arm on the end of a tube that was connected to an empty bag. It must have had some saline solution in it, Bailey thought, for the dehydration. He pulled out the needle and sat on the edge of his bed for a moment to get his bearings and let his body catch up with his brain. With his head clear, he stepped onto the lino floor and hobbled to the toilet adjoining his room.

His ribs, cheek and thumb were throbbing, but it felt good to be back on his feet. He was peeved that Doctor Peter wanted to keep him there. He was even more annoyed that Dexter hadn't come to see him. He wanted to know why.

Bailey was leaving. Checking himself out the old-fashioned way.

Someone had brought him a bag with clean clothes and a toothbrush. He got changed, gave his teeth a scrub, and crept out into the hallway.

He could hear the nursing staff discussing patients at the reception desk. He limped past without being seen, pausing only when he noticed a trolley loaded with food and drinks with the smallest bottles of wine he had ever seen. He helped himself to a bottle of red – it was meant for patients, after all. A short ride in the elevator and he was breathing the cool night air outside the Royal Prince Alfred Hospital, congratulating himself for the tidy exit.

Bailey knew the area well. The hospital was attached to the University of Sydney campus, where he'd signed up to play rugby but had spent most of his training sessions at the little student pub called The Alfred less than a hundred metres away. It was tempting, but he wanted to see Dexter.

'Shouldn't you be inside?'

Bailey turned and saw Ronnie Johnson lighting a cigar on the footpath.

'Visiting hours are over, mate,' Bailey said.

A cloud of smoke floated around Ronnie and he puffed until the tightly rolled leaves began to simmer.

'Yeah, sorry about that, bubba. They wouldn't let me in.'

Bailey stared at him, wondering what he was up to.

'I presume this is a self-checkout?'

'How'd you know?' Bailey was slightly unnerved by Ronnie's ability to know more than he should.

'Checked your chart.' He took another puff of his stogie. 'You're fine, by the way.'

Bailey couldn't stop himself from laughing.

'Drink, bubba?'

'Can't. Got somewhere I need to be.'

'Your special detective friend?'

'Maybe.'

'I'll drive you. Car's over there.' Ronnie pointed at the Toyota Corolla parked in the No Standing zone up the street, hazard lights flashing.

'That my car?'

Ronnie shrugged. 'You weren't using it.'

They didn't talk much during the short trip to Dexter's house. Old friends don't mind the silence.

But Bailey did want to know one thing. 'Are you going to retire for real this time?'

'What do you mean? I am retired.' Ronnie kept his eyes on the street.

'Yeah, yeah, so you've been saying. But we both know it's bullshit.'

Ronnie cleared his throat, as if he was going to say something else. Then stopped.

'Ronnie? What?'

'Here we are.' Ronnie pulled the car over by the white picket fence outside Dexter's little grey cottage in Leichhardt.

'What were you about to say?'

'Ask me again, bubba. Maybe in a few months.' That was the closest to the truth that Bailey was ever going to get.

'Okay, mate.' Bailey clicked open his door. 'You staying at my place tonight?'

'That okay?' Ronnie tapped his half-ashed cigar through the open window. 'I'll sleep on the couch, just in case.'

Bailey was surprised that, right now, he actually liked having Ronnie around.

—

Bailey was still standing on the street after his car had disappeared around the corner. He hadn't given much thought to what he would say to Dexter when she opened the door, or whether he'd say anything at all.

He opened the gate and walked the short distance from the fence to the patio steps. Another few feet, he could knock on the front door. Dexter would appear, she'd be happy to see him, they'd go inside and all would be okay.

Bailey stopped walking and started looking for reasons to turn around. It was late – almost ten-thirty – too late for a pop-in. It had been a traumatic few days for Dexter, too. She probably wanted to be alone.

Bailey turned and began to walk back towards the gate. Maybe he'd go and get that drink at The Alfred, after all. The old university pub, for old time's sake. A whisky – two-finger pour. Maybe a few beers to wash it down. Maybe. It's not every week that you almost get killed. Although, if you were John Bailey, the chances of it happening were higher than most.

Click.

There was a noise behind him.

'Bailey? Is that you?' Dexter was standing at the front door.

He turned around, embarrassed, looking for a reason to be walking the other way. 'Hi Sharon, I thought I saw the lights off. Didn't think it was, you know, didn't know if –'

'You're an idiot, John Bailey.'

In the semi-darkness, Bailey couldn't tell if she was smiling, or scowling.

'Yes,' he said. 'I'm an idiot.'

'Are you coming in, then?' It was a smile, not a scowl.

Bailey reached into the pocket of his coat and withdrew a small – no, a tiny – bottle of red wine. 'I didn't come empty-handed.'

'Did you steal that from the hospital?'

'Well, it depends on your definition of stealing,' Bailey said. 'Technically, it was provided.'

'And aren't you due out tomorrow?'

'How'd you know?' It seemed to Bailey that everyone was better briefed about his condition than he was.

'I visited you today. You were asleep and I didn't want to wake you. How else do you think that bag of clothes made it beside your bed?'

Bailey's heart sank into his chest. There was so much goodness in Dexter that he was frightened to step inside. She deserved better than him. She really did.

'Sharon?' He didn't know what he was going to say next. 'What . . . what are we doing?'

'You tell me, you silly old fool?' That was Dexter – strong, confident and willing to take a chance.

'I mean,' Bailey stumbled, 'are we, are we doing this? What do you want?'

Dexter sighed and stared at the complicated man standing in her front garden. Hopeless and brilliant. Full of love and full of shit. But the most *just* man she had ever known.

'What do I want?' Dexter paused. 'I can tell you what I don't want. I don't want to look past tonight. But tonight, I want you to come inside.'

'I won't argue with that.'

He walked through the door and handed her the tiny bottle of shiraz.

'You might want to give that some air.'

EPILOGUE

Matthew Parker loved the ocean. He loved swimming in the big blue pond, the waves and the creatures that thrived beneath. He loved the smell of salt and the cleansing layer of crust it left on his skin after the breeze blew it dry. The ocean was nature's bathwater, and the prime minister visited the beach whenever he could. To run, swim or surf. It didn't matter. The beach relaxed him. Helped him to rationalise his thoughts and sort through the crap.

Parker had spent most of his childhood on the sand at Manly Beach. His father had bought him his first surfboard when he was barely old enough to carry it from the car to the shoreline. That Aloha twin fin was his pride and joy and it was shaped to last. He was never much of a surfer and, as he grew older, the boards got longer. The longer the board, the easier it was to stand up. These days he surfed a ten-foot Malibu.

The problem with Manly was that it was always crowded. He couldn't put his foot on the esplanade without being stopped by someone with ideas about how he should run the country. He had always listened, or at least he had mastered the art of pretending.

When Parker had something serious on his mind he would find a beach further north where he could be alone with his thoughts. And so it was on this humid January morning when he climbed in his car, he headed for Palm Beach. He didn't care that his security detail had to make the forty-kilometre journey from Kirribilli House at five o'clock in the morning. They were paid to do a job – to protect the prime minister, no less – and they should have been used to it by now. This was Parker's sixth trip to Palm Beach in two weeks.

With parliament in recess, he was taking an extended summer break and he had a lot to think about. He parked his car on the thin strip of peninsula at the northern end of the beach that separated the surf from the Pittwater. This morning he would stick to the routine he had developed this summer and run the sand dunes below the lighthouse before taking a swim.

'Stay here. I want to be alone,' he told his security detail. Rob and Chris, or Paul. He could never remember their names. He didn't need to. It was his time and he didn't want anyone ruining his sunrise.

The sand crunched and squeaked beneath Parker's toes as his feet pressed into the track that led to the bottom of the sand dune. The sun had started to move on the horizon, bathing the top of the dune in a warm orange light.

The sand was still cool underfoot. By lunchtime, under the full rays of the sun, it would be piping hot. Today was supposed to be a scorcher.

Parker knew that the secret to running sand dunes was making sure your footprints were evenly spaced to create a natural staircase. You had to pound the same holes on the way up, while avoiding them on the way down. Eventually, the sand would stop shifting underfoot and you could get a rhythm. If you messed up your foot holes it wouldn't be long before your muscles ached and, at Parker's age, brought on a cramp.

Exercise helped him clear his head. But after a tumultuous seven months his trusted remedy wasn't working, and the stress was keeping him awake. Bo Leung was dead and Ambassador Li Chen had disappeared. The People's Republic was yet to provide an official explanation about Ambassador Li's absence, other than to say that he would not be returning to his post in Canberra. Corruption was not well received in the new China, and Parker knew that State Security had its own way of fixing problems outside of the judiciary.

He was also furious at Gary Page's stupidity and even angrier about the fact that he needed to protect him, if only to keep his prime ministership intact.

The evolution of Operation White Dragon from an ideological fraternity to a powerful reality was to be his crowning achievement in life. He was going to be the man who changed the world. There was nothing corrupt or treasonous about it. The re-balancing of the globe away from the idea that there could be only one lone super-power was a moral imperative.

The United States had inherited its throne through the ashes of the wars of the twentieth century. Now there needed to be a new world order, a genuine uniting of nations that could only be achieved through the creation of new partnerships – military, diplomatic, economic. One nation should not lecture the world about the merits of a capitalist system that has allowed bank CEOs to get paid fifty million dollars a year, while a cleaner is paid seven dollars an hour. The United States of America was faltering and failing its people. The world needed better leadership and more leaders.

But the mission had changed.

Page had broken the pact they had made back at Princeton. Matthew Parker's ambitions were stalled, but they weren't dead, unlike his old friend, Bo Leung. The only way back was to hold on to power, keep his government together, and wait.

America's new president was spending another fifty billion dollars a year to maintain his nation's military supremacy, even though the United States already had more nuclear weapons than every other nation combined. But global power wasn't about nukes any more. It was about territory and trade – two areas where Washington was floundering, and Beijing was growing.

Matthew Parker was preparing to do something no Australian prime minister had ever done before. He was turning his back on America.

He would not be supporting joint military exercises with the US and its allies in the disputed waters of the South China Sea. For China, this would amount to a declaration of war. And if America's president wanted to be the bully and follow through on a threat to make Australia choose, Parker would choose Australia's largest trading partner, China.

He climbed the sand dune for the twentieth time, his legs achy but strong, the sweat pouring down his back. He looked at his watch. He'd been running for thirty minutes, faster than yesterday.

He stopped at the summit, the dune all to himself, and looked down at the stairs in the sand. The foot holes were perfect. It was a shame that by day's end they would be blown away by the southerly.

Parker could see a group of runners heading along the track towards him.

Fuck off. The little voice in his head was snarling at them. *This is my mountain.*

The runners would want to talk to him as soon as they realised that the person building a staircase in the distance was the prime minister. Why wouldn't they?

Parker wasn't in the mood for small talk, not even at a moment like this when he knew they would be impressed by his athleticism. Find him another world leader who had just run twenty sand dunes at six o'clock in the morning.

He took off his singlet and began jogging slowly down the side of the hill towards the water. The big January swells were yet to arrive and the waves were small. North Palm Beach could be a dangerous place to swim because of the strong currents that pushed the water along the shore before pulling it back out to sea like an escalator alongside the rocky headland.

Parker knew this beach well and, in a two-foot swell, he wasn't worried. He spotted his two security guards hurriedly walking along the beach towards him. They didn't miss a thing.

He dropped his singlet on the sand and ran into the sea. The initial chill of the water tightened his skin and mellowed the warm fuzz of the endorphins from his run on the dune. He dived through the shallow water until it was deep enough to start swimming and it wasn't long before he was out past the breakers.

He swam towards the horizon, rolling over his arms in a freestyle stroke, the water getting deeper and darker the further he went. There were no shark nets at this end of the beach. He wasn't worried about that, either. There had never been a shark attack at Palm Beach and the thought that he might become a statistic hadn't even crossed his mind.

He stopped swimming about two hundred metres from the shore and turned onto his back so he could float and look up at the sky. He was truly alone now. The glassy water had relaxed his muscles and he was enjoying the moment, closing his eyes, listening to the gentle lapping around his body. Even if he had opened them, he wouldn't have seen the shadow lurking below. It was too deep. And the shadow was moving quickly.

Rob and Chris – and those were their names – were standing on the sand next to the prime minister's singlet. Both had their right hands raised to shield their eyes from the sun that was now shining brightly from the east. The glare on the water made it impossible to monitor their boss floating on the surface. It was so bright they missed the splash when he was pulled under.

It all happened so quickly that Parker didn't even get a chance to scream. In one lethal manoeuvre he was spun around and driven to the bottom of the sea, arms pinned by his sides, rendering him helpless. He could feel a heavy weight on his back holding him down, his face pushed into the sand. His lungs were burning, the saltwater stinging his throat. Parker kicked his legs and tried to wriggle free. It was no use. He could feel the water entering his lungs. Exhausted by the futility of the struggle, he stopped resisting. Through the darkness, he could see a pair of large hands locked together across his chest. Those big hands were the last things that he saw.

—

He pulled himself up onto the rocks at the back of the headland. He didn't have much time.

It had taken fifteen minutes to swim back from the beach and he knew the helicopters would soon be in the sky searching for any sign of the prime minister. They'd find him, unless the sharks got to him first.

He disconnected his oxygen tank and lifted it into the small dinghy that he'd jammed between two boulders at the base of the cliff. He tossed in his flippers and goggles, and unclipped the hunting knife from the holster on his wetsuit. Luckily, he hadn't needed it. They wouldn't find a scratch on Parker's body when they pulled him from the water. It was perfect.

He surveyed the rocky ledge to make sure he didn't leave anything behind. Tins of food, water bottles, tracksuit, the small bottle of whisky and the plastic survival blanket he'd brought in case the nights were cold. All were packed in the small bag that was fixed to a cable inside the dinghy.

He had prepared for a quick exit once the job was done. There could be no traces.

He reached down and picked up the cigar he had stubbed into the rock the day before, threw it into the boat and splashed seawater to wash away the ashes. Then he removed the steel peg he had hammered into the rock to secure the dinghy, tossed in the rope and climbed in.

The engine started with the first pull of the cord. He turned it to full throttle and headed northwest towards Lion Island. The tide was coming in. He should be able to make it back to Pearl Beach inside an hour, load up the boat on the trailer and keep heading north. After all, he was supposed to be on a fishing holiday.

There was nothing else on the water at the mouth of the bay. The fishermen had headed out to sea hours ago and he was too far north for the kayakers. He was alone out there, which was exactly how he had wanted it to be.

When his dinghy rounded the western side of Lion Island, he reached into his bag for a fresh cigar, sparked up and took a few deep puffs to calm the adrenalin.

Ronnie Johnson was a professional and he had taken an oath. Even so, this job had shaken him to his core. It was a shadow operation – an order straight from the president's desk. He'd done them before.

Ronnie had been watching Matthew Parker for months, looking for an opportunity to take him down. The Australian

Federal Police didn't protect the prime minister in the same way the Secret Service guarded the president's every move. The heightened threat posed by radicalised Islamists had led to tighter security around Parker, but he was still exposed to danger from someone who knew what they were doing. Someone like Ronnie Johnson. He just had to make sure that it looked like an accident.

By the time Parker had made his third trip to Palm Beach, Ronnie was up on the headland watching him. Parker kept the same routine each time. A run on the dune followed by a swim.

Ronnie had spent seven nights sleeping on a rocky ledge before he made his move.

It was a targeted assassination, ordered by a new president with a new way of doing things. For Ronnie Johnson, it was cold-blooded murder, whichever way he reasoned it. But he didn't care. He wasn't worried about being judged, because he didn't believe in God. He had nothing to fear but life itself. Raised by Oklahoma Baptists, he had heard all of the arguments about faith. The added richness in life and a ticket into heaven when you're done. He never bought any of it.

Ronnie believed in America. He believed in improving the world and he didn't mind getting his hands dirty doing it. When life called time on Ronnie Johnson, he was dust. He might as well change the earth for the better while he was still walking on it.

He had never killed anyone who hadn't deserved it. The means always justified the end. Ronnie Johnson didn't need forgiveness. He needed justification.

The greater good.

ACKNOWLEDGEMENTS

My father once told me that writers write. It's the best advice I've ever been given about the craft and it taught me to enjoy writing (and re-writing) every word, published or not.

I started writing fiction many years ago and I'm very grateful to my parents, John and Helen, and also to Neil Brown, for encouraging me to keep going.

A big thanks to Fiona Henderson, Dan Ruffino and the team at Simon & Schuster Australia for backing me, and to my agent, Jeanne Ryckmans, for believing in that very early draft, staying with me for the journey and helping me to get it right.

To Australia's most prolific thriller reader, David 'Mac' McInerney, for reading draft after draft and helping me believe that I had something good. And to my other draft readers, Gavin Fang, Chris Uhlmann, Chris Bath and Julia Baird – thanks for the kind words, advice and encouragement.

Family is a big part of my life and I'd like to thank my brothers and sisters in law, Matthew and Terri, Ben and Rachel and Sam and Sandi, for their love and support over the years and the same goes for Jenny, James and Caelia, and Nahum and Carmela.

I've always been lucky with friends – old and new – but I'd like to single out Dan, Marcus, Harry and Rob for their support and to my high school mates for always being there and for looking out for each other – you know who you are. And to the London crew – thanks.

Thanks also to my colleagues and friends at the ABC – it's such a tremendous organisation with so many passionate people who care deeply about what they do. I've been privileged to work there for the past decade.

And lastly, a special thanks to my wife, Justine, who read so many drafts of this book I've lost count. Without her love, support and encouragement this book would never have been possible.

ABOUT THE AUTHOR

Tim Ayliffe has been a journalist for almost 20 years and is the Managing Editor of Television and Video for ABC News. He was TV News Editor for ABC News and Executive Producer of ABC News Breakfast. Before joining the ABC in 2006, Tim worked in London for Sky News as a digital and television journalist. *The Greater Good* is the first book in a three-book series featuring John Bailey. The second, *State of Fear*, is available now. Tim lives in Sydney.